'A delightful novel that leaves the reader pondering its many subtle themes' Piers Paul Read

'The value and strength of this heartwarming book ... lie not so much in these grippingly interwoven plots as in the passionate and wholesome narrative style, enviably neat, snappy and lyrical ... The scent of newly-baked bread stirs the village women's appetite for gossip, and smoke from the Signorina's cigarette floats to the ceiling in two perfect circles like turtle doves. Indeed, the whole story, like its heroine, might be said to throb with a passion for life' *Spectator*

'Sensual, lyrical and as robust as a plate of spaghetti' *Daily Express*

'For her first novel, Cristina Odone has chosen an unusual, apparently naive theme: the fable of a young girl in an Italian village who is experiencing visions of the Blessed Virgin Mary. A quiet and serious young woman, Santarella also has the disconcerting gift of predicting events that turn out as foretold ... Underneath this seemingly artless story lies a more complicated text. *The Shrine*, though beautifully set in time and place, evoking the sights and sounds of its own world, is not really, or essentially about the plot to build a shrine at all. It is elliptically, but insistently, about the uncertainty of identity for modern women' *Literary Review*

Cristina Odone is Italian, and was brought up in both Italy and America before attending Oxford University. She lives in London.

The Shrine

CRISTINA ODONE

PHŒNIX

A PHOENIX PAPERBACK

First published in Great Britain
by Weidenfeld & Nicolson in 1996
This paperback edition published in 1996
by Phoenix, a division of Orion Books Ltd,
Orion House, 5 Upper St Martin's Lane,
London WC2H 9EA

A CIP catalogue record for this book
is available from the British Library.

ISBN: 1 85799 429 9

Filmset by Selwood Systems Ltd, Midsomer Norton
Printed in Great Britain by
The Guernsey Press Co. Ltd,
Guernsey, C.I.

*For my mother
and my father*

1

Dreaming on her hot terrace, the widow Lea saw her daughter speaking to a lady in white. She awoke with a start, to find Santarella at her side, eyes fixed and face pale as a bride's veil.

The widow stood up from her chair. 'Santa! Santa!' She shook the young shoulders.

Santarella looked up and smiled. 'What is it, Mamma?'

The widow didn't answer: as usual with her daughter, she didn't know what to say. What do you make of a girl who, since childhood, claims to speak to Our Lady? A girl who says she has seen the Child holding a Lamb in a field of snow on the Day of the Epiphany? What do you do with a girl who seems steeped in secret thoughts, a girl who refuses to be drawn into the tribulations of daily life? Nothing seems to touch that placid face – not worries about money, about customers, about the competition from Vanna's greengrocer's, or about the evil tongues that wag like dogs' tails about everything a still-appetizing widow says and does.

Widow Lea shook her head and wondered once again why of all His creatures the Good Lord should have chosen her to bring such a child into the world.

Already in the village her daughter was known as

Santarella, 'the little Saint' – and even she had begun to call the girl, whom she had baptized Marina, by that name. Ever since Santa's first vision, so many years ago now, a group of the older women had asked Don Luigi to write to the bishop in Torino and describe the wondrous happenings that were taking place in San Lorenzo, so that the insignificant little speck of a village would be transformed into the newest Marian shrine, attracting throngs of pilgrims from the four corners of the world.

But widow Lea had quickly put a stop to their scheme: she had forbidden Santa to speak of any further apparitions, and had scolded Don Luigi for filling her daughter's mind with such notions. The sighting, she told him firmly, had been brought on by the girl's Lenten fast rather than by any divine intervention.

She herself did not know what to believe any more. Her own life, a breathless rush from shop-keeping to money-pinching measures, of violent quarrels with her suppliers and brief encounters with her lover, the Mayor Battistini, left very little room for religious rituals. The dull Sunday morning Masses where everyone watched to see who took Communion and who didn't, the mantillas draped on bowed heads, the Mea Culpas whispered while kneeling in a dark pew: these rites were for old people who feared death, not for women who were still in their prime, desirable and full of fire, as she was.

That her daughter was different, that she was pure and pious, wrapped in her own mysterious world, filled the widow Lea with an awe leavened with guilt, so that she often approached her own flesh and blood with the shyness of a schoolgirl coming to the confessional.

She studied the beautiful face before her: she was

worried lest Santa felt it her duty to reveal all to Don Luigi in the confessional – the priest's mouth, everyone knew, was wider than the Atlantic and moved with the speed of an express train when it came to spreading news.

Now she ventured mildly: 'Did ... did you see Her? Did She speak to you again?'

Santa's smile shone sweeter still. 'Yes, Mamma.'

The widow took a deep breath of fear and excitement. 'What did She say?'

'She told me that Marcantonio Ferrati has just died. We must pray for his soul, Mamma.'

Widow Lea shivered and made a quick sign of the cross. Her daughter's prophecies were always fulfilled: had she not predicted the terrible drought that had scorched every field in these hills, three summers ago? And had she not warned of the influenza epidemic that had killed those two poor little children in Acqui, just last winter? And what of Bishop Guardini's death, and his replacement by Bishop Natti? Yes, Santarella had predicted it all.

The widow sighed, twisting one of her long dark curls about her finger: what changes would Marcantonio's death bring to her own life? Would the Mayor buy Ferrati's lands? Not, of course, that the expansion of Bettino's possessions would affect her directly, but she did hope that in becoming the greatest landowner of San Lorenzo her lover might swell with more generous instincts towards her than he had displayed so far.

Don Luigi's bells broke the afternoon silence: it was six. The widow shook her head: no time for dreaming, tomorrow was Monday, and the week would start all over again ... She smoothed down the tight wrinkles of her dress. 'I'm going inside, now, I have to bring up all those boxes from the cellar ... come along and give me a hand.'

She walked back into the shadows of the kitchen. Once inside, she looked through the window at the motionless figure on the terrace: the sun shone behind Santa's profile, and the girl's face seemed to glow. 'Mother of God, I didn't ask you for a saint!' The widow raised her eyes heavenward.

Outside, Santa stood still, breathing in the warm silent air and praying softly for Marcantonio Ferrati's soul.

2

'Signorina Ferrati, won't you go and lie down?' The nurse shook Alma out of sleep.

Alma opened her eyes. Above her, the pale Madonna and Child on the ceiling smiled down, benevolent, all-seeing. She rose from the armchair, crossed the terracotta tiles to stand at the open window, where hills and vine-yards stretched beneath the last of the afternoon sun. The faint rays shone blue, muting the countryside. She could see the turreted outline of the castle at Castel d'Oro, and to the east the ancient water tower of Susa, whose blurred black edges seemed charcoal drawn. Beyond, upon the hills, village roofs and spires cut into the horizon.

Beneath the window sill, the persimmon and walnut trees looked like dark clouds upon a heaven of grass and gravel. The orchard lay to the left, shadows stretching to take over more and more of the garden. To the right, over the blackberry hedge, she could see the white road that the mayor had had repaved. Every day of her childhood, of her youth, had been circumscribed by the tall hedge that then, as always, separated the Ferratis from the rest of the village.

The sounds of the evening bocce game came towards her: the men were playing earlier than usual. She could hear them argue over someone's throw, measuring distances with excited voices. Later their quarrel would be forgotten, as they grouped together at the counter in Vanna's bar, slapping each other's backs with the camaraderie found among bottles, glasses and men.

San Lorenzo: a handful of farmhouses, a cemetery, a church. A stretch of land among hills of vineyards, a dozen hidden courtyards, a cluster of familiar faces. San Lorenzo, where everything she touched set off an echo, and where a memory waited for her at every corner.

A Vespa roared down the road, dislodging a nightingale from the hedge. The bird flew into the dark fronds of the persimmon tree, Alma's gaze following. Suddenly, beneath the tree, a figure moved: Francesco sat there, holding a handful of pebbles that one by one he tossed back into the path. Alma watched her brother as his arm arched, slow, methodical, to throw each stone. He had immediately come, when she had called London last week: but his presence, which she had yearned for during the entire winter, struck her now as insubstantial – it had proved no comfort to see him, silent, pale, at their father's bedside. They had exchanged no more than a few words as they took turns beside the dying man, and this silent brother seemed to underline, in Alma's eyes, the loneliness she would step into when Marcantonio died. Why had she thought that her grief could be shared, and lightened in the process?

Greater comfort seemed to come to her from the village itself, from this garden, from the orchard beyond. She knew every change that would soon steal upon the window's view: the darkening of dips and hollows at the foot of the hills; the deepening of violet shades that would turn the vineyard ridges to wine; the appearance of village lights that, one by one, would nestle against the hills, like jewels on a woman's bosom.

Alma's eyes turned from the window to the bed where her father lay. Here the changes had caught her unawares – the darkened eye sockets, the shadowed cheek bones, the wrinkled yellow skin. 'Dear God, please help him,' she whispered. She did not know whether she was praying for his death or for an extension of his life here among the smell of spirit, the shuffling of doctor and nurse, the syringes and the bedpan.

She approached the bed. Nothing was visible: Father lay on his side, face turned from her. He had not changed position since he had fallen asleep, more than an hour ago. She laid her hand upon his shoulder. 'Father,' she whispered.

She stood beside the bed, watching over him, and wondered at the ease with which the natural order could be reversed: the children mothering the parent, washing him, spoon-feeding him, offering reassurances and attempting to note his progress. How confusing, this reversal. She, who had always studied her father's expression and listened to his words and tone before taking a step – she now watched his face fill with doubt in response to the slightest question, and his eyes seek hers for a lead.

The all-powerful Marcantonio Ferrati. Her most vivid memory of him was during the famous storm, more than fifteen years ago now, that had wrought devastation upon San Lorenzo and the neighbouring villages. Mother and Rina (whose headaches had predicted the storm days in

7

advance) hurried through the house, shutting windows and doors, calling to the children for assistance. Alma, disobedient as ever, had paid no heed, and had stared, from the kitchen window, at the rain that washed the garden and bent the trees in a humiliating way. Outside all was crazy, exciting and inviting. It took her a moment to dart out of the kitchen door and run beneath the rain. She lifted the hem of her dress to form a basin, and stomped about the garden, listening to the wind and the rainfall. She was standing under the persimmon tree when suddenly she saw her father rushing towards her. A loud crash deafened her: Alma, trembling now, saw her father before her, body and arms stretched to hold up, above her head, a huge branch that had broken from the trunk.

And now – death? Death was for others, for the old village men who sat in the piazza, for the tiny ancient women whose widows' weeds spoke of acceptance of all that lay before them. Death was for those who had nothing left to do, no one left to love.

She looked down now at the figure that lay beneath the sheet. Slowly, her hand stroked the curve of the fleshless shoulder.

Downstairs in the entrance hall the clock struck five: soon Don Luigi would arrive. The priest had insisted on coming once again, in the hope that tonight the dying man would consent to see him. Alma watched the nurse take out her knitting on the armchair: she looked calm and strong, her big brown hands and arms constantly in motion. Her father, Alma thought, had loved that type of woman.

Once more she stroked the covered figure that lay still

and silent beside her. Then she knew: she lifted the sheet and saw the grey face of the dead man. She pressed her forehead against his chest and wept.

3

No one in the village was surprised to learn of Ferrati's death. Many months had passed without Marcantonio's daily supervisions of his vineyards, beetroot and potato fields. Many months without the familiar figure appearing during the farmers' midday siesta, when in the shade of a tree they ate bread and salami, murmuring imprecations against a bee, trading jokes the women shook their heads at, while hands lazy with wine readjusted a kerchief or a cap as protection from the white sun. Marcantonio had liked to come down to his fields, to visit the men and women as they rested on the grass, to share cigarettes with one, to talk of last year's crops with another, towering above them all as he leaned his elbow against a tree trunk and looked over his lands.

Grillo, whose mother Vanna ran the village bar and the greengrocer's, brought the Ferratis their weekly supply of bottled water, but he hadn't laid eyes on the sick man since March: Marcantonio had kept to his bedroom, to which only his daughter (who now seldom returned to her studio flat in Torino), a nurse, and the doctor from Alessandria were allowed entry. And of late Don Luigi, with much shaking of the head and much swaying of his cassock, had been seen in the afternoon making his slow way to the Ferratis' house.

There was not much doubt as to what would befall the estate: Marcantonio's son and daughter would inherit the whole. But everyone knew that the Ferratis' fortunes were no longer what they once had been and that Marcantonio's children didn't have the money to maintain the property. And, in any case, both had their lives away from San Lorenzo and would have no interest in keeping all the family lands. The question was – how much of the property would they be forced to sell, and to whom?

Already, Francesco had been seen paying visits to Franca Felici's big farmhouse: did it take a genius to guess what that meant? Still, Franca was not the only interested party: the butcher Romeo had said over billiards in Vanna's bar that he would put in a bid for the lands; and the Mayor Battistini had for years cast longing looks over the potato fields and the beetroot rows that were part of the Ferratis' property.

Once the black-bordered posters lamenting Marcantonio Ferrati's departure were glued against the houses that lined the main road, the whole village settled down to watch the would-be buyers haggling over their prize. For days, the widow Lea's affair with Battistini, the possible saintliness of her daughter Santarella, the butcher Romeo's brand new Fiat – in short all the favourite topics that knitted together women's voices outside a shop's entrance, that brought men in clusters around the billiard table in Vanna's bar – were replaced with the sale of the Ferrati property and speculation as to its future owner. Whoever bought the Ferrati lands – not to mention, if it were to come up for sale, the house – would inherit the

11

family's undisputed place at the top of the village social hierarchy.

The old men, those who had known Marcantonio when he wore a sailor suit and sported muddy knees, were particularly excited by the forthcoming sale. Seated in a row outside the bar, their canes leaning against their legs, the old men warmed their wrinkled skin and their weak bones in the afternoon sun and swapped predictions over their card game.

'Franca will bid the highest and get the whole lot, you'll see,' said the Marshal Ciuffi, twirling his white moustaches as he watched Old Rocco deal out the limp cards.

'That woman's got more balls than all the men in this stinking village.' Old Rocco, the Sicilian, dark and puckered as an olive, spat on the pavement. 'But what's for sale, that's what I want to know: will they be able to hold onto the vineyards? The wheat fields that are adjoining to their garden?'

Gianni 'er Brutto' ('the ugly one'), whose brown birthmark spread like a pat of chocolate across an entire cheek, put forth his own conjecture now. He spoke in his low unassuming voice, with the timidity of one who has suffered insults throughout his life. 'The butcher, what about him? He told Vanna he wants to set up a wine distillery and he'd buy the Ferrati lands and vineyards...'

The marshal and Rocco shook their heads in unison at this, and the Sicilian shouted: 'Never in a million years! That fat ass may be rich but he will never set anything up, he couldn't even keep it up with his wife, we all know that!'

The others gurgled with laughter at the memory of that night when Romeo's wife, Filomena, had stood with her

12

suitcase outside their front door and screamed out his impotence for all the village to hear, before disappearing forever inside the night coach to Alessandria.

'What about Bettino? My money's on him. Our mayor's got a bank account that has more zeros than you've got teeth.' The Marshal Ciuffi tapped his cane upon the flag-stones as if to the beat of a military march.

Old Rocco grinned his almost toothless smile. 'That's not saying much, Marshal, when you're talking to the likes of us.' The old men chuckled. 'Anyway,' resumed the Sicilian coarsely, 'Bettino's energies are all being wasted inside her.' And Rocco jerked his thumb towards the widow Lea's shop.

The group snickered, and much elbow-nudging and winking followed. The widow Lea, lusted after by all the village men, had become so much part of their talk and their sighs and their dreams, that only to name her would set off a group session of bawdy boasts.

The cards were shuffled and dealt out once more, and the men bent close to the table for a better look at the numbers and figures. It was nearly four and one by one the blinds of the shops were pulled up. Nuccio the baker stretched outside his door in the sunlight, the butcher Romeo plaited the plastic strips that curtained his en-trance, and Vanna came out of her bar to water her basil pots.

Now the widow Lea appeared outside her shop: she was readjusting the hairpins that kept her long dark tresses coiled round her head, a soft frame to her perfect oval face and large black eyes. Once satisfied that her hair was in place, she began to bring out the cases of fruits and vegetables, the crates of bottled mineral water that each day flanked her door. The card players watched her in silence as she bent, lifted, lowered, crouched, her tight dark dress wrinkling on her body. The marshal gave a long low whistle and nudged Old Rocco.

At that moment Don Luigi passed by, black soutane flapping about his ankles. He slowed down and cleared his throat as he approached the ancient card players. He did not, however, stop altogether: he disapproved of the lot of them, men in their sunset years who did not attend Mass to cleanse their erring souls. Of course the late Ferrati himself had refused to call for him before passing away – and the matter still rankled. But then, Ferrati and his family had always contributed generously to his fundraisings – for the new church roof, for the painting of his sacristy, for the cleaning of the frescos.

'Good afternoon,' Don Luigi muttered towards the card players, smiling for a brief second at the toothless group. Unenthusiastic replies of 'Afternoon, Padre' wafted from the table.

Don Luigi moved on, almost tripping on his soutane and wished for the umpteenth time that Bishop Natti did not frown upon his parish priests wearing trousers. Still, this was not what he should be thinking of: what was he to do about the confession he'd heard this morning, that was more to the point. Had Our Blessed Mother truly spoken to young Santarella once again? Who could doubt the crystal clear voice that had come to him through the grille of the confessional, who could cast doubt upon so blameless a young girl? And, more important, why should he want to distrust such a wonderful miraculous event that might convert the whole heathen lot of them? Here was a sign from the Good Lord, an opportunity for his parish to be placed high above all others, a chance for himself to shine before Bishop Natti as the best of shepherds . . . and yet here he was, forced to remain silent, tied to his confessional secrecy . . .

The village housewives were beginning their rounds of last minute shopping. Unlike the morning visits to the baker's, the butcher's and the grocer's, the afternoon shopping could proceed at a leisurely pace: children had been fed, husbands had returned to the fields, the slipping sun was soft and pleasant at this hour.

The women strolled, as if they were tourists on the boardwalk at Ventimiglia, and stopped every now and then to chat with someone who crossed their path. They inspected one another's clothes and hairstyle; they examined each other's children for growth and dirty nails; they swapped advice on which grocer carries the freshest apricots and which the cheapest olive oil; they gave out recipes that would hide a less-than-best cut of meat and traded remedies for nausea, stomach cramps or fatigue. In the middle of the piazza, along the main road, leaning out of a window – from every corner of the village – you could hear the sound of women's voices and laughter, punctuated by their children's shouts and the weak ring of a bicycle bell: this afternoon stretch belonged to the women, and for an hour or so they would bask in this sweet late sun and in the knowledge that duties need not be unfolded till a little later, with the napkins and the oilcloth that protected the kitchen table during meals.

The old men watched all this and sat still in their chairs, caressing their canes and slapping down a card, leaving all other activities to those who had not yet come to the end of their days. The old men knew that they, after all, had now tumbled out of the youthful web of ambition, love and hard work in which the spider of life catches its flies. They could sit beneath the overhanging roof of Vanna's bar, over the grease of unwashed tables, and watch village life go by.

This is not to say, however, that the dust had settled upon the burial of all their quarrels, needs or doubts. The Marshal Ciuffi always spent a moment or two tugging at his fabulous moustache, mulling over his defeat in the race for mayor; he remembered it like yesterday, the wretched Battistini courting votes with promises of getting money from the Region to build a huge wine cellar – 'We'll start our own village co-operative, make millions out of our wines!' he promised – and fooled them all, including the great cynic, Old Rocco, whom the marshal had caught red-handed one night, pasting a poster on the butcher Romeo's wall: 'Want more vino? Vote Bettino!' The marshal shook his head at the bitter memory of this past treachery. Beside him, the traitor sat, small and dark, scrunched up in his chair, dealing the cards. Old Rocco himself had never forgotten the hostile silence that greeted him when he first set foot in Vanna's bar, newly arrived from Sicily, a peasant looking for work. Nor had he forgotten how, when he and Maria – may she rest in peace – had broken off their engagement after one of his scenes of jealousy, her parents had paid for Don Luigi to say Mass to St Anthony, 'for the danger averted'. Oh no, Old Rocco had not forgotten, and he still ground his teeth at night in memory of those ancient grievances.

In his corner, Gianni er Brutto closed his eyes in the afternoon light, and listened to the voices of his village. He basked in the warmth of the sun, and in the newly forged friendship with these two men, Ciuffi and Rocco who, in their younger days, had had no time for him. For years he had had to put up with being mocked, marginalized because of the great brown birthmark that covered his face. The villagers had approached him only when they needed something fixed – a bicycle, a stool, a bookcase. Otherwise, they steered clear of him, allowing their children to point at his birthmark: 'Er Brutto! Er Brutto!' their chants had wafted over the wall, into his courtyard, under the canopy of the walnut tree where he'd set up his worktable. Gianni sighed and studied his large, knotted fingers, studied their scars – all the wounds he'd collected with his sawing, hammering, filing . . . Now, age had marked all their faces, blurring their features into the same wrinkled form, reducing them to an equality they had never suspected before. Yes, Gianni mused, in their old age, the three men had discovered much that bound them: for waking up meant struggling to gain control of flaccid muscles, eating and drinking meant fighting down a choking sensation, coming to the piazza involved frequent stops while, trembling with exertion, they snatched at the air.

And despite their mockery and jibes at Don Luigi's skirts, they wondered now, in the wake of Marcantonio Ferrati's death, what lay in store for them.

'Blood will be spilt as they race to take over the Ferrati lands and, more important, that house.' Old Rocco rubbed his hands with glee.

'The village could use a bit of excitement.' And the marshal's cane tapped the ground at his feet.

'It's so Goddamned unfair – the rich are surrounded by excitement even at their death,' spat out Old Rocco. 'Marcantonio would enjoy the sight of them all at each other's throats. The way they flap about, trying to buy his lands and take over his position...'

'Oh, no one will truly be able to take the Ferratis' place.' Gianni sounded shocked at the mere idea of it. 'I'm sure that Francesco will make sure that they keep most of the property. And anyway – you're born into that name, you can't buy it.'

'Nonsense.' Old Rocco set him straight: 'Money buys it all nowadays.'

'Well, whatever happens, it will be fun to watch.' And with a loving hand, the marshal twirled his great moustache.

4

'Debts, what debts are they talking about?' Aunt Lucia whispered, furious, behind the short black veil that hung from her hat. Francesco stood silent beside her. He watched Don Luigi, on the threshold of the family chapel, draw a cross in the air: inside, the pallbearers were sealing Father's coffin into the Ferratis' sepulchre, their dark figures illuminated by the soft light of a red-paned lantern. Outside the chapel, in the hot sun, the black-clad mourners seemed to shine, as polished as ebony rosary beads. 'I distinctly heard' – Aunt Lucia was peering at the sombre gathering, neck stretched like a crowing roos-ter's – 'one of those della Rocca brothers warning Alma about your father's debts. The impertinence ... Mar-cantonio, may he rest in peace, was no saint. Some of those dubious business ventures he got involved with ... we were all worried. But he repaid his debts, of that I'm sure.'

Francesco followed her gaze now as it found the della Rocca brothers. What had they told Alma, these two men who had been his father's greatest friends? What gamble had his father taken that had alarmed them? Francesco wondered whether Father had confided in Alma – had they conspired to keep him in the dark, not to worry him?

He couldn't remember ever being taken into his father's confidence over business matters. Father had always been secretive about his 'investments' – lands bought abroad, construction sites he thought would develop into highly lucrative blocks of flats. Neither wife nor children had been told anything about the deals: the study door was firmly closed, and Father's voice lowered when Barbini, the family's accountant, rang from Torino on business. Immediately after Father's death, Barbini had asked for a meeting, darkly hinting at 'difficulties'. Francesco had postponed it – it had struck him as almost indecent to begin all the money talk before Father was even buried. But at lunch, he would have to confront the small red-haired man in his neat suit and sparkling spectacles, to learn how matters really stood.

Behind Barbini, Alberto della Rocca, impossibly cool and elegant in his dark suit, was whispering into Alma's ear; and Bernardino stood beside them, applying a handkerchief to his eyes, to his forehead, to his spectacles. Bernardino had shared shooting weekends and more than one woman with the dead man: Francesco could see that he was visibly shaken, his eyes fixed upon the marble slab and its fresh inscription: 'Is it my turn next?' they seemed to ask, filled with the panic of an unclean conscience. Francesco felt pity mix with dislike as he surveyed the sober-suited man now blowing his nose. He resolved to speak to Alma after the funeral about the brothers' warnings.

Francesco felt the sun burn his bowed head. He felt tired, thirsty, wretchedly out of place. He wished he could move away from his aunt and her whispers. She stood erect and proud in her role as chief mourner: Aunt Lucia was the eldest of his remaining relatives, and although she lived in Torino, she had organized the Mass, the funeral, everything with due decorum and the least expense, for which he knew he should feel suitably grateful. Yet he resented her curious myopic stare as it swept round the cemetery, her meddling in his grieving, her reminders that financial trouble loomed.

Don Luigi now entered the family chapel. In his wake, with slow footsteps, the living crunched the gravel path to pay their homage to the dead. Aunt Lucia pulled Francesco into the tiny vaulted space. Beneath the ascending Madonna of the frescoed ceiling, the lantern hung, its frosted red panes muting the light of a tiny flickering candle. As Don Luigi intoned the languid litany, Alma stepped into the chapel. Francesco studied his sister while the priest's singsong voice lifted and dropped holy words. She stood behind Don Luigi, locked in silence: her slim, black-clad figure seemed tense, as if unaccustomed to the stillness imposed by mourning. Francesco looked at his sister's bowed head, the long neck visible beneath the cropped dark hair, and felt her distance. His conscience chided him – she'd been left alone to care for their father, she had witnessed the illness from its onset, while he ... but as his thoughts began to search those last few months, he saw Alma raise her head, shake back her hair in the defiant, square-jawed fashion he knew so well. He needn't worry: his sister would survive, she was the heir to their father's lineage, to his strength. And while the likes of himself would vacillate, lose their balance in the struggles of life, Alma would stand stock still, unperturbed by the chaos around her.

Still, he thought as his eyes left her black figure, she

must come back to London with him, stay a while ... he grimaced at the thought of London, where Camilla lay in bed. 'Far too ill to face that horrific journey, I'm afraid,' she had moaned over the telephone yesterday, her little girl's voice taking on an offended tone when he had tried to insist that she come. He could picture her perfectly, lying back against the pillows, her pretty pouting mouth trembling with indignation at the thought of someone trying to force her to fly to Italy – for a funeral, no less. 'Darling, you know how unhappy I become surrounded by all that talk of death and those down-in-the-mouth expressions...'

In the chapel, the lantern shone upon the names of eight generations of Ferratis, black against the white marble slabs. As Alma stared at the wet cement of her father's grave, she thought of how she wished to leave the sombre flock of mourners and walk up the steep hill that rose, blue and distant, to the west. She would have liked to stalk through the long grass and air her loss alone. It was almost a week since her father had died, but she still felt the need for solitude: she did not want to rein in her grief, or to mute it in any way. Only Francesco seemed to belong to her unhappy present: and she had sighed with relief when his wife had rung to say she would not be able to travel, her cold having turned into bronchitis.

Alma stood in the family sepulchre and with her eyes followed the string of names that stretched across the marble, some dead for so long that she didn't even know their stories.

Don Luigi had embarked upon another prayer. Her thoughts returned to the man they were burying, whose dreams, whose hunger for more – more land, more women, more money – were still unsatiated, even at the moment of death. Father's talk had always been of the future – 'one day we shall ...', 'if it's the last thing I do ...' – but the illness had cheated him. Whereas Mother's death (befitting her life) had been a serene passing away, a soft handshake of farewell, Father's was the prising open of fingers that held on, nails digging into the wood of life. Mother had been so conscious, in her piety, of death as giving shape to life, that she had settled her accounts day by day, had done her penance for every evil she thought herself guilty of. But Father had placed all his bets on life rolling on and on.

She looked at Francesco, standing behind Aunt Lucia. He looked so much like their father, the same tall strong frame, the dark eyes beneath heavy brows, the large sensuous mouth. But whereas Father had seemed ever in motion, burning with the need to chase, to capture all that life held, her brother's handsome face was quiet, expressionless, his figure immobile. He seemed to see his role as standing still amidst the rush of life.

'In the name of the Father, the Son, and the Holy Spirit. Amen.' In the chapel, the cluster of mourners echoed Don Luigi's words as they crossed themselves. The priest led them out once again into the hot summer light. The doleful figures, whom her father would have dismissed as 'professional funeral-goers', all crowded round Francesco and herself. She watched them warily, the relatives, friends and villagers whom her aunt had found fitting to invite to share the Ferratis' grief: the sophisticated family friends from Torino looked uniformly elegant in their sober suits and well-polished shoes as they made their way to brother and sister, offering smoothly phrased tokens of grief; the villagers, instead, seemed uncomfortable, subdued, in their stiff black clothes. As if intimidated by the city mourners, they kept to themselves, drawing comfort from the proximity of familiar faces.

'Not everyone is here, I've noticed.' Aunt Lucia sniffed. Her black cotton glove clutched Francesco's elbow. 'Quite a few of your father's friends are missing – though I suppose that's something to be grateful for, when you think about some of those sharks my brother took an inexplicable fancy to ... that endless stream of seedy businessmen your poor mother had to welcome to her drawing room ...' She looked over the dark crowd as if she were casting about a fruit vendor's stall for the perfect product. 'There's that horrid mayor, Battistini, and his poor rag of a wife: look at her, he's wrung her dry, and now he's looking elsewhere for his fun.' Aunt Lucia tugged at her nephew's sleeve to urge him to do the same.

Francesco obediently glanced, with no real interest, at the well-fed figure of the village mayor, Battistini, who, with his haggard wife and son, stood at the forefront of the villagers, as was their due.

'They say he wants the lands.' Aunt Lucia pressed closer to Francesco, and her faint lavender scent for a bewildering moment took him back to childhood, to his mother's arms, so that he found himself staring hard now, at the black-clad throng, the better to remember where he was. 'He'd make a bid for the house, too, if it were for sale.' Here Aunt Lucia looked Francesco over carefully to test for his reaction. Satisfied that her family home was not at risk, she sighed: 'Our property ...'

'Not much left.' He answered her drily.

'My father would turn in his grave at the thought of

that big red oaf swanning about our lands ...' Aunt Lucia sniffed. 'Just how much do you think you'll have to part with? Not the vineyards, I hope – it meant so much to your father and grandfather, to have their own wines ... and the wheat fields – you must keep them, if you sell them to a jumped-up peasant who knows that he might not get it into his head to build some monstrosity right next to our house ... you know, don't you, that an acre was declared good for construction?'

'Yes, yes,' he murmured, 'but as yet I have no idea how much we can keep. I'll talk to Barbini at lunch ...'

'I don't see the widow Lea and her holy daughter.' She was determined to engage him in conversation, her whispers and nudges reminding him that the day ahead included a family luncheon with its predictable talk of spoils to divide, sales to undertake. Why were the dead so quickly disposed of? Where were the funeral pyres?

His eyes now searched the congregated villagers for Santa. Here, among the hypocritical grief, she would bring a stark note of piety. But he could not find her.

Aunt Lucia was moving still closer to him, and again he breathed in the faint lavender scent: 'I worry about your sister, Francesco. She's a difficult girl, you know. Your father was capable of dealing with her – but now ... all those artistic airs and graces put people off ...'

Francesco's eyes returned to his sister, flanked by the della Roccas. Now he spotted behind her Miso Brusoni, the notary's son who had been his only friend in the village. Summer upon summer Miso and Francesco had sat at the feet of the unknown World War II partisan in whose honour the people of San Lorenzo had erected

25

a statue in the midst of their piazza. While the village youngsters enacted their ritual courtship – the boys brazen and loud-mouthed on their motorcycles, the girls coy behind their younger sisters – and drove off to eat pizza in Susa, or to count the shooting stars on the hill by the cemetery, the two boys had talked, sharing their ideals, constructing a utopia they felt sure they would one day inhabit. They spoke of the absolutes – Justice, Liberty, Equality – that would inform their daily lives, and of the important struggle against the evils of greed, selfishness and above all conformity that they would wage. They unfurled great banners of oratory learned from their respective teachers – Benedictines in Miso's case, Jesuits in Francesco's – and when they sought an audience they would go to Gianni er Brutto's courtyard. There, among the tools, the wood chips, the metal scraps and sawdust, they spoke gravely of good and evil, of the meaning of life and of the need to hear your own voice amidst the babel around you. And Gianni er Brutto, bent over Pina the postmistress's bicycle, or one of Vanna's tables, would nod and smile. Every now and then, between the hammering, sawing, filing, he would look up and share with the two youngsters the wisdom gleaned during a lifetime spent watching and listening.

When Francesco had told Miso of his scholarship to the University of London, he'd seen a moment's jealousy light up his friend's black eyes: 'Some people have all the luck,' he'd laughed, looking away from Francesco, and then, 'but even in London, keep looking beyond the pat answers they give you and don't forget we're going to change the world ...' Yet neither had been convinced by his words. They exchanged a few rounds of letters, and

26

then lost touch. Now Miso stood there, his dark figure towering above the mourners, his heavy-browed face wearing a guarded expression. Francesco felt himself fill with a wave of nostalgia for their youthful forging of dreams: he must try to see him during his stay in San Lorenzo.

Don Luigi now made the sign of the cross in a large generous gesture that blessed the whole assembly, breathing and buried alike. Duty done, he moved quickly away, skirts blowing.

No one else seemed to wish to leave the cemetery, although the heat had grown oppressive and the meal hour was fast approaching. Francesco remained impassive as the well-dressed men and women took turns to spend a few moments with him, adopting him with their paternal embraces, their maternal caresses, as a temporary son. 'A real man, your father.' 'This death – it's the end of an era for me ...' 'They don't make them like that any more, do they?'

'May he rest in peace,' he heard a warm voice say behind him. He turned to find Franca Felici, encased in a shiny black suit. Her strong body seemed ready to burst forth out of the fabric, out of the cemetery, rebellious of all this homage to the dead. Life always tugged at Franca's apron strings.

'I hadn't seen you in church, Signora Franca. I'm glad to find you're here after all.'

'I was very fond of your father, Dottore.' Franca smiled, one tooth flashing gold. 'He and I ... we were made of the same stuff, you know: couldn't keep us down for long ... Not many like us left nowadays.' And she surveyed the mourners, the well-groomed important-looking men, the dry beauties in their middle years, the old village men hunched over their canes.

'Alma and I haven't really had a chance to discuss anything with our accountant. We of course want to part with as little of our legacy as possible...' Francesco began. Franca raised a hand to interrupt him: 'Let's not talk of that now. You and your sister are very dear to me.' She surprised him by wrapping him in a tight warm hug and her embrace, strong, confident, brought tears to his eyes for the first time that day.

Turning away, Francesco saw at last the widow Lea and Santarella. They stood on the gravel path, apart from the rest of the mourners. The mother looked as provocative here among the dead and the sorrowful as if she were in an unmade bed. Her curves and long-lashed eyes drew glances from everyone but the mayor's wife, who stared resolutely at her little son.

Santarella, eyes cast down, stood tall and lovely, a step behind her mother. Framed by long black hair, the girl's pale face shone bright. Francesco couldn't breathe as he watched her: memories of those summers when he'd been shyly, hopelessly in love with her rushed to him. She, blind in her innocence, had never realized what torture he underwent whenever he came upon her in her mother's shop (every day, on countless pretexts, staggering his mother's shopping into three or four phases, till she had been forced to send Alma in his stead). There, in the dim light, among the hanging salami and hams, with the smells of cheeses, vegetables and fruits, with customers' orders and the widow's chatting, there among the crates and the scales, the tins and the boxes, Francesco had adored the pale and silent girl.

28

He would stage chance encounters on the road to the river, where she sometimes went at dusk, to stroll alone on the moist banks. Or he would accidentally meet her in the piazza, when she helped her mother move in the crates for the night, and he would come silently to her aid, lifting the heavy boxes effortlessly onto his shoulder, flushing not with the effort but with her smile of gratitude. They had exchanged maybe three full sentences each summer.

He stood in the heat now, watching Santarella at her mother's side, and wondered how she had managed to preserve the same child-like air of wonder, that mystery of someone who can never quite be reached. How old was she now? he wondered: she had been no more than a child when he had first fallen in love with her, but that had been more than a decade ago. And yet, as he saw her today, the sun glazing her dark mantle of hair and the white profile beneath it, she seemed untouched by time.

The villagers came trickling towards him, contributing their polite, reserved condolences. The Mayor Battistini, who felt it his duty to make a speech about the loss of the village's most important landowner, launched into ponderous sentences of communal bereavement, speaking in a slow deliberate voice. But the mourners were growing restless, and no one listened to the mayor: noon had struck. Among the villagers, the housewives began to exchange gossip, heedless of the husbands who, uncomfortable in their tight-fitting Sunday shoes, muttered about hunger pangs. Francesco saw Miso lift a hand in greeting, but before he could move towards his old friend, the mayor came towards him, and Miso had moved on. 'Francesco ...' The mayor approached him.

But now as he drew closer to him, he seemed to grow suddenly timorous and to perform a strange two-step – taking one step back, another forward: this was how Battistini always approached those he regarded as his social superiors – a step back as he remembered his background, his poor insignificant father, the poverty of his childhood; then one forward as he reminded himself of who he was now, a man of means, the mayor of a village, first citizen among a thousand souls ... 'I know that I speak for all of San Lorenzo, my dear boy, when I express my most heartfelt condolences. Your father was a man in a million, superb example of a true gentleman ... He will be sorely missed ...'

The mayor droned on but Francesco was not really listening, as he worried instead about the financial uncertainty he must now confront.

The family friends were looking at their watches, calculating whether they could still be home in time for lunch. It was as though these thoughts of food and of daily rituals reassured them that they were still, thank the Good Lord and all the blessed saints, in good health.

'Francesco.' It was Alberto della Rocca. He placed his hand upon Francesco's sleeve. 'Just a word. Should you or your sister need any assistance – of any kind, financial or otherwise – don't hesitate to let me know.'

Francesco peered into the cool blue eyes, but did not reply. Alberto made as if to add something, but then turned away with a brief wave.

At last, Francesco drew close to his sister, who, face vacant, had stood alone as an identical procession of relatives and friends murmured condolences. 'Let's go, Alma. Hold onto my arm.' She clutched the arm he proffered,

and they moved slowly through the remaining out-
pourings of sympathy that fell about them as temporary
and tepid as a spring rain.

5

Alma closed the gates behind her aunt Lucia's car. She walked slowly back to the front door. The family friends and relatives had stayed on and on, devouring the cold luncheon, chatting about the future, seemingly oblivious of her. She had wished for their departure with all her strength.

She stared up, now, at the beloved face of her house. When she sat in her studio flat in Torino, she pictured the façade as glowing, warm-hued, almost golden. But today, she saw the house as grey-faced, a sadder, worn version of what she imagined in her mind's eye. There were cracks upon this, the southern wall, and dampness stained the paint beneath the window sills, beneath the roof. Some of the ornamental pilasters and window frames were chipped, and the paint had peeled back on the shutters, the balcony railing and the door frame. Towards the ground, the red bricks showed beneath the crumbling plaster – like the slip that shows below a dishevelled woman's skirt.

She stared up at the ancient façade. How she loved this house: even now, the day of her father's funeral, she could draw comfort from its presence, and from the mellow, curved landscape into which it nestled.

Over the hedge she heard a bicycle's bell, two women exchanged greetings: village life would go on, impervious to the changes that befell her family. And she too must go on, would go on...

She returned to the dining room, where beneath the crystal tears of the chandelier sat platters dotted with a few crumbs of prosciutto, salami and cheeses. The late afternoon sun beamed upon the ceiling's frescos, as if to resuscitate their faded garlands of flowers.

Francesco was stacking greasy plates. He had spent almost the entire meal talking, in low tones, to Barbini. While the family friends had eaten with a gusto intended to reassure themselves of their hunger for life, Francesco had learned from Barbini of his worries about the Ferratis' future.

He now approached his sister cautiously, dreading the conversation to come. 'Alma, Barbini is not convinced that he knows about all of Father's debts. He wondered if you had heard anything, whether he himself had ever confided in you about any money worries?'

She had joined him to clear the table, and was brushing the crumbs from the tablecloth into a bread basket. 'No.' She frowned. 'None that I know of. The accountant's told you about the outstanding ones – as far as I know that's all there is.' She spoke slowly, as if loath to clutter their mourning with such petty concerns.

'Aunt Lucia said she overheard Alberto della Rocca warn you about other debts...'

'Oh honestly, that woman's meddling instincts ... only she could turn a funeral into a gossip session ...' Alma shrugged, impatient with him. 'All Alberto said was that towards the end, Father had had to borrow quite a bit to cover some – some investments. Alberto was scared that Father died before he could settle all the debts ... But you know all that, isn't that what Barbini told you?'

'Yes. That's what Barbini said.' He watched Alma bend over the table to pour salt upon a purple wine stain. He spoke quietly, wary lest her indignation engulf him. 'Alma ... he said we'll have to sell all the lands to repay the debts.'

Alma stood up. 'What?!!!' Her dark eyes widened, incredulous. She brought a hand to the table as if to steady herself. 'We can't sell everything ...'

'We have to.' He wiped a tired hand over his brow. 'We need to repay almost 200 million lire. Neither you nor I have that kind of money: even if Camilla and I sold the flat, it would fetch less than that – and in any case, she owns half and she'd never agree to sell our home before the lands here ...'

'Our lands, Francesco!' Alma was shaking her head. 'Our legacy ... our family's owned those lands forever, they're part of who we are ...' She sat down in front of the stack of plates, and buried her face in her hands. She looked suddenly so vulnerable, her thin hands protecting her from the outside world, her black figure trembling. He heard her sob: 'We can't, it's as if we were betraying them ...' And from the linked fingers now came the accusation he had dreaded: 'Why don't you do something?'

Francesco felt the sense of failure seep into him, as remorseless as the rain that had slipped in through the roof tiles, to dampen the bedroom ceilings upstairs. Money. Whenever money talk began, he felt judged, and found wanting: it had been like that with Father: 'My son the philosopher!' Father would roll his eyes when

34

Francesco would come to him with yet another existential question. 'Don't you understand all these whys and wherefores won't keep you in the style I've accustomed you to?' And then, when, years later, Francesco had announced his decision to become a publisher: 'Why publishing, when our family's always invested in land?' He had turned to Mother, who sat reading beneath the persimmon tree, on the white and green canvas deck chair. 'This is all your fault. It's because you've been putting ideas into his head about your father who scribbledscribbledscribbled and died so poor he doesn't have a stone to mark his grave ...' And Father waved his cigarette like a sinister wand that might soon transform his son into a bird or a mouse.

But Francesco had been carrying out his silent rebellion since his youth when, at the foot of his mentors – the Jesuits at school, Gianni er Brutto in the village – he had sought something that could explain how life was to be lived. Implicit in his exploration, he now realized, was a rejection of his father's world. He could not lead life as a hunt, as Marcantonio did, or as a thrilling gamble against great odds. He could not content himself with the here and now, with the sensual pleasures that Father always sought – in his meals, in his bed, in his possessions.

He had gone into publishing, and stayed away from San Lorenzo, finding himself a home and then a wife in London. But in the end, even there, he had not escaped the grasp of money: Camilla always seemed to want something beyond their means, and to aspire to a lifestyle his salary could not afford.

Now he winced at his sister's unspoken reprimand: surely, had he been a man of his father's stature, the

Ferrati lands would never need to be sold. If he had been a man like Marcantonio, he would have been able to take care of Alma, to protect her from money talk and worries.

'We can't sell the vineyards ... they've been ours for generations. And the beetroot fields ... The Ferrati lands have always stretched from Susa to San Lorenzo.' She was looking at him now, from her seat across the table. Her eyes, almond-shaped, coal black, glistened with tears. 'We're no one without our property, no one.'

'Alma, it's no easier for me, I can assure you. But Barbini said if we could sell them for 250, we'd have enough money left over for us not to have to worry about selling this house...'

'Our home!' She shot up in anger, and strode to the end of the table where she had left her cigarettes and ashtray. She lit a cigarette, her back to him. Then she turned to face her brother, arms crossed, cigarette in one hand. 'If I have to beg for money on the streetcorners of Torino, I won't ever let you sell this house.' She flashed him a look so confrontational he dropped his gaze.

'Alma,' he murmured, 'I am not against you ... we both want the same thing...'

But his sister would not listen to him. 'Think of the pride our father, our forefathers took in this legacy, think of the sacrifices they made to keep the property in the family, for generations ... who are we anywhere else? This is where we belong, this is the beginning and the end of every Ferrati's life...' She drew heavily on her cigarette, one thin hand waving in the air.

'Barbini says...'

'Yes, what does that man propose?' She pushed her hair

back from her furrowed brow. 'Surely he's come up with some idea...?'

Francesco did not want to share with his sister the family accountant's indignant splutterings: 'Typical of your father, I must say: he was always high-handed with his creditors, as if in borrowing their money he were doing them a favour. The creditor's hopping mad, I can tell you. We'd best move quickly, I'm not sure he's got much patience left with the Ferratis ... your father really had no sense once he fell in love with one of his wildeyed schemes.' Francesco looked at his sister's hollowed cheeks, at her nervous fingers as they clenched the cigarette. He would spare her the family accountant's verdict. 'Barbini – what can he advise us? He's an accountant, not a financial genius. He said Father borrowed 200 million, to buy a piece of land down south.' Francesco paused. 'No one knows what happened with the project, but he hadn't repaid the loan when he died. According to Barbini there's no money for us to inherit – just the debt.'

Alma shot him a look. 'How do you propose we proceed, then?'

'We stand a better chance to get a good price from the people around here...'

'Yes. They'll see our lands as their status symbol,' Alma said bitterly.

'We could use that to our advantage – it will push up the price. We know that both the mayor and Franca want to bid for the lands ... and Barbini's been approached by the butcher Romeo.'

'Already! Before we could even bury Father ...' She stubbed out her cigarette in the ashtray before her.

'It's hurtful, I agree. Barbini, to his credit, didn't want

37

to tell me anything until later this week ... but I figured it was important to have all the cards before us now.'

Alma cast him a scornful look. 'You mean so that you could rush back home and leave all this behind.'

'Alma ...' he protested, but her anger was stronger than his instinct to defend himself. As ever, her outbursts shocked him into passive silence. He'd felt that same sense of powerlessness when he'd argued with Father – their passion, their energy spilled over to swamp him.

'Well it's true, isn't it?' Her voice rose till its strain was almost as painful as the words she cast at him. 'You talk as if this weren't your property, your legacy, we were putting up for sale ... you talk as if Father's death were just a prelude to our worries ...'

'That's simply not true.' He met her tear-filled eyes. His sister lowered hers, and again buried her face in her hands. 'I'm sorry, Francesco, I'm so sorry ... I feel so helpless, and so full of unhappiness ... don't listen to a thing I say.'

Francesco moved beside her. He took out his handkerchief and slowly wiped his sister's face dry of tears. 'Don't worry. I'll stay on ...'

Alma nodded, silent.

'I'll get you some water shall I?' His voice and look were anxious.

She nodded assent, but only because she knew he sought release from this confrontation. She watched him walk away, and withdrew to the open window. She stared out at the green garden beyond. The sun had slipped behind the curves of the hills. The evening breeze brought to her the voices of San Lorenzo: Don Luigi's church bell tolled six, the tractors rumbled in distant fields, the housewives, hidden by the walnut and hazelnut trees, exchanged greetings as they made their slow way towards the widow Lea's shop, or the butcher Romeo's, or the baker Nuccio's ... She heard the litany of the farmyard animals, the barking of watchful dogs, the chorus of invisible crickets.

Her home. How fiercely she resented her brother's talk of selling the lands. This was her own beloved refuge. Here she could seek solace from her dissatisfaction with life in Torino, where amidst bonds of faint friendships and half-hearted gestures of solidarity from distant relatives, she found herself ill at ease. Increasingly, over the past few years, she had found herself returning to this, the world she knew best: to this house, to San Lorenzo, to her home, where in endless conversations with her father, she remembered who she was and what she wanted to be.

'Here, have a drink of water.' Francesco stood before her.

She bowed her head, and suddenly the grief she had feared all day took possession of her, and the sobs that burst forth were so painful that she bent double before her brother's impotent figure.

6

Francesco could hear his sister whistling as she dressed next door. She seemed to have cast off – as indeed he had known she would – the grief that had stunned her those first days after their father's death. The funeral had taken place only a week ago, but already Alma had made her way back to the very centre of life, from where their father's death had torn her. They'd quickly buried the memory of her outburst, and had spent the week tiptoeing around each other, as if fearful of waking more quarrels.

A distant rumble drew his gaze from the garden to the road beyond: a row of caravans wound its way towards San Lorenzo. It was the gypsies, of course: every summer they moved from village to village among the hills, to set up the Ferris wheel, the tombola, the shooting alley, the wheel of fortune and the dance floor that made up the village 'festa' – to celebrate the day consecrated to the village patron saint. It must be the 10th of August, the day of San Lorenzo – and neither he nor Alma had remembered. How many summers he and Alma had waited for the 'festa': you were scrubbed by Mother and Rina, strapped into tight and proper clothes, forced into patent leather shoes, warned not to wander from the piazza. His heart ached now at the memory of Rina running about all day, locking the doors, shutting the windows, 'because you know what happens when those good-for-nothing gypsies are around!'; of Mother running a wet comb through his hair and then pressing a kiss upon his forehead; of Father bringing him into the garden to practise his horseshoe throw – 'I want you to win a prize – it's important you know, every now and then, to prove yourself.' And all those preparations would lend the summer evening an even more magical air, so that he felt intoxicated the moment he stepped out into the busy street, Alma's hand clutching his: the spinning of the Ferris wheel, the fireworks that exploded in the black sky, the candyfloss sold by women with hoop earrings and bright red mouths ... And even Father and Mother had come down to the piazza, to take a turn on the dance floor: for once, they seemed to belong to one another, pressed together in a slow waltz.

He turned from the open window and moved towards his bed. Above him a golden-haired Madonna was kissing her little son, oblivious to the plump-cheeked cherubim who looked on like winged orphans yearning for her embrace. How often he had lain back on this bed, stared up at the perfect rondo of those figures. How different, the earthy, curvaceous woman on his bedroom ceiling from the wife he had left behind in London. Camilla. His hand reached for the telephone: he would ring Camilla, see how she was: he only half-believed that she had developed bronchitis – her illnesses seemed to strike whenever she was required to do something against her will. But even before he'd raised the handset he had changed his mind: he had nothing new to tell her, after all, and her voice over the telephone would prove no comfort. He sighed, lay back on the bed. When had it changed: the giggling, pink-cheeked girl who hung on his arm and his every word; the proudly possessive fiancée who thumbed her nose at her father's disapproval of marriage with a foreigner? When had this Camilla disappeared to make way for the wife he had grown estranged from?

More than a year, now, of arguments about money, ambition, the future: 'Why don't you care,' she would burst out, 'that everyone else we know is better off than us? Oh God, if only I'd known what I was letting myself in for!'

Marriage. The silent fury, the snide asides, the spiteful words. And the stranglehold it kept you in. Even when she was not there, marriage's Saturn rings revolved around him, keeping him well within their sphere of influence, so that every deed and consideration was coloured by Camilla.

'Marriage,' Father had warned, 'means putting on spectacles to find that the young beauty you had seen through a myopic gaze is a hard-faced hag.'

'Marriage is like this,' Gianni er Brutto had told him, spinning the wheel of the postmistress Pina's bicycle. 'It can only work when both wheels move in the same direction.'

Had he and Camilla ever moved in the same direction? He no longer knew.

He heard Alma calling him: today they were to go to Franca's, to discuss her bid for the lands. The Ferratis had already received two formal proposals, one from the butcher Romeo, one from the mayor. He shook himself and went downstairs.

42

'Do you realize,' he told her as they locked the front door, 'that I just saw the gypsies making their way to the piazza? Tonight's the festa. It's San Lorenzo.'

'The festa!' For a moment, Alma was as wide-eyed with excitement as she had been when a little girl. 'Oh Francesco, to think we had completely forgotten the festa ...' But she shook her head. 'Though I don't think even I could muster the necessary enthusiasm tonight ... it's still too soon ...'

They walked in silence in the shade of the cypress trees, then out through the green gates. Franca lived on the other side of the village, but instead of taking the main road, brother and sister took the narrow path that bordered the south side of San Lorenzo, linking their vineyards with Franca's. The river flowed invisible beyond rows of blackberry bushes and silver birches: they could hear the soft movement of its waters, a cool continuous music amidst the silence of noon. They walked past a large brick farmhouse whose courtyard sent wafts of rabbit hutches, of chickens, of cooking. A woman, hair wrapped in a kerchief, was taking the linen from the laundry line that stretched between two apricot trees. Distant and blue, the hills rose against a light-filled backdrop that could be the skies or the Alps.

'Do you know how often I have painted this scene?' Alma's arm stretched before them as if she were ushering her brother into her rooms. 'I feel as if I've claimed this as my own, this landscape, this village. My comfort and my inspiration.' He saw her long, almond-shaped eyes fill with tears: he placed a hand on her shoulder. 'There is no place as beautiful, is there?' Suddenly she stopped and looked up at him. 'We must keep the house, Francesco. I understand we have to sell the lands – but never the house.'

'Never,' he repeated, imitating her decisive tone.

'Good day.' Pina the former postmistress pedalled past them, on her way to delivering a few precious nuggets of gossip to Vanna: Nuccio the baker and his wife had quarrelled so violently last night that he'd been forced to sleep at Miso the notary's house; and she'd heard from the mayor's poor wife that he was livid with rage because the butcher Romeo was bidding against him for the Ferratis' land; and they said Beppe, Franca's first-born, had been shown the door by his fiancée.

'Good day.' Alma smiled. She looked up at Francesco beside her. 'Village life goes on anyway.'

'Yes ... I sometimes wonder if this place doesn't hold all the most important lessons ... perhaps I should come back and learn anew.'

She squeezed his arm affectionately. 'You mustn't talk of coming back. You must move forward, always. There are so many good things still to come.'

'Well ...' He looked straight ahead, at the bleached path before them. 'I've closed a few doors behind me haven't I?'

'Gaining quite a lot in the process, seems to me – pretty wife, solid career prospects – most people would be happy to trade places with my big brother.'

He smiled at her calling him her 'big brother': though he was five years older, his protective manner towards her had always struck him as unconvincing. She did not need any assistance in her march through life – and certainly not from him. 'I want you to come and stay with us in London for a while.' Francesco's voice rose over the

44

tolling of noon. 'You could rest there, meet a few people.'

Alma nodded: 'Yesyesyes.' She kept walking. 'But you needn't worry about me. I am twenty-six, I can earn my living, I never feel lonely. I'll manage.' She shot him a smiling look.

'Yes. You always do.' And, as if in truth she needed no support from him, he lifted his hand from her shoulders, and moved slightly away from her.

'In a way' – Alma ran a hand through her short dark hair – 'it will probably do me good, you know, not being able to rely on him – I was always rushing back here from Torino every time I needed money or reassurance. I'll probably end up working far harder.'

They were approaching Franca's gates. Beyond them, tidy fertile land stretched as far as the eye could see. Well-tended, well-nourished, the fields of corn and beetroot broke the plane in rows of crops and earth. Kerchiefed women and cap-crowned men moved back and forth among the corn, among the beetroot leaves. The farmers bent to weed the soft earth near the plants, to inspect leaves for the fraying caused by worms, or for the brown splotches of disease.

Two lean guard dogs now cantered towards the visitors: they pushed their muzzles between the iron bars of the forbidding gate and then barked to alert the family and the whole village of the arrival.

'Here you are, Dottor Francesco' – Franca came out of the kitchen into her courtyard – 'and the signorina too, welcome, welcome.'

Alma studied the broad woman before her: from the round, ruddy face shone the sharp blue eyes from which there was no hiding; the black hair that was greying at

45

the temples was pulled back with the combs she remembered in Rina's small bun; beneath the large, masculine nose spread a wide grin.

Behind Franca, laid out on the gravel that skirted her house, rows of tomatoes ripened in the sun. She wiped her hands on her apron and opened the gates, all the while barking back at the dogs to keep their peace. 'You're not eating properly, signorina.' Franca shook her head. 'All skin and bone is no way for a pretty girl to be.'

Alma smiled but did not reply. Her brother behind her, she followed the large matron into the house.

'Come in, signorini, I was just finishing the sauce for lunch. Everyone's here, somewhere in the house.' And she made a large gesture, as though the house were much too big to be encompassed by a more restricted arm movement. 'But when I cook I don't want anyone peering over my shoulders, you know how it is. I won't allow even the girls to set foot in the kitchen, once I get started.'

Alma stood away from the stove, watching her brother and Franca chatting over the saucepans: every modern appliance filled the square room, gleaming hard and white next to the ancient fireplace, the low wooden table, the sturdy chairs. A calendar in which St Francis stood feeding some sparrows hung near the door, and above it, a crucifix sported dusty palm leaves from Palm Sunday. The tile floor, the window panes, the appliances: everything shone with the cleanliness achieved only by constant work. Garlic strings hung next to the stove, and dry herbs, pots of basil and a bunch of parsley in a jar of water lined the spotless counter. Beneath the large white towel that covered half the kitchen table she could make out the soft mounds of freshly made tagliatelle.

Franca lifted the lid off a pot, dipped a long wooden spoon inside the thickening sauce, and smiled at Alma. 'Why don't you have a taste, signorina?' She handed her the spoon. 'It's nothing sophisticated, just a bit of garlic, a few basil leaves, half a hot pepper thrown in and my tomatoes ... taste it and tell me what you think.'

Alma, obedient, bent over the spoon: she smiled at the sweet spicy scent that brought her back to her childhood kitchen and Rina's jealously guarded secret recipes. She carefully tasted the sauce, then issued every noise of approval she could muster.

'Good, eh?' And Franca turned to Francesco. 'You see, Dottore, I went to school until I was only ten, so I'm not much good at reading or writing – but cooking and a few other things I can manage.'

'Don't be so modest, Signora Franca,' Francesco laughed, 'we know that there isn't a farmer round here who wouldn't trade everything in the world to be in your shoes: you've bought more lands, more fields than the rest of the villagers put together.'

Franca took out one of her combs, pulled it through her hair, then fixed it once again above her nape, grinning all the while at the memory of all those deals she had single-handedly made since her husband's stroke, more than thirty years before. She smiled and displayed her gold tooth at the thought of the anger and the hurt machismo of her male competitors as they watched the noisy, pur-poseful progress of Franca Felici across acres of wheat, corn, beetroots, across hills of vines, as undeterred in her conquests as one of her tractors. And now, if she sealed the sale of the Ferratis' lands, what wouldn't they say in the village? And she clucked with satisfaction, like a well-fed hen.

'Come through, signorini, let's have a drink: a glass of my new wine, a bit sweet, but nice.' She led them through the beaded curtain that separated the kitchen from the living room.

This room was her pride and joy, and neither her children nor her grandchildren were allowed to set foot in it without her express permission. The shutters were always kept drawn, against the dust of the courtyard, and the room smelled of the beeswax with which, at the turn of every season, she polished the dark heavy arms of her tapestried armchairs. She'd spent more on the chandelier than on the lawn mower, as she never failed to remind her progeny. On the marble-topped chest of drawers sat a row of ancient photographs of her in-laws and her own parents, the laced kerchief that held the sugared almonds from her granddaughter Luisa's First Communion, and the silver harmonica which Tommaso had serenaded her with in their courting days. While brother and sister sat in silence, Franca took out glasses, a bottle, a corkscrew, her gestures big and generous, her voice unwavering. 'The best wine for more than two hundred kilometres, that's what they say, have a taste and see for yourselves.' With a quick strong jerk of the elbow Franca uncorked the bottle and poured the yellow wine. She handed them their glasses, then settled her broad body on a thin-legged chair between them. 'Eh, Dottore, it hasn't been such a good harvest this year. The Good Lord, he didn't think we had enough troubles down here, so he poured down rain and hail all winter. My fields were as stiff as shirt cuffs.'

Alma listened to Franca as she served up the warm soporific rite of hospitality, speaking of crops, prices, weather. It was, she knew, merely the overture: Franca was like the mother of a bed-ridden child who plumps the pillow behind his fevered head, tucks in the blankets round his limbs, freshens his brow with a damp sponge, and then finally tells him just how long his confinement will be.

'Eh, when my poor Tommaso had his stroke' – here Franca turned her eyes heavenward, to ask the Lord once again for his reasoning – 'only Jesus knows how much I cried. There I was, with six children, tiny tiny they were. . . . I was still weaning Tino, with a farm to run, and a husband flat on his back upstairs with a face that looked like Death itself had kissed it . . .' And she crossed herself at the memory. 'I could have filled the well in my court-yard with my tears, signorini. But who can afford to mourn like that, eh? You have to keep moving, you dig here' – and she tapped her heart – 'and here' – her index finger touched her temple – 'and you pull out all the strength you have. No one gives you a hand, you're all alone in your misfortunes. No one likes to look unhap-piness in the face: they're nice to you when your hus-band's healthy, when you've got a roof over your head and money under your mattress, but God help you if you've got misfortune in your life.' Franca shook her head. 'You stand alone when your luck runs out . . .' She allowed them a pause here. And then she placed her hands, thick fingers linked, on the table. Her eyes stared into Francesco's. 'Well, shall we discuss our business then?'

Francesco and Alma looked at each other: gone was

the chatty manner, gone the echoes of past troubles and present wisdoms. Franca's heavy face and body revealed the tension of clever bargaining: eyes steady upon Francesco, voice warm but determined, she swept through the flaws of their lands with the same unwavering fervour with which she would have cleaned her house for a guest's visit. The wheat fields were practically worthless, because for years they'd gone untended; the beetroot fields had suffered visibly from last winter's frost, and would yield only half a crop this autumn; there were also predictions about the forthcoming winter being a particularly difficult one ... all in all, Franca let them understand, the lands could not fetch a great price. 'I'll take them for 220 million lire. Not a lira more.' Franca placed her hands palms down on the table.

Francesco, cheeks slightly flushed, set down his glass. 'I'm not sure we agree on the price, Signora Franca ... perhaps the best thing to do now is for us to hear what the other prospective buyers are offering.'

Franca spread out her great golden smile: 'Of course you must hear out all the bidders. But I can tell you here and now how much each is prepared to offer you.' She savoured their attention with the same expression with which, after throwing a few basil leaves and a few chopped garlic cloves into her pot, she would have tasted her sauce: 'The mayor talks big, but in fact he can't afford more than 200 million – and that's if he tightens his belt and settles down to a difficult year. The butcher could probably offer a little more, but the man never knows his own mind, and before he would decide to match my offer we'd all be toothless and white-haired. The truth is, signorini, the only one around here who can afford to buy your lands at a suitable price, and who will do so now, is me.'

Alma stared at her brother: she could read in Francesco's face the sudden anxiety, and could see his distaste at having to bargain over something they loved.

'I don't think,' Francesco began, cautious, articulating each word as though it contained a chain of difficult sounds, 'that Alma and I wish to postpone the sale of the lands. However, 220 million is quite a bit less than we'd decided upon. We had estimated 250 – the beetroot fields alone were priced at 180 by Franzoni from Susa last year . . .'

'How would Franzoni know the true value of a piece of land, anyway?' Franca shrugged. 'The man's never had anything but soap under his fingernails.'

'Be that as it may' – Francesco lowered his voice, kept it free of emotion – 'that's the figure he came up with, and the figure we're going by.'

'You drive a hard bargain, Dottore.' Franca's gold teeth gleamed. 'But I like you both and I cared for your father, so I'll come up – 230, and that's my very last offer.'

'But . . . !' Alma exploded, angry eyes upon her brother.

He frowned at Alma, and pressed his index to his lips. Franca stood up. 'I'll give that sauce of mine another stir while the two of you have a think . . .' She stepped back through the beaded curtains.

'She's mad, it's far too little, we can't let her get away with it . . .' Alma's anger had blanched her face.

'Shshsh.' He nodded towards the doorway through which their hostess had disappeared. 'Calm down.'

'I won't calm down!' his sister exploded again. 'We

decided we wouldn't sell at under 250. We mustn't give in to these people ...'

'But remember what the mayor said only last week – he won't go above 200. The butcher was even lower, and don't forget that Barbini warned me that this year land prices have taken a knock. We also cannot delay paying back the loan ... the man in Genoa's rung Barbini twice already.'

'Francesco, it's a big difference: 20 million ...' Alma kept shaking her head.

'Let me see what I can do ...' But he saw she did not look any more convinced than he felt. His father's ghost hovered over the room, judging him: would he, could he, stand up to the indomitable Franca?

Franca returned, eyes smiling, face beaming. 'That sauce is going to be delicious, if I may say so myself ...'

Francesco cleared his throat: 'I'm afraid, Signora Franca, 230 strikes both me and my sister as unacceptable. We shall wait a while longer before selling the lands ... We can afford to wait, after all.'

Franca smiled pleasantly, wiped her hands on her apron. She slowly removed one of her combs, patted her hair, pulled the comb through it and pinned it behind her ear. 'Yes I can imagine that you can wait. Tell me, dottore, what if I came up five? We could make it 235, and seal a bargain.'

Francesco didn't move. He felt Franca's irresistible will pulling at him, tearing down all resistance. His eyes sought his sister: Alma was staring at him, face set. 'No,' she mouthed, her eyes boring into him. He felt as if they were children again, and she, the younger one, was as usual pulling him in her wake, impatient with his slow, deliberate steps. Slowly, he said, 'No.' He felt himself swell with the look of pride he saw on his sister's face.

'Dottore, Dottore …' Franca shook her head. 'How can I hope to satisfy you without forgetting that I have to feed my brood, keep a roof above our heads, and keep a bit under my mattress to see us through a bad winter?' But her jaw jutted forth: brother and sister saw that she meant to have their lands. '240 then, dottore. And not a lira over.'

Francesco looked over at Alma, who gave an imperceptible nod. He turned back again to Franca and smiled. 'Done.'

'Done!' Franca clapped her hands in delight. Then her wide grin appeared, its gold tooth shiny with glee. 'And remember, Dottore, that should the time ever come when you might consider selling the house …' – from her seat Alma made a motion, as if to interrupt – 'I shall offer you the best price for that, as well. That house is almost as much a landmark of my days here in San Lorenzo as it is for the two of you … when I was struggling to make ends meet, I would pass by your father's house – and in my eyes I suppose it will always be his house – and think: this is what I want, this is where I can get to …' She looked over at Alma, her blue gaze kind. 'Don't misunderstand me, signorina, I would be the first one to wish that the great house remains in Ferrati hands – but it's always been one of my dreams. And' – here she lowered her voice to a whisper – 'you never know, you can never predict what fate will bring. There may well be a moment in your lives when to sell the house is your only alternative … But for your sakes' – she beamed at them her gold-toothed smile once more – 'I hope that moment never comes.'

Francesco shook his head. 'Let's not place the cart

53

before the horse, Signora Franca. The lands are one thing. The house ... it's a different matter ... we were born there, we spent every summer there. If the two of us can manage without selling it, we shall ...'

'We'll never sell the house.' Alma interrupted him, and her dark eyes were cold and hostile as they rested upon the woman before her.

But Franca quickly smoothed down the ruffled feathers: 'Of course, signorina, of course.' Her voice slipped into the cosy warmth of the humble housewife receiving honoured guests. 'Let's drink a toast to our friendship, the three of us then!' And she poured more wine into their glasses. 'Cin cin.'

As if a mealtime gong had sounded, the house suddenly filled with echoing footsteps, cries and laughter, and the Felici clan poured down the stairs, ran in from the courtyard, rushed in from the vineyards to surround their mother and the two guests. Franca's four bull-like sons in their undershirts, her pregnant daughter, two timid, weary daughters-in-law: all congratulated Francesco and Alma, as though the deal they had just agreed to were to their great advantage. They helped themselves to the wine, cooed their best wishes, asked a million questions about Francesco's life in London and Alma's days in Torino.

Then, above the din, the plaintive voice of the paralysed Signor Felici rose from his hidden domain: 'Come and take me, Beppe! Gigi! I want to come too!' The two largest sons disappeared upstairs, to return with their father in their arms, his woollen cover trailing the floor.

The villagers heard of Franca's latest acquisition within hours. Beppe Felici went to play billiards that evening, and boasted to the butcher Romeo of his mother's deal. The butcher moaned about the matter to Vanna the innkeeper, who in turn told the Marshal Ciuffi, who lost no time in telling the Mayor Battistini, who that night, above the widow Lea's gleaming body, screamed out his anger.

7

The year following Marcantonio Ferrati's death brought turmoil to the habitually peaceful life of San Lorenzo. It all started one Sunday, a few weeks after the sale of the Ferrati lands to Franca Felici. Standing in his pulpit, portly body framed by ethereal winged angels, Don Luigi clasped his hands and joyfully intoned: 'My dear brethren, after some careful review, and following great deliberation, I have decided to share with you some momentous news. Santarella, whom all of you know to be a girl of supreme goodness, honesty and sterling virtue, has for some time now shared with us the magnificent news that Our Lady speaks to her.' Here the priest drew himself tall in his white and black cassock and paused, for extra emphasis.

'Yes, one of our own has been chosen by Our Lord's Mother to be the channel of her messages. This is indeed glorious news for our little village: not only is it a blessing upon our heads, but, more important, the visitations offer us, the faithful, a wonderful challenge: we have been invited to honour Our Blessed Lady. How can we do so?' Again he paused for effect, and his eyes swept the upturned faces assembled before him. There was an audible intake of breath. The older women stopped their fans, the men cocked their heads the better to hear and even the children stood quite still, at attention. 'We can build a shrine in the name of our Mother.'

'A shrine! A shrine!' The word echoed beneath the vaults, floated like incense under the newly restored frescos, rose like the ascending blue-veiled Madonna on the triptych beyond the altar.

'We shall build the shrine to honour Mary, Mother of God, and in so doing, we shall earn ourselves happiness and glory.'

After Mass that morning, as the widow Lea was locking up behind the notary's widow (as a favour to Carla Brusoni, she had opened her shop and sold her a quarter pound of Fontina for her son Miso's lunch) she found herself suddenly surrounded by a group of excited, gesticulating villagers. 'Lea!' The former postmistress Pina, still holding her rosary beads in her tiny little hands, addressed her first: 'Lea, Don Luigi's told us the wonderful news ... about your daughter's visions ...' A murmur of happy expectation rose from the group.

The widow turned to face them. Her worst fears had been realized. Hands on hips, she spat: 'Go away, the lot of you, and tell that priest to stop using my poor innocent daughter to get himself noticed by his bishop!'

'But Lea! We shall build a shrine! There, in San Lorenzo!' Nuccio the baker stepped forward, a joyful expression on his flour-white face.

'Oh please!' The widow raised both arms heavenward, and shook them at a God who was having his fun at her expense. 'Can't you dimwits see that Don Luigi's just chasing a bishopric? He's known about Santa's visions for years, and only now that Bishop Natti is looking for an auxiliary does he decide to reveal all. Can't you see that all he wants is to use the shrine to become even more puffed up with self-importance than he is already?!' And with that the widow turned on her heels and disappeared into the low-ceilinged shop.

Despite the widow's attempts to cool their ardour, the villagers' enthusiasm grew unchecked. Since Don Luigi's revelation, nothing seemed the same. New alliances were forged, strange betrayals took place, new heroes emerged.

Everyone, it seemed, stood to profit from the holy girl's miraculous conversations: a shrine would attract pilgrims the world over. Throngs would come and feel the Grace that had touched this corner of the earth.

In the evenings, when houses trapped the heat, the men slipped away from their wives to the coolness of the piazza, and plans and dreams of a wonderful new future took over from their daily chores.

'Do you realize,' the butcher Romeo addressed the men outside Vanna's bar, 'that I'll have to multiply my stock tenfold if all these pilgrims arrive? I'll have to get myself a new freezer ...' And the butcher's big hands rubbed together at the prospect of feeding the multitudes.

'The faithful will feed on manna from heaven. They won't need your meats, fool!' Old Rocco, sitting next to Gianni er Brutto, spat his cynicism onto the pavement.

'Vanna and I are drawing up a list of all the supplies we'll have to order.' Claudio ignored the Sicilian. 'More of everything, not just food but toiletries and picnic stuff ... and last night I had an idea: why not sell plastic mementoes – you know, miniature Madonnas, small vases for the blessed water, rosary beads.'

'Claudio, you and your Vanna can buy all the supplies

you want, but once the pilgrims find out that the widow Lea is the visionary's mamma, they'll storm her doors not yours.'

'Rocco, you're nothing but a bird of ill omen!' The baker Nuccio thumped a hairy fist onto the card table and the creases in his dough-like face deepened. 'Do you understand how important this whole thing is for us all? Take my case for instance: why, I'll need to open a new oven, just to keep up with the orders ... Jesus Blessed Mary, we'll all become millionaires!' And Nuccio rocked back and forth in his chair with a happy smile.

'The shrine's just like everything else – the only ones who'll make money are the ones who already have it ...' and Rocco shook his head at the foolishness of the men around him. 'God help those responsible for filling your heads with dreams like this one!' the old Sicilian shouted, and pointed at the principal architects of the future shrine.

There they stood, as was their wont, in a little cluster, slightly apart from the rest of the villagers: the Mayor Battistini, the Marshal Ciuffi and, an imprimatur on the enterprise, Don Luigi. Not a day passed without this trio laying down some new plan for San Lorenzo. So much to do, so much to change ...

Every day you could watch these men of ambition stroll through the village, walking its length and width as though they were tailors casting a measuring eye upon a difficult client's shape. You could see the mayor, squat, fleshy, red-faced, striding along between his comrades: fist in hand behind his back, head held high, the mayor strolled through San Lorenzo as though an empire's fate had been placed upon his wide shoulders. He listened to his advisers' words, now nodding assent, now raising an eyebrow in disagreement. No matter what doubts may have followed him to his wife's and mistress's beds, the mayor's public face never betrayed any anxiety. To his advisers he confided that 'In politics, nerves are weakness. And weakness means defeat.' Rocking back and forth on his heels, the Mayor Battistini would explain that 'slowly slowly the shrine will unite the people of San Lorenzo behind us.'

At the mayor's side waddled Don Luigi. The priest's heart beat with joy at the miraculous happenings that had occurred in his parish. And, may God forgive a little personal pride, Don Luigi welled over with satisfaction beneath his flowing cassock. Had he not told those faithless farmers that they should pay as much attention to the spiritual stuff of life as they did to the seeds, rains and soils? Had he not warned them that Cain, too, had been a tiller of fields, and that with such ancestry they had best watch their ways? Had he not pleaded with them – or rather, with their wives, who attended his sermons while their husbands spent Sunday in Vanna's bar, watching football on television and quarrelling over the billiards table – to pray and attend Mass, lest the burning flames of hell meet their coffins as they were lowered into the ground?

What sweet satisfaction Don Luigi gleaned these days, when the little church filled at the calling of his bells! What smiles he wore behind the grille of the confessional as he recognized more and more voices from the village, voices he had not heard whisper guilt for two decades and more! And when the collection baskets made their rounds, how rewarding to watch these stingy parishioners drop notes and coins inside! 'The Good Lord has waited patiently,' Don Luigi would explain to his faithful housekeeper Rosina, 'and so have I: we are both reaping the benefit of our wisdom. The people of San Lorenzo have had their faith renewed by the miraculous occurrences, and their new-found belief will fuel our joint enterprise – the shrine.'

But, of the trio, it was the Marshal Ciuffi who seemed to have benefited the most from recent events: his eyes shone bright as medals these days, his moustache seemed fuller, and his cane seemed a mere decoration as the old soldier's stride regained its determination. He listened to every word that fell from his general's lips, and encouraged every plan of Battistini's. When news of San Lorenzo's visionary spread to the villages of the nearby hills, the marshal busied himself with reading each new article to the village men, before gluing it into an old stamp album. 'Our campaign will succeed!' the marshal would exclaim at every new article on Santa. 'Victory is round the corner!' And his voice, once tremulous with disappointed hopes – his eldest son had proved such a good-for-nothing, his campaign for mayor had brought him only humiliation at the hands of Bettino – now shot out like a rifle's bullets.

Harmony and camaraderie, the special friendship that buds among those men who share the beginning of a profitable venture, linked the three men, fortifying them against hapless cynics. And their energy and optimism cast its net over most of the village, so that, like so many fish, the farmers, grocers, innkeepers allowed themselves to be trawled into the plans.

And, despite the scorn of a smattering of non-believers (Old Rocco and his cronies) and the indifference of a few

(Franca Felici and her brood), the atmosphere of contentment and optimism that the triumvirate bred began to infiltrate the narrow roads and inner courtyards of San Lorenzo.

By the arrival of the first snows, the dream of the shrine had spread a thick protective mantle upon the day-to-day life of the villagers: hardships were now dismissed with gaiety – 'Don't fret now, soon the shrine will be up ...' – and disappointments muted by talk of future success. The people of San Lorenzo, who were used to looking to their past for clues of their own future; to the weather for predictions of what they would reap this year; to weddings, christenings and the patron saint's feast for their celebrations, now found, in the prospect of the shrine, a new focus for their efforts and hopes.

Their common dream seemed so vivid to the villagers, that already the shrine was as real as the inn, the piazza, or Don Luigi's church. It took the triumvirate's greatest efforts, therefore, to explain to their excited followers that Mother Church worked at a leisurely pace, and that the shrine could not be built overnight. It took centuries to canonize a saint, decades to join the ranks of the blessed: how then could they hope to receive an instant authorization for the building of the shrine? Why, they would first have to convince Bishop Natti in Torino, then the other bishops in the archdiocese, then Rome itself as to the truth of Santarella's visions. How long before the young visionary's state of grace convinced the men of the cloth that yes, a miracle had occurred in that insignificant village, San Lorenzo?

'It might take years, maybe our whole lifetime, before the bishops recognize Santa's words as true ...' explained

Don Luigi in the warmth of Vanna's bar to those men who, huddled round the tables with their glasses of grappa, sought his view. 'The bishops must be certain that we, the people of San Lorenzo, are not interested in mercenary activities, but rather in honouring Our Lady and Her Church.'

'Well, mercenary or not,' the mayor quickly interrupted, little eyes shiny, 'I can tell you one thing we've got to start doing right now and that is to collect money for the shrine and all the facelifts we need to give this miserable place before it is fit to be a pilgrimage site.'

At this talk of fund-raising, the card players retreated behind their hands, the drinkers behind their glasses, and the billiard players began to study their cues with the greatest attention.

Once the triumvirate was safely ensconced in the white-washed mayoral office in the Municipal Hall, Don Luigi ventured to cool down the mayor's hot talk of collections and pledges and promissory notes: 'We must proceed with caution, Bettino, we cannot collect money before we have Bishop Natti visit us here and speak to Santa. Once we have Bishop Natti on our side, then we can rest assured that an enquiry into our case will take place ... And then, but only then' – here the priest raised his index finger in warning – 'can we collect money from these poor people.'

'Poor people, pshaw.' The mayor pounded the desk before him. 'These villagers sleep on mattresses stuffed with money. Anyway' – here the mayor's bright brown eyes rested upon Don Luigi – 'if you don't want to collect money from the poor, my dear Padre, why not approach the Signorina Ferrati? She's got plenty of money and no husband and no heirs to spend it on ... you were so close to her mother, you go and ask her, Don Luigi.'

Despite the poor priest's yelps of protest – 'But Bettino, Alma Ferrati, she's so difficult!' – the mayor stood his ground and pledged that he would not continue to work on the erection of their shrine until the priest had fulfilled his mission.

8

It was with a trepidation that sat as heavy in his heart as Rosina's agnolotti sat in his stomach that Don Luigi made his way to the Ferratis' house. He hated to ask for money, and especially from a sophisticated city woman like Alma Ferrati, who, as far as he could make out, took more from her father's hard-hearted approach to the Church than from her mother's generous piety. With the son, at least, he had always felt at ease: a serious boy, always courteous, and the Jesuits in Acqui, he had heard, had even thought he might have a vocation, such were the questions he posed and the fervour with which he attended his classes.

Alma Ferrati had been seen only rarely in San Lorenzo since her father's death and the sale of the land. She came on the weekends, mostly: he had seen the shutters fly open on the second floor, and the smoke twirling from the chimneys. But she never set foot in his church and hardly ventured into the village, except to buy bread rolls at Nuccio's bakery. He wasn't even sure that she knew of the great undertaking of the shrine.

Don Luigi pushed the heavy green gates open, stepped onto the gravel path that wound its way through the cypress trees to the great house. The orchard and the garden, stripped of leaves and fruit, trembled in the winter air. Rain puddles had collected on the uneven ground, and Don Luigi was forced to pick his way carefully up to the huge grey house. As he stood silent before the heavy oak door, and a hollow echo answered his ringing of the doorbell, he felt his courage shrivel up. At times like this, in front of so much money, he remembered his own mother, who had worked as a cleaner in the wealthier homes in their mountain village, and who had often brought him along to the houses she 'did': he had hung on her skirts, gaping wide-mouthed at the luxury of the landowners she worked for, and so shy before them that he would not utter a word.

'Signorina Ferrati . . . !' he called out, and then, thinking it ridiculous that he should thus address a girl he'd known since she was so high, 'Alma . . . !' he said. The gentle afternoon sun shone upon his bare head, and he stood waiting before the door for what seemed to him an eternity. Finally, the doors of the balcony above him opened, and out came Alma, dressed in a paint-stained smock. Behind her radio music blared.

'Good morning, Alma!' Don Luigi was perspiring: no Romeo had trembled more at the sight of a young woman at her balcony.

'Well, well, Don Luigi, what a pleasant surprise.' Alma waved a brush at him. 'Wait a moment, I'll just put the brushes in turpentine and come and open the door.'

She disappeared, and minutes later he was following her into the dark, cold entrance hall, through to the drawing room. How well Don Luigi knew this room! How often he had come here, on Thursdays, to pick up the work that the ladies of the sewing circle had completed – timing his arrival with that of the silver tray bearing Rina's homemade amaretti ... What a different woman, the Signora Ferrati, from this tough and independent young lady.

'Would you like a coffee, Don Luigi?' Alma removed her smock, uncovering a red twinset and skirt. She smiled at him, but Don Luigi felt the unease cling to him: there was nothing meek and soft about that smile, it held no resemblance to the humble sweetness with which her mother had always greeted him. It was, he thought, a victor's smile, a taker's smile, confident and strong. 'I come here only on the weekends, so all I ever have is coffee and cases upon cases of bottled water – I don't have the heart to tell Grillo to stop his deliveries ...' She smiled, ran a hand through her short hair. Then, with one hand she was switching off the advertising jingle on the radio, with the other she was folding her smock. Her movements were quick, purposeful, and Don Luigi felt suddenly exhausted. He wasn't sure he could go through with this task, after all.

He looked around at the darkened room: bright-coloured canvases filled with swirling bold colours and no intelligible shape, stood against the walls. A plate with the remains of a bread roll sat on the floor beside an unfolded newspaper and an ashtray filled with cigarettes. In the fireplace, the wood was burning low. 'Ah of course!' Alma dashed out, then returned, a large flowered box in her hand. 'What about some chocolates, Don Luigi, handmade from Switzerland ...' She lifted the top, for him to admire, and he saw her eyes shine like a little girl's. 'Ooooh ... who could resist these?' And she laughed.

'No, no, Alma, I've just finished my lunch.' He waved her away with his hand. Alma reluctantly shut the chocolate box and placed it on one of the damask sofa pillows. 'Rosina outdid herself,' the priest continued. 'I had two plates of agnolotti with her special cream and mushroom sauce ...' Then, embarrassed, he gave a dry little cough. 'I find you looking – very well, yes, very well, my dear Alma. I worried about you after your father's death ...' Here he coughed again, because he caught Alma's cool look with its question, 'Then why didn't you come and see me before?'

But Alma merely turned away from him and said in a low voice: 'When the person who understands you best is no longer there, it tips you off balance ...' She turned back to face him, and he saw the eyes shine with tears. 'He was also my great friend, so I miss the laughs and the bickerings we used to share ...' Suddenly, she couldn't help a smile at the memory of how often Don Luigi himself – 'that long-skirted, boneless wimp' Father had called him – had set them off laughing, in this very room.

'I see you are working ...?' He pointed to the ladder and pot of paint by the window casement.

'Yes.' Alma nodded. 'I like to have a few house projects going while I come here to paint my own pictures – the window frames all need redoing, and I thought I would start on them now ... so much work, to keep up a house like this, and since we have very little money, I thought I'd do as much as I could myself...'

'Ah yes, money ...' The priest looked away from the pretty and animated face. Alma took a packet of cigarettes from the mantel over the fireplace, lit one, returned to his side, cigarette dangling from her left hand. 'Money is a terrible worry for all of us ...' The priest fixed his eyes upon the black and white tiles at his feet.

'Yes. I always took it for granted and now look at me – worrying about selling my paintings in order to lead a comfortable life and not worry about ever having to give up this house.' Alma, cigarette in hand, crouched to stir the embers with an iron spade. She picked up the bellows and began to blow into the ashes, chatting over her shoulder all the while: 'It's terrible, isn't it, when you think one particular place is sacred and holds all the meaning of life ... I'm sure that's a blasphemous thought ...' She grinned mischievously as she stood up, the fire reawakened behind her.

'Yes, well ...' The priest was at a loss for words.

'I mean, I have a studio in Torino, I live there too, one big room – but oh, Don Luigi, it's not the same thing at all. This place – this place is my home ...'

'Yes, San Lorenzo has been the home for generations of Ferratis ... Our village and your family – their fates have been linked for hundreds and hundreds of years.' The priest now slipped into his homily voice, piety laced with warning. 'Your family has always been the head of our community, the single most important land- holders ...'

'Not any more, you can look to Franca for that,' Alma said, and her eyes darkened with regret.

'Yes, well, Franca's just a jumped-up farmer isn't she? We can't look to her for a lead. Whereas you and your brother, Alma, you should see yourselves as our first citizens ...'

Alma laughed and shook her head. 'But Don Luigi, how can that possibly be – Francesco lives in London ...'

'But returns here every summer,' the priest interjected.

'Yes, but only for his holidays – and my guess is, very much against his wife's wishes ... her visits are getting more and more infrequent. She couldn't even come for our father's funeral.' For a moment, bitterness coloured her voice. Then she shook her head and resumed: 'Francesco loves the village for what it is, for the people in it – but me, the San Lorenzo I know and love is there' – she pointed to the bright red and green canvases along the wall – 'and it has very little to do with the real village. I hardly set foot there, hardly remember people's names ... I don't come here to be part of a community, you know ...'

'Be that as it may ...' The priest was losing patience and he linked his fingers upon his ample stomach now. 'We regard you as very important. With this in mind, Alma, I want to share with you some happy news. We are to build a shrine.'

'A shrine?!' Alma looked puzzled.

'I came to let you know that a miracle has taken place in our modest little village' – here he saw an eyebrow rise, lips move slightly – 'yes, a miracle: Our Lady has come to speak to young Santarella ... and we hope, Alma, to build a shrine on the very spot!'

'A shrine?' The voice rose in disbelief. Don Luigi dabbed his forehead with his kerchief.

'Yes. Santarella has revealed her visions to me. Our Lady has chosen her as a messenger for her words of hope ...'

'The widow Lea's beautiful daughter ...' Alma murmured. She remembered the pale figure as the object of Francesco's youthful passion.

'A virtuous, pious girl. A girl so modest she doesn't wish to bask in the glory of her role as Our Lady's chosen one ... But I cannot overlook the wondrous occurrences that take place in our little village, Alma. No, I believe we must let the whole region, the whole nation know about our blessing. And Bishop Natti in Torino first of all. Once he gives his approval – of which I am as certain as of your standing before me – we shall go ahead and build a beautiful shrine on the spot where Our Lady appears to Santa.' Now he drew closer to the young woman before him. 'Though of course, to do this we need to collect some money, a few contributions …' Here his eyes filled with longing, and his voice grew soft with hope. 'I was wondering, Alma, whether you would help us … you know how our villagers are: if they see someone give first, they follow suit.'

'You've come to me for a contribution?' Alma exhaled the smoke from her cigarette in two perfect circles that floated like grey turtle doves up to the ceiling.

'Well, I thought you would want to lead the way in this matter – think of it, a shrine on our hill …'

'Don Luigi.' Alma's voice and eyes were cold. 'You don't seem to understand. I am worried as it is about money – and here you are asking me to give a donation to a village shrine!'

'But Alma, just a small token …' He heard his voice whine unpleasantly as the slim figure moved past him.

'Don Luigi, I am very fond of you, I would like to give you a hand …' Alma stubbed out her cigarette in a porcelain shell. 'But not in this ridiculous enterprise … I don't believe in shrines, miracles, in visitations … I think of Santa as a childlike lost soul, not a visionary. I think of this village as the backdrop of my childhood and now of my paintings. The notion of converting it into a miniature Lourdes or Fatima sends shivers down my spine …'

'B-b-b-but,' Don Luigi spluttered.

'No buts.' She pulled back the woollen sleeve from her right arm, glanced at her wristwatch. 'And I have to leave for Torino in an hour. I need to change, wash ... I'm afraid I'm going to have to draw our conversation to a close, Padre.'

As Don Luigi walked down the path away from the Ferrati home, he thought he could already hear the abuse that the mayor would hurl at him for failing in his mission.

9

In the widow Lea's shop, the widow stood on a step-ladder, cursing under her breath because once again Santa had been late back from Mass. Every evening she went off, mantilla covering her head, rosary beads in hand; by the time she had reached the piazza, a cluster of women materialized out of nowhere to follow the young vision-ary towards Don Luigi's church. 'Santa,' they pleaded, heads bowed humbly, 'Santa, tell us of your visions!' But her daughter merely smiled at them, and proceeded towards the steps that led to the church.

'Ah, what a saint you've been blessed with,' the women would tell the widow, as they chose their lettuces, or watched her wrap half-a-dozen eggs in newspaper. 'What an honour that He should have sent her among us ...' They would shake their heads as they handed over their money.

'What a pious girl, what a shining example to us all ...' whispered that gossip-monger, the former postmistress Pina, whose head hardly reached the counter. And the widow could read in her mischievous raisin-black eyes the tiny woman's wicked thoughts: for, with her window facing the widow Lea's shop, you could be sure that Pina had spied the mayor through her shutters as he skulked by her door at night, waiting for the widow to throw down the keys. The widow bit her lip, lest she answer the former postmistress with a few homespun truths of her own.

Every evening Santa would return to her mother's shop wearing her secret, sweet expression. 'Mamma, let me help you.' She would stand, head bowed, ready to obey her mother's instructions.

'Oh, Santa, Santa, you'll drive me mad one day with this piety of yours . . .' The widow shook her head. 'Surely Our Lady would wish for you to spend more time with your own mother and less time with Don Luigi and those scarecrow women who hang about you hoping that they'll catch a glimpse of Our Lady?!'

But the girl's perfect lips merely parted into a smile of such joy that the widow swallowed her scoldings. 'All right, Santa, all right,' she sighed, 'just give your poor mother a hand with these tins . . . hand them over and I'll range them up on the shelf . . .' Slowly and carefully, her mantilla and rosary beads now in the pocket of her white dress, Santarella lifted the tins of coffee, meat, peas, beans, two at a time, her cool fingers briefly touching her mother's hot hands.

They worked in silence, the widow stretching high towards the last shelves that sat directly beneath the ceiling, stopping only every now and then to ascertain that her footing was steady. Winter plunged the shop in darkness by four in the afternoon, and beneath its green concertina shade, the electric light shone upon the hams, salamis, cheeses that swung beside the widow. Outside, Don Luigi's bells tolled eight.

'Lea!' The shop door burst open, sending the little bell

pealing with laughter, and in strode the Mayor Battistini, with the bold step and the confident smile of one who is intimate with the home he's just entered. But the sight of Santarella's pale figure and the clear eyes that met his gaze robbed the mayor of his aplomb and now he stood in the middle of his lover's shop looking for all the world like a schoolboy awaiting his headmistress's rebuke. 'Ah ... ehm ... Santarella ... our heroine ...' But as usual with Santarella, he grew flustered, and fell silent. He looked at her in the mellow light of her mother's shop, against the row of tins and packets and bottles, beside the baskets and crates heaped with fruit and vegetables: how still she stood, how forbidding she struck him, head held high, her tall, graceful figure almost luminous in its white dress. The mayor filled with embarrassment as the lovely pale face turned to him now and the clear eyes sought his: God spare him from those all-seeing eyes, that crystalline glance that seemed to see into every nook and cranny of his heart!

Up on the stepladder the widow asked the good Lord why oh why He'd sent her so many trials all at once: a daughter with her head full of visions and a lover who only heard his own needs. 'Wait there, Bettino, I'm coming down.' The widow climbed slowly down, fully aware that her hips swayed just so, and that her black dress rode high to reveal the solid whiteness of her thighs as she descended.

But for once Battistini felt no surge of desire at the sight of his mistress's curves: all pleasures of the flesh sank, like his heart, into the depths of unease as he felt himself watched by the strange child-woman.

'Well, it's a good thing you're here, Santarella. It's about you I've come to see your mother.' And here the mayor coughed, uncomfortable with the lie that seemed already to have been pierced and deflated by Santarella's clear gaze.

The widow, moved to pity by her lover's discomfiture, smiled at him. 'And what nonsense do you have to tell us now about that shrine you keep dreaming of?'

'Don't call it nonsense, Lea: I can tell you that your own fortunes will benefit greatly from the shrine ... if we ever have one ...' he added, with a doubtful glance in Santarella's direction. 'I've sent off a huge document listing all the sightings Don Luigi tells me that Santa's admitted to' – here Santa flushed, and made a movement as if to stem the mayor's flow – 'and also all the data we have on your daughter, the miraculous prophecies she's made, the miraculous cures that have taken place because of her ...'

'What ... ?' whispered Santa, suddenly pale.

'Have you gone mad?! What miracles?!' The widow's voice rose in disbelief.

'Well ...' Battistini felt suddenly hot. He ran a big broad hand through his greying hair, and took a great gulp of air. 'Well, it might seem like we're stretching it a bit, but there is reason to believe that your daughter's prayers have effected a number of miraculous cures ...'

'But,' whispered Santa, 'I have not prayed for anyone in particular ... I haven't tried to cure anyone at all.'

'Of course not, my dear girl.' The mayor took a step closer to the pale figure. But Santa drew back, as if fearful of his proximity. 'I know that you had no intention of becoming a miracle worker, but you see, you are so close to Our Lady that your prayers bring about the most won-

derful things ... Don Luigi's Rosina, whose son had men-
ingitis, for instance: well, she swears that Pippo was cured
because of your intercession. And Nuccio the baker's
Marta – the plain-faced daughter, not the pretty little one –
the doctor in Susa was certain that she would die of that
fever last summer, but when Nuccio and his wife prayed
that you might grant her health, apparently she got well
immediately. And ...'

'That's enough out of you.' The widow wrapped her
arm protectively about her daughter's shoulders. Santa
stood completely still, head bowed, as if the mayor's list
had been a series of accusations. 'Can't you see that you're
upsetting her with this string of lies? Shame on you for
trying to pull the wool over the bishop's eyes and for
trying to ruin my daughter's life because you can smell a
profit at the end of it. Pick on someone else to carry out
your sleazy plans.' The widow stamped her foot.

But the mayor had not risked his wife's wrath or a cold
plate of risotto in order to go away empty-handed. He
hunched his shoulders now, raised his hands in a beggar's
palm-upwards plea: 'Santarella.' His voice seemed
unsure, soft and low. 'Santarella, all our hopes lie in your
hands. It is now up to you to decide our fate: if the bishop
comes here, as we are certain he will, he would want to
meet with you, to learn from you directly about your
visions and your prayers and the cures ... Don't let us
down, my girl, I – we have such faith in you.'

Santa did not look at the mayor. Instead, her tear-filled
eyes searched her mother's face beside her. 'I don't want
to lie, Mamma.'

'You don't need to lie, Santa. You don't need to take
part in this sham at all.' And the widow cast a killer glance

past her daughter, at the mayor. If only she weren't so lonely, and didn't set such store by the lovemaking, she had a good mind to break it off with him right then and there.

'I'll go now, Mamma, and fix our supper.' And without another glance in Battistini's direction, Santa had gone upstairs.

'Now look what you've done,' the widow whispered, furious.

'Well, what can I do? I need her to be her own witness. I need her to testify to the visions – and yes, the miracles ...'

'Witness? Testify? My daughter's not on trial!' The widow pushed away the hands that were reaching for her waist. 'Don't you dare make her suffer like this!'

The mayor hung his head, sheepish. 'Oh Lea, please, I want you to be happy, I think of you all the time ...' He watched the effect of his words upon the beautiful face before him: yes, Lea's expression was softening. 'I want only the best for you ... and you know that I try to help you any way I can ... who's blocked Vanna's attempt to get a tobacconist's licence, so that you could have a monopoly here?' He raised his small brown eyes and lowered his voice, lest he could be heard upstairs. 'I want you so ...'

'Hmmmm.' The widow, pleased despite herself, allowed the hands to caress her hips. 'Well, we'll see about that. Pretty speeches are not enough ... you'd better go home to your wife now, before she comes looking for you here ... and I have the last tins to stack up there.' She pushed him off, but not before he kissed her throat, and watched him leave.

Alone in her shop, surrounded by her vegetables and

fruits, her meats and cheeses, the widow Lea sighed: why must she spend her life thus, torn between her instinct to protect this strange daughter of hers and her need to fill the loneliness that made her heart ache so? But then, as usual, she shook herself and went slowly upstairs, where in their small kitchen Santa was heating the soup for supper.

10

'I think you ought to come, you know. Lots and lots of potential clients, and Marisol always throws a great bash.' Alberto della Rocca stood watching Alma as she put the finishing touches to his portrait.

'Oh, this is useless – there's no light left ...' Alma was talking to herself, frowning at the pale man on her canvas. The sun still hovered in the winter sky, but already darkness had taken possession of great areas of the study. She had worked at this portrait for two months – Alberto had called it his 'bait' in the ironic tone he always adopted when referring to his courtship of her. But she was not fooled by his attempt to make light of his feelings for her, and the certainty of his love had steadied her in the wake of her father's death. Alma cocked her head to study the seated figure whose cool elegance she had tried to capture in icy greys and blues. Yes, she was satisfied with her lover's portrait – the long figure lay back in a pose that somehow managed to convey control rather than indolence; the slim, long hands seemed ready to take possession of anything desired; the patrician white head, almost silver on her canvas, sat erect and proud upon the strong neck; the cool blue eyes evaluated, compared, measured everything and everyone. She nodded, pleased.

He had been an interesting subject – and an excellent sitter: she could always trust him to retain his pose without protest – he seemed unflustered by the self-discipline stillness required.

'We could have a quiet dinner afterwards ...' Alberto continued. Their eyes met for an instant, but quickly she looked away: the intensity of his desire never failed to shock her.

'I really don't feel like it, Alberto. These people sit for me for hours, I don't particularly want to spend my evening in their company as well ...' She shook her head.

'You have to be sociable to be a portrait painter, you know.' She felt his eyes still fixed on her, and stared resolutely at her brush as it stroked blue oil upon the shoes on the canvas before her. 'You have to meet lots of people, get them interested in you.'

'I'm very sociable. If I'm not seeing you, I go out dancing, go to dinners and the cinema ...'

'You know what I mean. And in any case, I thought you had outgrown that bohemian set you used to see.'

'Well, at least they're my age group.' Immediately, she regretted the words. She set down her brush, rushed to him, wrapped her arms around him and beamed him a great smile. 'I'm sorry, I'm being beastly, and for no good reason.' She pecked him on the forehead and brought a smile to his lips. But before he could restrain her she'd moved back to her easel, which she now covered. She placed her brush in turpentine, removed her smock and tried to comb her hair with her fingers. 'And it's not that I want to spend every night with the black polo-neck brigade and their posturing, their wine drinking and their back-stabbing comments and false praises ...'

Alberto glanced at his watch. 'You are positive, then? I ought to start out now – the fog was terrible on my way here this morning.'

'Positive.' She smiled, certain of her victory.

'Trust you to snub a roomful of useful people.'

'Useful is in business, Alberto. And business is not every hour of the day. I walk out of those drawing rooms feeling as if I've been sipping tea all day with my little finger turned up just so and my knees pressed together like Mother taught me ladies do. I can't fit into that world, you know.'

Alberto stood up now, unfolding his long legs with the casual grace of a man completely at ease with himself. He came up close to her, a glint in his eyes and a half-smile on his lips. 'I wanted her to tell you herself. But as you won't go there ... Marisol was very impressed with your paintings. She rang me to let me know that she's ready to take you on in her gallery – she's talking of a private view this summer.'

Alma threw her arms round him. 'A private view! I can't believe it!' She clapped her hands while he looked on, amused. 'A private view ... how could you sit there for hours and not tell me ...? Oh Alberto, I'm so happy so happy! And so grateful.'

'It was your talent that impressed her, not my eulogies.'

'You're wonderful, nonetheless. Thank you thank you – oh my God, all the work I still need to do ... oh Alberto, tell her I'll be up in Torino tomorrow, pronto, ready to receive any instructions ... my dream come true!' She was near tears at the prospect.

'Well, I'm glad to have been the bearer of such glad tidings. I'm off now. Take care and – come and see me after Marisol – we could spend the afternoon together.'

'Yes, yes,' Alma said quickly.

She saw him off, and allowed herself to sigh only once she heard him start the car. Once again, she owed so much to Alberto. Ever since her father's funeral, his constant solicitude, his ready encouragement had offered her solace amidst the solitude that engulfed her. These past few months she had discovered she wasn't the Alma she thought she knew. She had attempted to live according to the so-called truths that she had taken from her past: Alma is strong, Alma will always survive, Alma knows what she wants from every moment of her life. But each attempt had failed, for the world of her childhood had not prepared her for her parents' deaths, for the days and nights of cold loneliness that filled her studio, even this beloved home.

She felt as if since her father's death she had slipped into a life of loose, unconstructed forms, like a woman who suddenly loses confidence in her looks and takes to wearing shapeless smocks. The only fixed points she could see were this home – this house, this village – and her painting. And the painting more and more seemed to feed on this home, pulling her back here to render its beauty and capture its magic again and again in her canvases. It was as if only here, in the generous forms of the distant hills and in the brilliant expanse of golden fields, in the handful of houses and scattered farms, the turreted church and flowing river, she could find her own voice.

Her dedication to her work had succeeded in discouraging the young men who had sought her company. But Alberto della Rocca had persisted in his attentions. He had rung every day, offering suggestions for this prospective sitter, for that gallery owner; he had invited her to exhibitions, to tête-à-tête dinners where he sometimes spoke of her parents, of the art world, but mostly of her. 'Why must you insist on bearing every burden on your own? Lean on me in times of need.' He had watched over her every step, examined her every plan. Soon she asked him to guide her through her difficulties, to comfort her in her grief. Her gratitude burned fierce and melted all scruples. Alberto had seen her need, and answered it.

She often wondered what her father would have said, what Francesco would say, were they to discover that she was involved with a man who for decades had been a friend of the family, a man more than thirty years her senior, a man she did not love. Father, who had thought her indomitable, such a free spirit; and Francesco, who thought her so strong, so brave: how could they possibly forgive her this?

Slowly she climbed the stairs, walked into her bedroom. Through the bare branches of the orchard tree she could hear the voices of the Daughters of Mary as they prayed before the statue of San Lorenzo that stood guard over the village, at the crossroads. In the alcove sat the plaster statue of brown and gold, and a little brass lantern hung above the flowers that the pious ladies brought to it almost every day. Once a week they congregated here, at the roadside, to say their rosaries, led into their Aves by Don Luigi. Alma heard the priest's voice, as it intoned the Our Father of the First Joyful Mystery. Their voices rose and fell like the evening breeze that lifted then dropped the branches of the persimmon tree outside her window.

Alma sat on her bed and lit a cigarette. If only she had grown up like these black-clad women who held onto their ivory beads and left all cares behind. She could have entered the life of the sewing circle, where pious ladies sewed altar cloths and prie-dieu covers and offered their every suffering to their Lord.

'Ave Maria . . .' The words stepped into the room, wove their holy spell from wall to wall as they had done when in her childhood she had sat in the family pew at the front of Don Luigi's dark humid church. She took a puff of her cigarette, drew up her knees to embrace them. The women at the crossroads were certain of the way. They accepted the life of their ancestors, with its pious rites and its limitations. They were happy to drown their voices in the chorus of domesticity and tradition.

She stared now at the angels that held hands up on her ceiling among garlands of faded flowers and leaves. In the darkened air, the cherubs did not smile but floated up above her like all-seeing critics of a life that needed to be shaped into something new. 'Come along, Alma, pull yourself together.' She stubbed out her cigarette and drew a long strong breath.

In the garden, the branches trembled in the evening breeze. Alma lay back against her pillow and watched the evening from her bed. How beautiful, the sky above San Lorenzo.

The women, beneath black mantillas, filed down the street. Before them, rocking gently with his new sense of importance, Don Luigi intoned the last prayer. It was time for supper, and the village mothers called their children, and the tractors entered wide-arched courtyard doors, and windows banged shut to keep out the cold and doors closed against strangers.

Loneliness entered Alma's room: slow, determined,

certain of its place. It seemed as comfortable here among her childhood memories as it was in the studio in Torino. Alma rose, moved to the window that for years had been her view on the world. Days and nights, year after year, had appeared framed by this window. She stood and watched the windows of the only house that you could see from the Ferratis' – and then, only when winter had torn leaves from their branches.

The house belonged to the Signorina Teresa. There she was, the signorina. She walked to her drawing room where every night she ate the same meal: a slice of pale yellow cheese, a bowl of clear soup, sometimes a pear or an apple. She sat alone, at the head of her long table, her hands politely to either side of her plate.

The signorina held her head high as she sipped from her water glass, as she brought knife and fork together upon her plate, then a forkful to her lips. Sometimes, Signorina Teresa listened to the radio programme when she ate: most especially if they played Mozart. She loved Mozart, as she told Alma's mother when she came to visit and sip tea; as she told Alma when she saw her at the widow Lea's or at Vanna's.

When she finished her meal, Signorina Teresa carefully put her dish (it was never empty, because the signorina's digestion was not what it used to be) and the glass on a lacquer tray, and then carried it into the kitchen. Now she could sit back in her flowered armchair, place her reading glasses on her nose, and take out her wool: a pot holder for her niece, a jumper for her nephew, a doll's dress for her daily's little girl. Soon, Alma knew, she would see the tiny head fall to one side. Then the signorina opened her eyes once more on the matter at hand. But soon, down fell the eyelids again, down dropped the head, and it was almost half an hour before the signorina was woken up by her own mild snoring.

Time for bed. The signorina replaced her wool and needles in the big straw basket beside her armchair, and performed the ceremony of the lights: first in the kitchen, then the little pink-shaded lamp by the chair, then the chandelier in the drawing room. Alma could follow the figure into the bedroom: beyond the white curtain's gauze, she watched the shadow as it glided from the cupboard to the bed, and the signorina now looked young and graceful, her movements as smooth as a ballerina's. Alone the signorina slipped into bed.

Had she ever loved, was she ever loved, the signorina? Had her every night followed this solitary pattern, or was she once gay and much-admired, tiny and beautiful as a porcelain doll?

Alma retreated from the window, drew back into her own dark room. Tomorrow she would go to Torino, see Marisol, begin to work towards the exhibition ... but as she switched on her bedside lamp she felt the tears streak her cheeks.

11

Alma Ferrati's refusal to contribute to the glory of their village took the architects of the shrine by surprise. For weeks, after Don Luigi's unsuccessful mission, the triumvirate tossed and turned the issue between them. Finally, the mayor's capacity to discern the silver lining even in this unexpected cloud triumphed. 'If she's got no means, my dear friends' – and here Battistini rubbed his hands with delight – 'it means she'll soon be forced to sell the house. And if she's pressed to sell, she'll sell at a low price. And if she sells at a low price – well, my friends, you see before you not only the architect of the shrine of San Lorenzo but also the future owner of the most important house for kilometres ...'

'Yes, yes.' The marshal tapped his cane impatiently upon the ground. 'But what about the shrine now?' He had thrown himself into the building of the shrine with the stubborn conviction of a zealot in his belief. His life had suffered enough defeats already – what with the race for mayor, his oldest son's imprisonment for fraud, his late wife's terrifying fight against the cancer that finally took her: he couldn't bear to think of yet another loss.

'We can't rush anything, Marshal, we can't rush anything.' Don Luigi wagged his index finger. 'Sooner or later the bishop will make up his mind and come to see our Santarella.'

'Well, I believe we ought to ensure that the bishop makes up his mind sooner rather than later,' Battistini snorted with disgust. 'I don't mean for the shrine to be erected in San Lorenzo when I'm lying beneath the ground ... I suggest that we send another letter to Torino, a letter so perfectly worded and wonderfully moving that Bishop Natti will have no choice but to come to our village.'

'Oh, I don't know how we could go about such a thing, Bettino ...' Don Luigi poured his rosary beads from one hand to the other, as if measuring the sands of time. 'It's no good putting pressure on Mother Church – and certainly not on Bishop Natti.' Don Luigi looked worried.

'It will be a beautiful letter. We must make sure it's a beautiful letter ... moving and candid and ...'

But the marshal's flow was stemmed by Don Luigi. 'Who'll write such a letter?'

The three men fell silent. It was true: who in their village would be capable of such an all-important task?

'But of course!' the mayor burst out. 'The notary, Miso Brusoni. He writes documents, letters, contracts from dawn till dusk. If he can't do this no one can!'

The marshal looked dubious: 'He's not the most accessible of men, Bettino. And he's been heard condemning our dream for a shrine as commercial exploitation ... and that mother of his she talks and talks and talks ...'

'Never fear.' The marshal twirled his moustaches. 'Whoever said our campaign would be easy to win? We always knew there would be a few obstacles to overcome on our way. Come: let's go and see him.'

* * *

The trio marched forth one fine Sunday morning. The Brusonis – Miso and his elderly widowed mother, Carla – lived at the edge of the village, in a large modern brick house overlooking the river. It was early and only the rooster seemed awake in the silent winter courtyard. The mayor rang the bell. 'Let's hope that tiresome woman doesn't come to the door,' he whispered to the marshal who nodded.

The notary himself came to the door, in his undershirt, newspaper in hand. 'Well well, to what do I owe this honour?' Miso's voice was slightly singsong with teasing.

The mayor stepped into the darkened living room, his companions at his heels. On the little table by the armchair before them sat a coffee cup and a packet of cigarettes. Upstairs, they could hear the radio's newscast. 'Brusoni, sorry to disturb you on a Sunday, but this is important.'

Miso's eyes, to Don Luigi's great discomfiture, twinkled with amusement. The priest felt the same unease that had overtaken him in the presence of Alma Ferrati – and unlike his previous visit, this was to someone whose moodiness was well known, and whose large frame, he registered with alarm, dwarfed even the mayor.

'We need a letter to be written, in the name of the people of San Lorenzo, inviting Bishop Natti to come and see our visionary for himself. We' – here the mayor gestured towards his companions – 'immediately thought that you should write it. After all' – Battistini now adopted a jovial tone of praise – 'who better than our trusted notary to express our plan?'

Miso crossed his arms and grinned: 'Flattery will get you anywhere, Battistini. Usually. But the problem here is that I don't like what the three of you threaten to do to my village; I'm not too fond of bishops; and Sundays are my only days off. So I'm afraid I won't be much use to you in this ecclesiastical enterprise.'

'Now look here, Brusoni, this kind of attitude won't do.' The marshal tapped his cane upon the red tiled floor. 'This desperate village of ours could change overnight into a thriving community. Money will finally flow in – and percolate from the top down. Surely we share a concern for everyone's welfare?'

Miso shook his head: 'Money, Marshal Ciuffi, has an odd way of sitting at the top, like scum on the river's waters. I'm not sure it ever percolates to all those who need it . . .'

'Miso . . .' Don Luigi tried now, a faint plea issuing forth.

'Don Luigi, you know my position. If I can help my native village in any way I will – but in the end, I think your scheme to build a shrine in San Lorenzo is ill-advised, to say the least. And be careful not to get too many people's hopes up. I don't want my poor friends to be peddled a lot of far-fetched plans – only to have their dreams shattered.'

The mayor looked cross and was about to retort, but a quick glance at the tall figure in its undershirt convinced him not to waste his breath. 'Well, Brusoni,' he sighed dramatically, 'if you must be selfish, you must. Not everyone in this poor little village of ours has done as well out of life as you have.' Here the mayor indicated the large living room, its television set, its crystal chandelier, its velvet armchairs. 'But I suppose you cannot be expected to understand how the other half lives.' Here the mayor shrugged. 'We'll be off then.'

The trio, sulky in their defeat, set off.

'An arrogant bastard,' the mayor spat once they were safely out of earshot.

'A good-for-nothing jumped-up peasant,' Marshal Ciuffi snorted.

Don Luigi merely sighed. They strode forth, into the piazza: there wasn't a soul about, and the village seemed still asleep, unimpressed by the mild attempts of the winter sun to draw them from their beds. Don Luigi did not have to say Mass for another three hours, and was just about to suggest a cup of coffee and a slice of Rosina's apricot tart to the two men beside him – he'd finished writing his sermon, unusually, last night – when he spotted the former postmistress Pina bicycling like a fury towards them, one hand waving in the air to attract the men's attention. Obediently, they stopped in their tracks: 'Don Luigi! Signor Mayor!' The tiny woman was practically falling off her bicycle in her excitement. 'It's Santarella!'

The mayor felt his heart skip a beat: had something befallen the visionary upon whom rested all his hopes? 'What is it, Pina?' he barked, fear making him brusque. 'For God's sake, woman, speak!'

Poor Pina was trying to catch her breath. 'Oh the tragedy! The terrible tragedy!'

'What, Pina, what has happened to Santa?' Don Luigi, truly concerned for the young girl's welfare, was tense with anxiety.

'She won't speak, Father. Her mother's just told me. Santa has not uttered a word since yesterday. I couldn't believe it myself, until I tried asking her a thousand questions, and she said nothing! Not a word!'

'Dear God!' Don Luigi whispered, and immediately

asked his Lord's forgiveness for uttering His name in vain.

'How could she hope to get away with this?!' asked the marshal, pulling at his moustaches as if in their length and lustrous thickness he might find some comfort following such an announcement.

'I'll go and see Lea now!' the mayor shouted.

'I wouldn't do that, Signor Mayor.' Pina shook her head, relishing each moment of her importance. Upon her two-wheeled throne, she cast a commiserating look upon the three architects of the shrine. 'I'm afraid the widow is convinced it is your fault – she yelled at me that it was because her daughter was being forced to say things she didn't believe that Santa had chosen to remain silent ...' The tiny raisin eyes scrunched up with mischief. 'I don't think even you' – here she looked meaningfully at the mayor – 'could persuade your ... could persuade the widow that Santa has not been forced into this ...'

'Oh Lord, what have we done to offend You?' asked Don Luigi of the cloudless skies.

'Not another defeat!' moaned the marshal into the kerchief with which he was wiping his face, upon which cold sweat had broken out.

'I'll kill her!' the mayor burst out. And no one knew whether he meant his mistress or her daughter.

The indefatigable Pina lost no time in spreading the news of Santa's retreat into silence: within an hour, it seemed as if every man, woman and child knew that their visionary no longer uttered a word. For days, for nights, the villagers tried to coax the young woman, then her mother, to break her resolve. But despite their pleas, Santarella seemed determined to maintain her silence. In vain, Don Luigi attempted to coax the girl into answering his quivering queries in the sacred quiet of his church: Santarella merely smiled and looked beyond him at the altar and the crucifix above it. In vain Battistini begged his lover to use her influence with her daughter: the widow, never a demonstrative mother, now suddenly assumed a fiercely protective stand at Santa's side, and threatened the mayor with expulsion from her bed each time he began his nightly sermons on Santa.

Santarella's walks through the village and by the river continued, and she could still be spotted at her mother's shop, meek and quiet behind the counter. But throughout, the pale visionary maintained an absolute silence, as though her lips had been sealed by a Divine Order or by a personal vow to Our Lady.

'No bishop worth his salt will give permission for a shrine when the visionary won't swear that she did indeed see, and speak to, Our Lady!' Don Luigi moaned, handkerchief flapping like a white flag surrendering all hope. 'If on top of all the delays we have this silence to contend with – we'll never build the shrine!'

'We must not give in, Padre, we can't yield to the enemy, can't stop in our tracks before the very first obstacle we encounter . . .' The marshal tapped his cane upon the flagstones.

'The marshal's right, Don Luigi: I'm going to use all my . . . powers of persuasion with the widow Lea.' Here the mayor gave a sharp little cough, and studied for a moment the carpet at Don Luigi's feet. 'She'll make the girl talk sooner or later . . . meanwhile I see no reason why we couldn't write a convincing letter ourselves, a letter worthy of attention, and perhaps – here's a thought! – we

94

could send the good bishop a crate of our finest wines, yes, I'll contribute the crate myself, we'll sweeten the bishop's palate with some nice Barolo ... and no need to mention the unfortunate silence to the bishop at this point.' The mayor winked at the marshal.

But that evening, as the trio bent over the mayor's desk and went through seemingly a thousand drafts of the all-important missive, Don Luigi decided they would have to send at least two crates of the very best wine – and pray that the bishop consumed quite a lot of it before reading their plea.

12

Brother and sister sat at the kitchen table, finishing their breakfast. Francesco had arrived late the previous night by taxi. He'd found his sister still up, adding yet another canvas to her inventory.

She had been coy over the telephone about the private view. 'It's nothing very grand – only a couple of pictures. And you really shouldn't feel you have to come...'

'But of course I'll be there. Don't I always take August off to come home?'

They'd hardly talked last night – he had been too tired, she, too preoccupied with the exhibition. Now sun filled the kitchen, gleaming upon the copper pots that hung above the fireplace, bleaching the dark wood of the table and chairs, ripening the fruit – peaches, plums, apricots – plump upon the grape leaves that lined an ancient wicker basket. In his childhood, the kitchen had always smelled of cooking – some extraordinarily elaborate concoction was always either just out of the oven or boiling away in a saucepan on the stove, with Mother and Rina hovering over the two. Today, there was only the faintest smell of coffee, lingering from Alma's earlier cup, which she had taken here alone, while he had slept off his journey.

He looked up at his sister: she looked well, not as thin

as in the wake of their father's death. The blue shadows beneath her eyes, and the hollows beneath the cheekbones had disappeared. 'How's it going?' He felt as if he were circling her warily.

'Oh all right.' She stood at the stove, busied herself with the coffee pot. She lit the gas beneath it, then came back, wearing a smile. 'This exhibition' – she gestured towards the canvases that stood in rows along the kitchen wall – 'has kept me busy. In the end, I painted quite a lot this past year ... it was a good way to cope with Father's death.' She squatted now by one canvas, her index finger pointing out an undulating blue horizon. 'Do you recognize this view? It's from your bedroom window – I painted there in the autumn, you can see the Alps from yours, mine faces west ... and look here.' She was excited, showing him now one canvas now another, smiling up at him from her squatting position, sharing with him her vision of the landscape they had in common.

Francesco looked down, obedient, at the vivid colours, the wild curves and sudden planes of the landscapes. 'They're all very good,' he said. And although he didn't like these solid, brightly lit scenes, where figures lay, or danced, naked and bold, he felt admiration fill him. He envied her this ability to forge a wholly personal universe, to arrange her images so that they ebbed and flowed before your eyes.

He found himself holding his sister in the same awe that, long ago, he had felt for Gianni er Brutto, whose storytelling had filled his childhood summers. Among the strutting roosters and the rabbit hutches of his courtyard, Gianni er Brutto had fixed broken bicycles and chairs, rewired ancient lamps, sanded newly made wooden furniture: and all the while, he recounted long tales, hammering out stories with eagerness, while Francesco listened and wondered at this source of magic and adventures. Gianni's tales would unfold like a farmer's knapsack, to reveal bits of folklore, of wisdom. A wisdom that rose from days and nights spent observing, as the village outcast, what people said and did.

The same desire for magic had drawn Francesco to his publishing profession, and made him approach writers with delighted trepidation, as if they possessed incredible powers, were privy to mysterious secrets. 'We're all vain, brazen creatures, you know,' one of his authors had once told him over the wine with which they'd sealed a contract. 'We're always issuing our small challenges to God above – we're always telling Him: "See what a world You created: ugly and full of misery ... look instead over here, at the world I've created, and see how much better it is!"' And at this the author, a ribald satyr who loved his wine and his words and his women in equal measure, had chuckled and grinned at Francesco, as if conscious of the latter's fascination with the craft he had just described.

And today as he studied his sister's paintings he knew she belonged to the author's race: to those who had found their own voice, and with it issued their challenges to all they encountered.

'The coffee!' Alma rushed back to the stove. She poured milk into a saucepan and stood watching it heat, arms crossed.

He looked up from the canvases. 'It'll be a spectacular success, this exhibition. The first step on your path to glory.' He replaced the painting and resumed his seat. As he watched her pouring the coffee and hot milk in the porcelain bowls they had used since they were little, he wished he had not come for next week's private view, had not taken, so readily, a spectator's seat in her life. But immediately he felt guilty; this was her achievement, and of course he should participate in its celebration.

She stood beside him now and handed him a bowl. 'And you ... how are things in London?'

'Oh ... this year's gone by quickly.' He shrugged as if to shake off her interest in himself and his life away from here. 'Camilla is well. I can't complain about the job, either – every other house is being bought up while we keep our head ... What about you – I mean, apart from the painting?'

'Oh, I see all the usual suspects, still go out dancing until all hours, though I suppose at my advanced age I should stop acting like a teenager ...' But she was laughing and he could see she felt full of youthful vigour. 'And I spend an increasing amount of time worrying about where my next commission will come from.'

'And this life makes you happy?'

'Are you happy?' she snapped.

'Sorry. What I meant was, no thought of settling down? A man, a home, a child or two?'

Alma laughed. 'Please, Francesco! You sound like one of our well-meaning elderly relatives who keep inviting me to drawing rooms that remind me of a mausoleum.' She ran her fingers through her hair, gave him a wide smile. 'What's the rush? Despite Father's death, the shock of having to sell the lands, and a couple of difficult clients who want you to flatter them rather than present them with the truth, I'm happy. Sometimes a bit lonely, yes, but all in all happy.' She repeated herself with conviction.

'I suppose I always imagined one found happiness in the bosom of the family – I'd rather see you fat and happy behind a stove with two children at your knees and no time for your painting than to hear you talk of being lonely.' He paused. 'Maybe it's too conformist an image.'

'It is.' She nodded, impatient. 'You can't possibly see me fit into a tidy scheme of marriage and children, with my life punctuated by square meals, the sewing circle and tea with other housewives, can you?'

Francesco said nothing. The heat from the window fell on his arm, in stripes. He felt tired from the flight, yesterday's rush. And the quarrelling with Camilla. He'd asked her to join him for his sister's private view. But he'd known full well that she would refuse. 'I don't find a little village in the hills of Piedmont a very amusing holiday spot,' she'd sniffed, for the umpteenth time. 'I mean really, Francesco, it's not even Tuscany!' She would go off to stay with friends in the south of France instead. He hadn't insisted: they'd had a bad year, full of quarrels, tears and Camilla's complaints about their lifestyle: 'I long for glamour, you know I do ...' She brushed her hair and pouted in the mirror at him. 'Oh if only our life held some excitement!' He'd tried to bury his unhappiness and her recriminations in long hours at work, but by the summer his managing director had called him in. 'You need a holiday, my boy.' He'd given him an avuncular pat on the shoulder. 'We all go through a bad patch at some point. You need a break. A change of scene can do wonders for a marriage.'

Francesco wrapped his hands around the hot porcelain.

'Oh Francesco, look at you!' She set down her bowl of caffelatte and laughed: her laughter was like Father's, hot,

100

thick, erupting from a smoker's throat. 'You look like a glutton doing his Lenten fast! Stop wearing such a martyred air ... who is the lucky one? You've got a good job, solid prospects and a loving wife ...'

Francesco smiled: 'It's not quite as you see it.' He sipped the caffelatte. 'The job is nothing more than peddling other people's talents, and for the rest ... Camilla ... I don't know. Anyway we needn't explain everything to one another.' He took another sip, scalded his tongue and set the bowl down with a clatter.

'Well, at least it's not too despicable an arrangement, is it?' Alma's voice mocked.

'No.' He shouldn't have been so eager to step back into this world of fields and hills, of farmyards and family ties. He studied his sister's face before him with the panic of a pharmacist who has mixed well-known liquids in order to produce the medicine he seeks – only to find that something altogether different has resulted.

'Well, here we are ... Drinking caffelatte in the morning, both concentrating on not burning our tongues and not drinking the milk's skin: just like when we were little.'

Francesco smiled: Mother busy shelling peas for lunch, head bent in womanly complicity with Rina. Alma half-sitting half-slipping from her chair, burning with her impatience to be outside. Upstairs Father rushing about, in search of his keys, his cigarettes, involving the whole household in his frantic urge to be out of the house and driving into town where God alone knew what bargain he would strike or what deal he would make.

Francesco closed his eyes and focused his senses on the porcelain bowl, the warmth of its coffee and milk.

'Father ...' he murmured.

'Don't.' Alma set down her bowl. 'The time after his death ... I've never felt so alone. He was my greatest ally: I used to come here and visit, moan to him about the competition, about the dealers and the gallery owners.'

'I told you to come to us ...' he began, his voice defensive. 'Camilla and I – we would have loved to have you stay.' She looked away from him, as if she knew that this was not true. 'So tonight we'll go to the festa.'

'Of course. I mean to dance the polka till dawn.' Alma grinned. She cocked her head. 'If you listen carefully, you can hear the gypsies calling out to one another as they set up the Ferris wheel ...'

'Tell me. What news in the village?'

'Oh my goodness!' Alma pushed away the bowl and rolled up her sleeves. 'I'd forgotten! I was so preoccupied with this exhibition, I completely forgot to tell you about the shrine! Though no doubt if things continue this way, they'll soon be talking of nothing else even in England.'

Francesco shook his head. 'What ... ?' He waited.

'Our village is threatening to become a miniature holy city, with pilgrims, vendors' stalls, grottos and the like. And the focus of it all, you'll be amazed to hear, is Santarella.' Alma's voice was full of mirth, and she smiled at her brother's puzzled face. 'You see, about a year ago, our Santa told Don Luigi that the Madonna was coming down for regular chats with her. And Don Luigi, never one to respect secrets, immediately informed the villagers. He and the mayor have been building great castles in the air about the hordes of pilgrims who will descend upon San Lorenzo to witness the visitations, to drink the water that our Santa drinks, to walk the streets she walks, and so forth. And the poor villagers, needless to add, have been bullied into accepting the whole thing.'

Francesco shook his head in disbelief. 'I've never ... but how could they convince Santarella to take part in all this ... she was extraordinary, above everyone around her, untouchable ... I can't imagine her playing a role in this farce about the shrine ...'

'Who knows what she thinks? In any case, I feel for her,' Alma interrupted him. 'I wouldn't want to be spending my afternoons amidst incandescent Madonnas and gilt-winged angels.'

'Well, I shall be standing there, side by side with the pilgrims, trying to catch a glimpse of the visionary ...' He laughed and stood up. 'I'll go and unpack. I need a shave as well.' He rubbed his cheek with the back of his hand. At the door he turned. 'Don't worry about the exhibition – I am certain it will be a great success.'

Alma listened to her brother's footsteps as they receded up the stairs. Francesco. She was always disappointed by their reunions: it was as if, after a year apart, too much had been done, said, thought in their separate lives to have left anything for their time together. She had meant to tell him a thousand things – that she had loved his Christmas present (a book on El Greco); that she had kept for Camilla one of Father's silver cigarette cases; and, most important, about Alberto ...

Today there would be Alberto's luncheon. He had insisted that she go: he was leaving for Rome tomorrow, only to come back in a week's time, for the private view. She had ended their affair in the spring, but they still saw each other frequently: he had been as generous in accepting her dismissal as he had been in his tutelage of

103

her. Lunch with Francesco might prove awkward, though: dread filled her as she saw the white table beneath the pines, the laughing faces and one of Alberto's friends or colleagues making some reference to their past alliance. What would Francesco think of her then? All along, she had known that his was the judgement she feared, his the only voice that echoed that of her parents. And she knew, as if he had spoken them out loud, the words of disappointment with which he would greet the revelation of her affair.

Still, she couldn't very well leave Francesco behind – he'd be hurt, or ask a thousand questions ... But as she walked slowly upstairs to her bedroom, Alma resolved not to tell her brother about her affair.

13

Francesco stood silent in the bedroom of his childhood. The three windows were shut and bolted, so that the air hung dark and heavy about the furniture. In the sombre half-light he looked over the thick curves and broad planes of the ancient prie-dieu and the marble washstand, the faded pastels of delicate garlands upon the ceiling. Everything was the same, and brought him bright memories of summer nights spent with open windows, of mornings when he'd rush from the bed to be down in the garden.

He slowly opened the suitcase, then laid it flat and open on the bed: rows of ties, three ironed shirts, a pair of shoes and fist-like socks; an old pair of trousers, and underwear. He had packed while she had looked on, her gaze indifferent.

He began to undo a window's bolt. He pulled open the wooden shutters, twisted the old-fashioned iron handle, pushed open the glass panes: everything now lay ablaze before him, the sunny fields beyond the green orchard leaves, the brick well in a far-flung corner, and the girdle of vineyards to the west. Above the dark waves of hills, the sky stretched pale and shiny. San Lorenzo. After all these years, it was still home. Perhaps ... perhaps he should have come back, years ago, when all was still possible. Perhaps he would have done it all differently, now. Now that Mother was dead, that Father's shadow no longer fell across the fields and vineyards of San Lorenzo, now that Camilla hungered for money he wondered whether it had been, in the end, the right choice. Had he stayed, would he have tasted the dissatisfaction that lingered, like yesterday's kitchen odours, between him and Camilla?

He wondered if he shouldn't retrace his footsteps, come back to San Lorenzo, lead his life against an undulating blue horizon, against a backdrop of orchard trees and fields. In the certainties of a life shaped by the seasons, by tradition and by the connections of generations, he might find the serenity that eluded him in London.

He turned from the window sill: he must try to see Gianni er Brutto. And Miso Brusoni. He wanted to talk with them, listen to their words over a glass of wine in front of Vanna's bar. He hadn't seen them last year – there had been too much to preoccupy him, with Father's death and the funeral, the sale of the lands and Camilla's calling him back to nurse her. But this time he would.

He went back to the bed and rummaged through his case for his razor and shaving foam. He hurried now, with his shaving: next door he could hear Alma move about her bedroom. Alma had not changed. Thank God: he had been afraid to find her lonely and vulnerable. But the girl he could hear whistling was the same strong proud girl of before, mocking everyone and everything, full of life, a clear, untroubled echo of their father.

'May I come in?' Alma rapped the door and let herself in without waiting for his answer. She sat on the bed and

106

smiled into the mirror: 'Just like Father, can't bear to shave in the bathroom ...' She shook her head and crossed her arms. Francesco continued to shave but looked now at her reflection: nothing of the admiration that had filled his eyes as he watched his father perform this rite could be found in Alma's brown eyes now. He almost smiled at the thought. He splashed water on his clean- shaven face, dried himself with a linen towel at the corner of which his parents' initials lay linked in tiny blue stitches.

'Today – it's rather a bore, I'd forgotten that I'd been invited by della Rocca and a few of his friends for lunch ... at Lino's in Castel d'Oro – remember, we used to always go in September for their truffles...'

'Della Rocca? Bernardino or Alberto?'

'Alberto. The serious one. He's been awfully kind, has recommended my portraits to a couple of influential gallery owners, forced a couple of rich industrialists to sit for me ... basically it's difficult for me to cancel. I told him you were here, he said he'd love to see you ... can you face it?' She was studying her hands, head bent over them.

'Why not? It will be fun to see the old place ...'

Alma jumped up from the bed: 'It's such a nuisance really.' She moved away to the open window. 'I'd rather have had you all to myself ... just because he's so terribly helpful I'd never risk offending him ...' She addressed him over her shoulder. 'Well, at least we'll get a sumptuous lunch out of it: you know how they are, these middle-aged tycoons and faded beauties – only the gullet can give them pleasure now.'

Francesco laughed: 'I don't really frequent these people,

you know.' He took off his shirt, then bent over his suitcase and chose a clean one.

Alma's voice rose in teasing: 'Pristine shirts, silk ties, crisply creased trousers and balled up socks in the four corners: a perfect testimony to my brother's neat and proper life, packed with care and wonderful skill by a loving wife's dainty hands. Hmmmm ...' She laughed now, behind him, and Francesco felt himself flush in anger.

Slowly he took out one shirt then another, keeping them neatly folded over his knee, pretending to choose between them. Finally, he stood up and faced his sister. 'Don't be so silly, Alma. You're beginning to sound like a sour-mouthed spinster.'

He watched her eyes turn to the open window, then heard her sigh. 'Sorry, let's not quarrel.' She leaned out, her elbows pressing on the hot sill. 'Look, did you see, one of our old hazelnuts died last winter and through the gap we can see right into Signorina Teresa's rooms. Now there we have a blameless spinster, the lonely old lady without a soul to care for her in her last years ...' Alma's voice lowered now. 'I have been studying her quite a lot, you know...'

Francesco buttoned the last button of his shirt, rolled up the sleeves and placed a hand on his sister's shoulder. 'Come away from there.'

Alma turned from the window, a wide smile on her lips. But Francesco saw the tears that sparkled in her eyes, and pecked her forehead. 'I'm sorry ... Lack of sleep makes me irritable. I was thinking: shall I ring Aunt Lucia?'

'Whatever for?'

'Family obligations and all that.'

Alma made a face. 'Oh Francesco, she is such a bore ... but of course you must do as you please. She's bound to come to the private view in any case.'

Francesco frowned at his sister. 'I know, but it would be more polite ... She's family, Alma. Remember what Father always said: family's like a mattress – no matter how lumpy or how hard, it's always better than sleeping on the floor.'

Alma laughed and raised her arms as if yielding to the enemy. 'Oh all right, all right, do as you please.' She made her way to the door. 'I'll go and change.' Then, at the door, she turned and beamed him a smile. 'I'm glad you're home.'

Francesco sighed when the door was shut behind her. He took his address book from the case. Alma was wrong to turn from the solace of family ties. He found his aunt's number in Torino. Aunt Lucia: he wondered which questions would greet him first – 'Why's your wife not with you?', 'Why still no children?', 'Still happy far away from home?'. Questions only family would dare ask and expect a truthful answer to. Questions which he had feared from Alma, but which she had spared him.

He picked up the telephone, dreading now the arrogant rich voice, the curiosity that would submerge him. How would he explain anything, hide anything from the prying relative? What excuses would he be forced to offer, in order that her curiosity might be fed? He replaced the telephone, and stood up, feeling suddenly disheartened, tired: he could avoid Aunt Lucia's prying today, but not at Alma's private view.

14

Beneath low-hanging pines, the piazza of Castel d'Oro lay protected from the midday heat. Lino's restaurant, famed for its truffles and its veal cutlets, took up a wide stretch of the town square, competing on Mondays and Fridays with the market stalls.

For years, Francesco and Alma had accompanied their mother and Rina to the market here. They had listened to Mother ask for their favourite fruits, to Rina haggling with the stallkeepers, listened to the arguing between the big men and women who stood behind the crates of fruits, vegetables, flowers and straw baskets. They had watched as rinds, leaves, pulps and over-ripe fruits were swept into heaps, sucked by flies, trodden by careless feet, to be pored over later by the town's paupers.

Today, brother and sister arrived as the market was being dismantled. The vendors rushed about, jostling their way past the lingering last customers, lifting with ease huge crates of unsold plums, apricots, cherries, lettuce, tomatoes, aubergines, all the while calling to one another in thick Piedmontese dialect.

The generous sticky odours of fruits, vegetables and blossoms lifted from the stalls. The scent filled the pores of the ancient buildings, the nostrils of those seated at the restaurant, the mouth of the scavenging mongrel whose muzzle, buried in a pyre of bruised plums and melons, had sniffed out a chicken wing.

The square overlooked a green stretch of land – the vineyards and hills of San Lorenzo, Susa, and in the distance the flat plain of Alessandria. Behind Lino's restaurant, medieval houses stood cheek by jowl, their windows open: the radio's commercial crooning and last night's football results came down in snatches, as did the sound of a pot cover crashing to the floor, of a baby's hungry wailing, a couple's quarrel, water rushing from a tap. An old man came out onto his balcony and sprinkled crumbs on his railing. He leant briefly out, to watch the mess of colours in the piazza below, then retreated back into the darkness of the kitchen.

'Ah here they are . . .' Alberto della Rocca stood up from the long table beneath the pines and came towards them.

Francesco shook the dry warm hand: Alberto looked cool and elegant, despite the harsh midday sun. His smooth silver hair was combed back to reveal the clear blue eyes that endlessly appraised everyone, everything. His smile hovered briefly across his slim suntanned face, and Francesco heard him speak in a pleasant, non-committal manner that assured you that, really, he had very little time or interest to devote to making a good impression.

'Welcome back, Francesco. You look well.' But Alberto's eyes were on Alma. He took her hand now and drew her close to him. 'Alma, no greetings from you?'

Alma placed her lips on his left cheek, then on his right, her eyes fixed on something behind his head.

'Come, Francesco, let me introduce you to the others.'

Alberto led him to the table where two women and two men, well-dressed, well-combed, gleaming in the half-light that fell from the branches above, sat and talked. Everyone turned to appraise the new arrivals. 'This is Francesco Ferrati, Alma's brother. He's here on loan from London, but only for a couple of days, so we should be honoured to have him among us.' Alberto adopted the thinly jocular tone of the humourless man.

Alma turned to Alberto. 'Where am I to sit then?'

'Come here, come here: I've saved you a chair beside me!' Rosso d'Arrighi, whom she knew from previous outings with Alberto, patted the chair to his right and gave her a rogue's wink. Alma obeyed and settled down next to the big burly man. 'Hello, beautiful.' With a loud smack Rosso's thick lips kissed her forehead.

The conversation, which for a few minutes following the brother's and sister's arrival had embraced them with questions about their welfare, about London, about Alma's exhibition and Francesco's view of Italy's economy, now resumed its earlier fragmented way with each end of the table discussing a different topic.

Francesco sat back in his chair: with Alma there across from him, with the white tablecloth garnished with dishes full of antipasti, the dark bottles of wines sporting expensive labels, the voices and laughter that rose and scattered like a flock of birds beneath the pines, he thought himself back at one of those long hot luncheons that Father used to organize here in Castel d'Oro 'to celebrate'. And there was always something to celebrate – some business venture, some land sale or simply a good mood. Alberto's presence (cool, every action and sound reined in) seemed to confirm the impression of travelling back in time:

Alberto and his brother Bernardino had always sat at one end of the table, with Father between them. The three of them would trade jokes and business tips, talk of land and crops and cast admiring glances at a pretty passer-by – sharing the well-being of men who have a great deal and know that few others do.

Today, the same talk filled the air, settled over the table. Rosso d'Arrighi complained about the shoddy work and high salaries he was forced to put up with in his glass factories, whilst the man to his left, a squat dark man with meagre grey curls and a shirt open halfway down his chest, spoke sadly of the disbanding of his ancestors' great estate, all the while caressing the perfectly suntanned arm of the beautiful young girl beside him. These were landowners and small industrialists, thought Francesco, with well-groomed wives – or mistresses – and middle-aged confidence: they were moneyed men and women and he felt ill at ease among their smooth ways and words.

'Bussola,' Rosso d'Arrighi called out to the man with the grey curls and the open shirt. 'Stop losing sleep over having to sell your lands. If you'd taken my advice, you would have sold those hectares long ago, made a tidy profit, and invested in that mill I told you about.' Rosso d'Arrighi was speaking in the loud voice of those who believe others should listen. 'Don't you know by now that Rosso here can sniff out a profit like a trained pig truffles?' And he poured himself another glass of wine, to toast his business acumen.

'Ah well ...' Bussola sighed. 'Some of us are not so lucky as yourself, Rosso. You've managed to go into business, but me ... I was brought up thinking that your land is your livelihood ... such beautiful vineyards, splendid wine ...' He sought consolation in his beautiful young mistress beside him. She sat immobile, perfect face expressionless amidst long blonde waves, as she allowed him to caress her shoulder.

'Of course, of course, Fernando.' Rosso d'Arrighi's voice once again took over the table talk. 'We all love our fields and vineyards as much as the next man. Why, my parents and grandparents owned more land than almost every other family in the Monferrato! But we have to all learn how to bend with the winds ...' Rosso laughed and raised his glass once again, this time to toast his own pragmatism. 'Here's to those of us who know how to land on our feet.'

Francesco frowned at his menu: money, money, money seemed to stain every word and gesture of the man. Money fed his masculinity, nursed his middle-aged pride, quenched his thirst for others' envy. Nothing else seemed to interest these people, nothing else seemed to satisfy them.

'Haven't seen you in ages, my dear girl.' Alma felt her shoulder squeezed by one of Rosso's large hands. His quick brown gaze swept her figure. 'Last time, you were dancing with my son for ages at the Sonninis' fancy dress party! I told him to watch his step with a sophisticated young lady like you.'

'Stefano's perfectly able to look after himself!' From her end of the table, the Contessa d'Arrighi raised her sunglasses to crown her dome of bleached hair. 'It was a super party!' She waved her cigarette in its ivory holder.

'And your son a super dancer.' Alma laughed. She was in a good mood, despite Rosso's overbearing exuberance. And the sun was shining, the wine tasted cool and golden, the food promised to be glorious. Over the rim of her glass she ran her eyes from one face to the next around the white table: yes, here they sat, the members of Alberto's world – and of her world, too, should she so choose. How easy it would be to close one's eyes and hand over the reins to Alberto once again, so that she could spend her days in search of pleasure and amusement, sit back at al fresco luncheons and sip drinks at evening salons, slightly bored, slightly complacent, safe. She met Alberto's eyes. Quickly she turned away.

'Food! Food! What should I have today, my dear Lino?' The Contessa d'Arrighi patted her bouffant hair-do with a pensive bejewelled hand, then threw up her menu and beckoned the restaurant owner. 'Take me by the hand, Lino, you know how I hate to make decisions ...' she moaned, and took up her ivory cigarette holder and fitted a new cigarette into it.

The restaurant owner, fat and white-faced, bent over Sofia d'Arrighi's middle-aged shoulders, paid her the attention she once received from men, now only from shopkeepers and restaurateurs. At the other end of the table, Fernando Bussola, Rosso's friend, chose his young mistress's meal, while the girl smiled and nodded and smiled again.

Francesco held up his menu for perusal, but his eyes slid to the pretty young girl at his side. She smiled incessantly, certain that her youthful beauty would smooth her sailing through any gathering such as today's. Such a pretty face, he thought as his eyes moved from the Risotto alla Milanese on the menu to the delicate lineaments she offered, from the Scaloppine al Marsala to the golden brown of her eyes, from the Truffles-and-Parmesan

Tagliatelle to the slim long arm beside his own. As if sensing approaching danger, Bussola's hand captured the girl's once more. Francesco cast off his incipient lust with only faint regret.

'And you, Francesco ...' Alberto turned his cool eyes onto Francesco. 'Did it break your heart to sell your father's lands last year? Or is there no sentiment for land among you men of the younger generation?'

Francesco blushed beneath the blue gaze that his father's friend turned upon him. 'Selling the land was difficult, yes. But if it was the only way to keep the house, we knew we had to do it.' Once again he felt he had to justify his behaviour.

Alberto was nodding. 'Nowadays only a handful of farmers and a few of the old guard like ourselves' – and here he overlooked d'Arrighi's indignant protestations of youth – 'feel any bond with the lands of our forefathers ... I don't know what else exists today to give these young people a sense of belonging and background – but I'm sure' – here he laid his eyes upon Alma who sat immobile, staring straight ahead – 'that they have found some worthy replacement.'

Alma felt Alberto's eyes rest on her face and throat, and she threw a look in her brother's direction: no, he had not jumped to any conclusions yet, and seemed more interested in the food before him than in any stories of his sister's past. Thank goodness.

'Beautiful!' Sofia d'Arrighi clapped her hands as the food arrived: in baskets, on platters, in bowls carried forth by waiters in white. With quick hands and a smile here, a nod there, the waiters served Alberto and his entourage, and the gathering fell into hushed anticipation. Red,

116

yellow, green, white: the food platters, soaked in sauces, bedecked the table. Risotti, spaghetti, salads, veal cutlets ... an endless array now covered the cloth.

'This is what I call a serious meal!' And Rosso dug into his spaghetti's truffle sauce with the same gusto with which he would negotiate a business deal.

Now everyone bustled about their food, swapping plates, passing a favourite dish from one end of the table to the other, exclaiming with pleasure, groaning with guilt. Some took to their plates with forks as eager as farmers' pitchforks to a haystack; others simpered like bashful girls at their first dance as they prodded one bit here, one bit there.

'I knew your father only a little, but I was so upset by his death – a man full of life ...' Bussola was leaning close up to his bowl of spaghetti, a napkin knotted comically round his neck, to protect his half-open shirt. He turned to Francesco. 'There were rumours about his debts ... I hope you've sorted all that out ... I have a cousin who found he had to sell every bit of his inheritance because his parents had borrowed above their heads...'

Francesco frowned. 'Yes. We've settled everything.' He resented this squat grey-haired man in his ridiculous napkin probing into his father's deals.

'Make sure that you go through all his papers,' Bussola, impervious to Francesco's irritation, would have proceeded, had not Sofia d'Arrighi cried out: 'A new arrival! Well, well, well, Alberto, what have we here?' And then, in a loud aside to the rest of the table: 'Far too good-looking to belong to our troop...'

The big, sun-bronzed man had made his way to Francesco's chair. 'Miso!' Francesco, delighted, leapt to his feet. 'Come and join us ... here, let me introduce you...'

'Over here, you fool, over here, don't get stuck at that end of the table! The beauties are perched right beside me!' And Rosso d'Arrighi stood up, big arms wide in an embrace that welcomed not only the new arrival but the whole of the restaurant, the waiters, the courtyard. 'Come here, young man, come here and meet the most charming girl I know.' He placed a large hand on Alma's shoulder. She smiled over her glass: it was Francesco's friend, the notary. She hadn't seen him in years. She looked at him in his expensive sober suit, and thought him handsome – large and dark, with gleaming dark eyes in a bronzed face. As Rosso reached over the table to shake his hand, Miso cast Alma a long appreciative look.

'Miso Brusoni.' Miso shook the hands proffered and ignored the booming commands being issued from Rosso's end of the table. He pulled up a chair to sit beside Francesco. 'I was having lunch inside with a client and I thought I recognized you ... I came to your father's funeral, but I didn't get a chance to speak to you. I haven't seen you properly for years...'

'I come for my holidays every August.'

'I go away for my holidays every August.' Miso grinned. 'But this year, I took my mother to a mountain resort at Christmas – so here I am.'

For a moment, the two men's eyes sharpened with mutual evaluation – more than twelve years had passed since Francesco had gone to study in London on his scholarship. Where did they stand now, in relation to one another, which worlds did each inhabit, how many turns had they taken from the road of their common past?

118

'The prodigal son ...' Miso smiled and squinted in the sun. 'Will he ever come home for good?'

'Well ... nothing's impossible.' Francesco set down his fork. 'But meanwhile I come back to stay in the family home, to see Alma ... you realize her exhibition opens next week.' Francesco poured Miso a glass of wine and leaned across to his sister. 'You'd better invite him to the private view – you see how smart his suit is and you heard the talk of a client ... he'll buy up the whole lot of them I bet.'

Miso raised his glass to Alma. 'Nice to see you again.' He smiled. 'I never see you in the village, but my young friend Grillo keeps us posted as to your movements. You have a devoted fan.'

'I'm very grateful. Though I could do with a few more. Preferably of the kind who commission paintings ...'

'I've heard all about the exhibition. There was even a piece in the *Gazzetta* about it ... photo too. Very impressive ...' Miso's voice teased.

Alma smiled, her eyes on her brother. 'You must come, Miso. It'll make it less of a trial for Francesco.'

Miso turned to Francesco. 'Married to a foreigner, eh? You know what they say, oxen and wives should hail from your native lands ... I bet you're settled into a successful career and earn more than enough money to feed your heirs with.'

'You still speak such rubbish.' Francesco grinned. 'What about you? Gianni er Brutto told me you didn't go into politics, as you'd threatened back then. I remember your impassioned speeches about the exploited masses ...'

'No politics for me I'm afraid. I bowed to the great indifference of this stagnant country. All those speeches of innocent idealism never amounted to anything. I got as far as trying to become a professor at the university but then – I didn't shine at exams.' He shrugged. 'So I decided to opt for something less ambitious and took over my father's business instead. Being a notary doesn't inspire anyone, and hardly sets off sparks for the revolution, but it's easy and you can make a good enough living.' Beneath the flippant tone, Francesco heard the faintest of melancholic notes: when they'd been young, who would have expected defeat?

A scream of laughter deafened them both as Sofia d'Arrighi relished some sally of Lino's.

'Then we've both let the side down.' Francesco sipped his wine.

'I suppose we have. But things aren't as bad as all that – look at what we could have turned into ...' Miso waved his hand to encompass the table and the seated company.

'I want you to paint my portrait, my dear girl.' Rosso placed his arm round Alma's shoulders.

Alma shook herself free of the big brown paw. 'You wouldn't sit still long enough, dear Rosso. But come to the private view and you can see all the people you know ...'

'True to life?'

'Heaven forbid – what do you think they pay me for? I'm to iron out every wrinkle, remove excess weight, fade away age spots ... I'm a miracle worker!' Alma laughed.

'What of my Filomena, why not paint her, she needs no miracles to look beautiful?' And Bussola raised his mistress's pretty hand to his lips.

Alma's gaze fell upon the girl across the table: hand captive in her lover's paw, Bussola's mistress smiled at the gathering. As if muzzled by her idea of femininity, she meekly waited for the males around her to cast their opinions and questions onto the table. She slipped into the silence that her mother, her grandmother, an entire bloodline of female ancestors had taught her. Watching the girl's passive expression, Alma winced: here she sat, the role model for every sweet companion, obedient mistress, pliable object of desire. With her voice never raised above a murmur, with her eyes so meekly downcast, Bussola's friend seemed to wish only for protection, for an assurance that her beauty need never decay with worry and the struggles of survival. How different this young woman was from herself...

'Yes of course, when I've finished setting up the exhibition...'

Miso and Francesco continued to ignore the rest of the lunch guests, engrossed in their own conversation. 'Do you know that every now and then Gianni er Brutto and I drink a toast to you?'

'Gianni...' Francesco smiled, moved. 'I plan to see him for a proper chat before I return to London...'

'Still full of sound advice. And, of course, he's taking no part in that nonsense that has blinded the rest of the villagers – you've heard I suppose? Santa as visionary, the village as shrine: it's all like some twopenny operetta. And saddest of all is the knowledge that the only thing that galvanizes these people into some form of action is profit. Talk about rights, freedoms and the pursuit of happiness and they wouldn't lift a finger. Dangle a purse of coins before their greedy eyes, though, and you could get them to move mountains.'

Francesco nodded. 'Though surely they don't think the bishop will say yes, do they? He would need to be convinced that Santa really had seen the Madonna but from the sound of it, Santa is not proving a co-operative saint.'

'It will take a lot more than that to put a stop to the villagers' plans.' Miso shook his head. 'They're determined to go ahead with the whole business. They're pleading with Bishop Natti of Torino to come to San Lorenzo and see things for himself ... as if there were anything to see. We haven't exactly got healing waters and there certainly has been no miraculous cure to speak of. But they already see the vendors' stalls, the throngs of pilgrims, the mementoes and T-shirts...'

Rosso d'Arrighi caught the tinny echoes of money talk, and immediately jumped into the conversation. 'What's wrong with a bunch of peasants making a bit of money from selling their little saint?'

Alberto, watching from the sidelines, saw Miso's frown, and like a good host he prevented the budding altercation. 'Rosso, don't always think of one thing...'

Rosso shook his head, and the rebuke slipped unheeded from his shoulders. 'I've got a good mind to invest some money in the scheme. Bussola, how about it – we buy ourselves a few years' indulgence by sinking funds into the holy site!'

Bussola nodded happily, his head of grey curls bobbing up and down: 'I'll join you, Rosso, I'll join you!'

'Good: a high-rise hotel, a big restaurant with some pretty waitresses...' Rosso snickered.

'How heart-warming to find that the spirit of enterprise is alive and kicking despite all the gloomy predictions that the country is going to the dogs.' Miso's voice was low but his face had darkened with anger. He stood up now, and pretended to check his watch. 'It's a shame,

Francesco, I've got to go to another appointment. I ... I might see you then at the private view ... if I may, that is?' He cast Alma the widest of grins. She nodded, suddenly embarrassed by Rosso, by the luncheon scene he'd witnessed.

'Oh no, look! He's gone! Look what you've done, Rosso! I told you to watch your drinking.' The contessa threw out her accusations while she blew clouds of smoke from her cigarette.

'Ohlalala ...' Rosso spoke in a loud stage whisper. 'If I get any mercy from Him up there, it will be because it takes a saint to live with that harpy!' And he placed an arm around Alma's shoulders.

Sofia d'Arrighi, now slightly tipsy, stubbed out her cigarette and laid aside the ivory holder. 'Stop pawing Alma, you fat old bear.'

'Did I ever tell you,' Rosso d'Arrighi placed his large soft-palmed hand upon her arm, 'that you're the most tantalizing woman I know? The most tantalizing woman in this country in fact.'

'For God's sake, Rosso!' From her end of the table the contessa slapped the table.

'Alma, Alma, let's get drunk so that I may forget the mill stone about my neck!' Rosso winked at her and poured them both more wine. 'A toast to Alma!' He raised his glass to Alma and then to Alberto. 'You let the best one get away!'

'Don't talk such nonsense.' Alberto remained composed.

Bussola shook his grey curly head at Alberto. 'Alberto, you'd better put a stop to this – your former girlfriend is causing a marital squabble that will upset our digestion!'

Francesco stared at Bussola, at Alberto, at Alma's blushing face. He set down his glass, wine slopping within, spilling over onto the white tablecloth. He made as if to speak, but the contessa had turned to him, eyebrow arched, voice cold. 'You should move back to Torino, my dear boy, and come and keep an eye on your sister ... not even Alberto was capable of managing her, and he's famous for the hard line he takes with...'

Francesco didn't hear the rest: he could feel the wine rise in his throat, swaying inside him as it had done in the glass. The heat beat down despite the shade, and he stood up, almost upsetting the chair and disturbing the pretty girl beside him. 'I'm sorry to rush off like this but I've suddenly remembered something I ought to give Miso ... please forgive me ...' He slapped some money on the table, which drew a frown from his host, and walked away.

15

Don Luigi strode, beneath the sun, down the dusty path that circumscribed the village – he didn't want a thousand eyes to follow his mission, and a thousand questions to greet him once he returned.

It was mid-afternoon, but no one seemed to be taking their siesta today. The piazza was bustling with the gypsies and some of the village youngsters setting up the wooden floor for tonight's festa, the fortune-teller Morgana flouncing about her stall, black and red skirts swirling, eyes and earrings shiny. And children were everywhere: on bicycles they scooted round the partisan's statue, round the men at work, exchanging excited cries with one another; on foot they ran and hopped, getting in everyone's way, mimicking Grillo who was strumming his guitar outside his mother's bar.

The festa ... each year, it required the same preparations. And to think that perhaps by next year's feast-day he would be able to announce that San Lorenzo had been recognized by the diocese as a holy site, worthy of a shrine...

Don Luigi sighed and took slow slow steps towards the Felici property. 'Why, dear Father, does Bettino persist in sending me out on the most difficult assignments? First,

Alma Ferrati and now ...' He shivered despite the hot sun. 'Oh dear Lord, lend me Your help to convince Franca: let the Holy Spirit melt her heart, let it melt her hard pride, Oh Father, so that by the time I reach her kitchen, I won't need to argue with her ... you know how that big woman frightens me, Lord ...'

Above the hatless padre, the sun shone behind a haze. A tractor rumbled past Don Luigi and a farmer waved his hand in greeting, but the priest only saw big broad Franca's face. 'Eh, I am worried, good kind Lord ... have I been too optimistic with the shrine? If Bishop Natti refuses to come down and begin the enquiry, Father, if he doesn't even set eyes on our Santarella, if he refuses to be moved by our people's appeal ... what will happen then?'

But he had arrived now at the tall black gates, and he felt his heart shiver as the Felici guard dogs (undernourished, mean-looking creatures, Father!) began their alarm.

One of Franca's sons opened the gates and ushered in the fearful priest. He found Franca in the kitchen, rolling out dough for the dinner's tagliatelle, whilst Beppe her first-born read out the latest profits from a black book and Rosa her daughter-in-law suckled her baby.

Franca betrayed no knowledge of the purpose behind Don Luigi's visit. She continued to push and pull her dough, to sprinkle her rolling pin with flour.

'Eh Franca, you prosper and prosper, and your family always looks happy and strong,' the priest began, fanning himself with his breviary. It was hot in the kitchen, with sun in the windows and the oven roaring.

'Yes, Don Luigi, praise be to God for looking kindly down on me and my brood.' Franca slapped the dough now, hard, harder, till Don Luigi winced as though his own pastry-white body lay beneath Franca's wooden rolling pin.

'Yes, Franca, yes: you do well to praise Him. And Our Lady, too, must be pleased with you, Franca, that she makes your motherhood such a happy and fruitful one. Perhaps...'

But Franca now called out orders, left-right-left-right, like a general in command of lazy troops: 'Quick, Rosa, grab the napkin, the babe's wetting your skirt. Beppe, that can't be right: we sold Moscone much more than two tons of corn last year. Check again. What were you saying, Don Luigi?' The priest began to mumble once more, but Franca's voice soared high: 'Ah there, there's your mistake, Beppe: you forgot to take into account the Bruna fields ... we harvested a ton of corn in those fields alone ... but go on, go on, Don Luigi, I interrupted you, continue, continue.' And Franca set aside the first sheet of dough, now ready to be cut into strips.

'I was just saying, Franca, that when we are blessed, as you are, with all this wealth, all this good fortune ...' Don Luigi fanned himself faster.

'I wasn't blessed with anything but my heart, my head and my strong constitution, Don Luigi: everything else you see here I made myself, with sweat and sleepless nights.' And Franca took a thin-bladed knife to cut her dough. Don Luigi felt slightly faint.

'Of course, of course, my dear Franca. Of course. But, nevertheless, we must all remember to pay tribute to Our Good Lord. He who has placed us on this earth. And with the shrine that we plan to build in our village, we hope to honour Him, and Our Blessed Lady, Franca. But the shrine needs money, and I thought perhaps ...'

'Ah.' Franca stared straight into Don Luigi's eyes, set down her knife and wiped her hands upon her apron. 'I'm going to be needing all the money I can save to buy the Ferratis' house, and as much of the contents as I can, Don Luigi.'

'But – but is it for sale?' Don Luigi wiped his gleaming brow with a kerchief.

'Not yet, Padre: but one of my farmhands comes from a village near Genoa where all they talk about is the debt that Marcantonio, God rest his soul' – here both Franca and Don Luigi crossed themselves quickly – 'owes one of their trouble-makers. He's had to go abroad, made a mess of it somewhere I shouldn't wonder, and maybe he'll have to keep a low profile for a while longer … but my reckoning is that if he ever decides to come and claim the money owed him … well, those two young people don't have much money left. They'd be forced to sell the house, wouldn't they? And I could outbid any of the other inter-ested parties, I could beat the lot of them!' Franca was lining up the strips of dough upon the table. 'And I'll tell you something else, Padre' – and here she dangled a strip of dough from her hands, so that it looked like a snake she had mastered – 'once I move into the Ferrati house, I shall have accomplished everything I've ever wanted to. Anyway …' Franca cast him a broad and generous smile. 'I'm grateful to the Good Lord, Don Luigi, I don't want you thinking that I'm not. But He knows full well that I need all the money I can save: I want my children and grandchildren to lead the lives of signori – in a beautiful house, surrounded by beautiful things. As for the shrine – the village can do very well without me, just as I've always done very well without them.' Franca began to cover the strips of dough with two kitchen towels. 'In fact, Don Luigi, you may think this arrogant of me, but I have a feeling that the Good Lord has chosen me to put things in their place down here in San Lorenzo. He saw the way all these men fought among themselves with greed and envy, and He said: "I'll fix them now, I'll send them a woman who's worth a hundred of them. She'll buy all the lands and the vineyards from right under their noses." I don't want to blaspheme, Padre, but that is how I see my role in God's plans for San Lorenzo. No, no, sit there, don't mind me, I'll just get the rabbit from the oven ... Beppe, give the padre a glass of wine, he doesn't look well. This will revive you, Don Luigi!'

16

Lino's was emptying: customers had retired to their siesta, and the waiters hung about outside the restaurant, lighting a cigarette, swapping stories they had all heard before. In the lull of the mid-afternoon, with the sun piercing through the blue skies above them, even the waiters – overworked, underpaid, swollen-footed – felt that life could be pleasant.

'Well?' Alberto studied Alma over his second cup of espresso. They had been left behind by the others, and sat alone, ignoring the loud ribald tales being told in the doorway.

Alma felt the heat of the wooden chair beneath her, of the table upon which rested her arms: rays, filtered yet strong, reached her. The rays made the empty glasses sparkle, the cutlery shine, and turned Alberto's hair into silver. The placid drunken mood she had attempted to preserve had melted, and every breath she took felt too hot, and every word came out with difficulty.

'You're upset?' Alberto replaced the cup upon the saucer.

'Not really. It's in the past, after all. He would have found out at some point in any case – I mean, I would have told him.' Alma drew little squares upon the tablecloth with her finger. 'Well, I'd better be off, just in case he's waiting for me at home.'

'I rather doubt he's waiting for you at San Lorenzo ... he looked like he needed a long walk to purge some excess emotion ...' And Alberto twisted his lips in an ironic smile.

Alma shrugged. 'It doesn't matter. I want to go back home, be alone a while ...' Her voice trailed off in a whisper. The waiters moved back amidst the tables, whistling and barking orders to one another in a mock staging of the lunchtime customers.

'Don't be silly.' Alberto laid a hand upon her arm. 'It's not some major scandal. And everything will be forgotten by tomorrow. Why don't you come back to Torino with me now, so that you can check everything is as it should be at the gallery?'

Alma sat in silence, looking through the darkness that stretched beneath the pine branches, at the blue of the skies beyond. She remembered so many other lunches here, or in similar places, with Alberto and his friends, and her feelings of unease. Alma looked down at the hand on her arm. That hand – cool, dry, smooth: made to hold a steering wheel, to lead an elbow through a room full of strangers, to pull you in its wake. Silently that hand moved to take possession, so quiet in its approach that it never drew your eyes, till you lay in its grip.

'Alberto – I'd really rather be alone now. We'll talk soon.' Alma heard her own distant voice. 'Thank you for a marvellous lunch.'

Alberto turned in his chair so that he faced her fully. 'I'm beginning to lose patience. You're not a teenager, I'm not a lecherous octogenarian. You're making all this fuss

131

for nothing. And you were on tenterhooks throughout the lunch, I saw you.'

'Well, at least that added some spice to an otherwise dull meal.'

'I wasn't aware that my friends were so repugnant to you.' Alberto's voice remained cool and dry, but Alma didn't dare look at his expression. 'They certainly were good enough when it came to commissioning your paintings.'

'Oh Alberto, I'm sorry. Of course you're right. I'm grateful for everything you have done for me – you know I am. But ... you didn't see the look in his eyes. I've disappointed him. And he's the only person left who can judge me ... Francesco has always seen me the way my parents did – I was strong, self-confident, determined to forge ahead ... They would never have recognized me as the Alma you know. They never thought I'd slip, never thought I'd tumble.' She freed her hand gently from his grasp. 'And you were Father's great friend ... in Francesco's eyes, that makes my fall all the greater...'

Again the stealthy hand took hold of her arm. 'And in your own?'

'I suppose ...' She had difficulty speaking. 'I suppose in my own as well.'

'I enjoyed putting things right in that messy life of yours. And you know that I believe it needn't have ended. I think I could have made you happy. Still could.' Alma watched the sun skid along the cobblestones, tables and chairs. She said nothing. He lifted her chin, to look at her. 'You'll be lonely, Alma. Loneliness is terrible.'

'Compromise would be worse. As I am now – thanks to your help during my darkest hours, I'm the first to acknowledge it – I feel that I know who I am and what I want.'

Alberto's cool blue eyes bored into her. 'You want too much, Alma . . .'

'Do I? All I want is to paint, to keep my beloved house from crumbling, and to find a man with whom I can be myself.' She flashed him a sudden grin. 'And, Alberto, I have great faith that very soon I shall have it all . . . great faith in what the future will bring.'

'I'm not putting any pressure on you – I never have. You know how I feel about you. If you won't change your mind, I can accept that. But I think I should warn you that you'll have a difficult time ahead. People won't know how to deal with you. Most people lack the imagination to understand anyone who is the slightest bit different.'

'I'll be fine, don't worry.' She blew out the words as if they were a wish. She leaned towards him and pecked his cheek. 'You've been lovely. Thank you.' Before he could say another word, she was off.

While she drove back to San Lorenzo, through the hills and the sunlight of the afternoon, she felt a great sea of voices swelling inside her, telling her to feel finally free of that smooth, possessive hand, to rejoice in the resolve she had taken, sitting there beneath the pines, never to return to Alberto or to his world; and then, as this great tide of relief ebbed, she heard other voices whisper their fear that, without Alberto, she had no one.

17

Francesco walked through the hills of vineyards and corn fields that led from Castel d'Oro through Susa, to San Lorenzo. He walked fast, trying to distance himself as quickly as possible from the luncheon table beneath the pines where he'd left his sister and her former lover. Alma: how could she have had an affair with Alberto? He felt as if she had betrayed not only their father's memory but also his own image of her as strong, independent, the great survivor. He strode along the narrow pathways, white with dust, where the heat rolled in waves upon his head and neck: he walked them slowly, distracted from the luxurious gaiety of summer's green, red, yellow by the thought of his sister. He brushed against far-reaching branches, trampled upon the grasses that fell upon the path from the verges, limp, yellow-ended.

What kind of woman was his sister? They had grown up between the same intimate walls of Father, Mother, summers in San Lorenzo, winters in Torino, of collective rites and rituals. He, the quiet one, had surprised them all by rejecting their father's legacy and turning to publishing, in a foreign land. But Alma ... Seeing her at Father's side, their voices a unison of teasings, insults, praises which revealed that here sat two true friends,

Francesco had always regarded her as the spirited heir to that world. Now, remembering her shame-faced and silent beneath Alberto's gaze, he wondered.

The song of crickets grew louder as he crossed the tall field of corn, where stalks and husked fruit swayed in the new breeze: the afternoon was slipping away, muting colours, shading great stretches of land, crops, trees.

Mother had often come for walks here in these hills. She loved the world that lay rooted in damp earth, beneath green foliage, soft under foot. She came here with her children, and during their walks Alma would run ahead, prancing in the grass, calling to mother and brother to hurry. But Francesco felt bound to Mother's side by a long leash, and never ventured far from her without feeling a tug, a series of gentle pulls that led him back to her. They walked, mother and son, with a slow gait that allowed them to admire and breathe in the countryside. Here she seemed happier than at home, where she read alone at the drawing-room window, where she stood next to Rina at the stove, listening to their daily's cascade of gossip. She was happier here than in the salons of fashionable Torino, where her beauty won her admirers that her timidity soon lost. Happier than in the afternoons at San Lorenzo when she spooned out charm and sorbet to the village women who came once a week to sew together in the Ferratis' drawing room.

Francesco climbed now the last hill before San Lorenzo: the village lay below him, gilt-edged by the late afternoon sun. Soft, smelling of warmth, the breeze moved the cemetery's cypress trees, the walnuts and hazelnuts, the slim silver birches by the river. And the river itself, broad and fast-moving through grasses and birches, shone as bright as the silver crucifix above the church door. He had loved this world for its visible, well-known boundaries, for the familiar faces that peopled it, for the way everything began at sunrise and ended at sunset. The rites and rules of the land were like those he found at school, with the Jesuits: they ensured that continuity and predictability would wrap him in a habit of certainty. In the structured universe of San Lorenzo, as within the grey courtyard of school, Francesco knew who he was, where he fitted and where he was expected to go.

He walked on, but decided not to take the main road and go through the piazza, where he could see the Ferris wheel stretched high above the municipal hall and the bell tower. He took the road by the river, on the south side of the village. The Ferrati lands that were now Franca's prized possessions stretched golden on his right. Again, his heart filled with disappointment: had he not also betrayed his family, by selling the lands?

But he recognized now the grey wall that he was approaching: it was the back entrance to Gianni er Brutto's courtyard. Without hesitation, Francesco pushed open the wooden door, stepped into the small courtyard. On the gravel sat squat tubs of basil, zinnias, petunias, geraniums. A rooster stomped imperiously about, his hen resting in the shadows of the house. In a corner, rabbits pushed their noses through their hutch.

'Well, well, what an honour, what an honour. My dear boy.' Gianni came smiling towards him, one hand extended. He clutched Francesco's elbow and drew him towards the chairs that stood beneath the walnut tree. Here in the old days Gianni had had his worktable, spilling over with wooden boards, a saw, a hammer, nails and sawdust. Here he had mended and fixed and unravelled a tale and advice for his audience – Francesco and Miso most frequent of all.

'Do you remember?' Gianni's birthmark creased as he smiled. 'It broke my heart when I couldn't work any more ...' He looked down at his old freckled hands. 'Just can't hold a hammer with this arthritis ... And who could see a nail with my poor weak eyes?' He shook his head.

'It's nice to see you ... last year I had so much on, I didn't get a chance...'

'Shshsh, should be doing all the apologizing. I should have made an effort to come and see how you were, offer you my condolences ... but I felt embarrassed ... wasn't sure really how to do it ...' Gianni smiled and patted the big strong man's hand as if he were still a child. 'You look well. Very well.'

'I saw Miso at lunch. He really does look well. As for me ... I'm not too happy with things, to tell you the truth. The job, the friends, the marriage – nothing seems quite right, nothing seems to give me any great satisfaction.'

'Give? I think you're supposed to find aren't you?' Gianni smiled at him. 'It's not always just sitting there.' He stretched his hands out before him as if to study them in the dappled light. 'Don't you think that we are all worried about finding the heart of things? Of course we are. Sometimes there are so many layers on top though, you can't even hear it beating.'

'Gianni.' Francesco leaned back in his chair, looked up at the dark green dome of the walnut tree. 'I think I should come back. Live here in San Lorenzo. Here I have the time, the silence ... I'm always rushing about in London, running after copyrights, profits, running scared of my

boss's reactions, running scared of my wife's moods ...
Here I don't feel so separate...'

'No place, no friend – not even a spouse – can take away
that separateness, Francesco.' Gianni brought a hand up
to his face, and lightly touched his birthmark. 'And what
of your wife, your life in London? Making a choice means
renouncing. Are you prepared to give up so much?'

'I think I could convince my managing director to let
me run their subsidiary in Milan ... I could commute
from here ... as for the marriage ... I'm not sure it will
survive even if I stay in London.'

'Francesco, be careful. Your life has so much. You feel
restless, but would escape lead you to any greater peace?'

'I'd be returning not escaping,' Francesco interjected,
sitting up. 'I came away because I could not live in
Father's shadow – or accept his world.'

'I remember it well. You were always torturing yourself
about living up to him and his expectations for you.'

'It was impossible.' Francesco shook his head. 'His
whole being seemed bent on the pursuit of being the best –
the best at purchasing lands, at making investments, at
having a good time ... I was never convinced that I would
find happiness in that life – I always felt buffeted by that
whirlwind of energy and eagerness.'

'Marcantonio loved life. He was driven into doing a
thousand different things by a thousand different
impulses. But I'm not sure,' Gianni continued, careful to
pick his words, 'that he took care to listen to those around
him.'

'How could he? He was always generating excitement,
always surrounded by a great deal of commotion ...'
Francesco laughed. 'Whenever you came close to him,

you couldn't even hear yourself think! It was very different here, beside you – when I watched you mend and fix other people's things ... I felt contented. You remember how you used to tell me and Miso that doing good was as important as doing well – that struck a chord.' Francesco again leaned back. 'I thought I had a very different vision of the way life should be lived – but somehow I've lost sight of that. Here in San Lorenzo, I feel as if I could regain a sense of what I should do, and where I should be moving to.'

'Hmmm ...' Gianni stared up at the skies: the Ferris wheel's steel arms shone against the late sun. 'Don't move too quickly, Francesco, or you'll lose your balance.'

'There is no balance, right now, in my life. For that, I think I must come back.'

Above them the air crackled. Gianni cocked his head. 'They must be trying out the air guns at the shooting alley ... will I see you tonight, at the festa?'

'Yes ... possibly ...' But Francesco sounded dubious: the lunch had left a bitter taste in his mouth and he did not want to be subjected to the villagers' curious glances. He was in no mood to celebrate. 'I'll be off, then ...' He rose, placed a hand on his old mentor's shoulder. 'I'll see you again before I go ...'

Once again he made his way to the back entrance. The sun was drawing closer to the line of the horizon, and the faintest moon had now appeared to one side. A breeze stirred the trees and the blackberry bushes through whose branches he could see the river shimmer. He walked home, leaving behind him the fading noises of the shooting alley, the excited voices and children's laughter of the villagers who were getting ready for the night's festivities.

139

He had arrived at the edge of the orchard: in the twilight, with the moon drawing light from the sun, the trees, the grass, everything shone gold. He moved past the fading roses that drooped above the path where gravel and grass fought for dominance, to walk between the untidy rows of fruit trees. The crickets' last song, and the breeze that moved the leaves filled the green caves beneath each tree.

He walked on. The breeze suddenly dropped and all around him a hush fell, as if everything – leaves, grasses, clustered fruit, slender branches – that had previously stirred, trembled, rustled, now lay quiet. This new stillness seemed to have softened the light, too, so that as it fell through the trees it gave more room to shadows.

Now among the trees, half-hidden by fruit-laden branches, he saw Santa. She stood completely still, a frail white figure illuminated by the sunrays beyond. Francesco felt his heart beat fast at the sight of her. 'Santa,' he called out.

The pale face before him lifted, but she did not move. He dared not move, or speak further, lest she disappear. He watched her thus, standing as if wrapped in the last sunlight. He felt suddenly humbled, as if her mere presence brought a sacred element into his profane existence. Everything – his worries about Camilla, about Alma, about his work – seemed to melt into insignificance before the glowing white figure. Francesco felt as if he were once more the young boy spending his summer here in San Lorenzo, considering this world and its hints of rewards, and the world beyond, with its eternal promises. Santa. She seemed as mysterious and untouchable now, among the ripe fruit and gilt-edged leaves, as she had done in her mother's grocery shop. He still felt that her presence drew him to consider some ancient truth, and led him away from the anxious bafflement of everyday life to the unseen and the eternal. Santa: his existence suddenly seemed precarious and meaningless.

'Santa,' he called out again. But she drew away from him, as if her body had been lifted by a soundless breeze. Helpless, he watched her disappear.

Francesco retraced his footsteps. The sun had now dipped behind the crest of the hill. On the road beyond the hedge, he could hear the tractors coming home after the day in the fields, and in the distance Don Luigi's church bells tolled the Angelus. He suddenly wanted nothing more than to come back to San Lorenzo, to live here with Santa, and Miso, with Gianni er Brutto among these hills and vineyards. Perhaps he would be able to forge his new life here.

18

Francesco knocked at the kitchen door. For a brief moment he looked up at the placid sky, at the moon that had become the colour of acacia honey. They would confront one another. Lights came on in the stairway, and the door opened.

'You've been gone for so long ...' Alma's voice strained for lightness and cheer. 'I managed to finish painting one of the window casements ... I was beginning to worry about you.'

'No need to worry.' Francesco strode past her and threw his jacket on a chair. 'I'm capable of looking after myself. Which is more than I can say for you.'

'Please: let's not quarrel.' Alma remained by the door.

'I've no intention of quarrelling.' He sat at the table and hid his face in his hands. He was whispering something she couldn't hear.

'What are you saying?' Alma used the staccato voice she adopted whenever obstacles rose before her. 'I can't hear the insults, since your hands are covering your mouth.'

'I said' – his voice rose in fury – 'how long were you with that old man?'

Alma blinked. 'A few months.'

'Why? Why?'

'I was lonely.'

'Lonely? You thought that man a good cure for lone-liness?' His eyes clung to her face like an unpleasant, heavy air. Alma remained immobile, expression vacant. 'Do you think it natural for a girl of twenty-six to choose a man who could be her father – indeed, a friend of her father's – as her bedfellow?'

Alma moved away from the door, stood by the fireplace and stared at the ashes that she had left there since May's cold nights.

'If you thought it so matter of fact, why not tell me? If you found your behaviour so blameless, why not write me a letter about it? You could have added it as a casual by the by, a postscript in one of those letters about "getting back on my feet", about "living a normal life again", etcetera. You could have told me this morning, instead of allowing that old roué to have the pleasure. Why didn't you?'

Alma leant against the mantelpiece, arms crossed, head bowed in the same position she had adopted as a child when she had knelt in the family pew. 'Why why why why ... I was so alone, Francesco, so alone ...'

'I wonder what Father, what Mother would have said.'

'Stop!' Alma hid her eyes in her hands. 'I've been living with all this – I don't need you to remind me.'

Francesco stared at his sister's bent head. His voice was low: 'Why, Alma?' He saw her start, but she remained silent: 'Alberto. Couldn't you have turned to someone else for comfort?' His voice now rose till it became a shout: 'Couldn't you?'

Alma turned to him, face red with anger, tears visible

143

on her cheeks. 'Shut up. How dare you scold me like this when you stayed away? Where were you when Mother died? Where were you when Father was so ill he'd cry every hour?' Francesco stood still.

'I was at their bedside, there beside them, through it all. Where were you?'

'I have Camilla to look after, I have my job ... I'm tied down in London ...' He answered slowly, wary: 'I wanted to be of help ...'

'No. You could have come, just as in the beginning you could have stayed here. Stayed at home, as they both wanted you to.' He made as if to reply, but she carried on, shaking her head. 'You who ran away from responsibilities, you of all people have the nerve to come here and condemn me! You who turned your back on us!'

'Alma, I never did that.'

'Couldn't stand up to Father, could you? You couldn't bear the comparisons we all made between the two of you. So you ran off.'

'Do you think it was easy to leave home?'

'Easier than staying here to live in Father's shadow. Easier than staying here and facing their deaths. You left me, damn you. You left me alone ...' She sobbed.

'Alma, what are you saying?' His voice lay flat, tired, as if levelled by her outburst.

'I'm saying that I've shouldered the burden you fled from. I'm saying that the loneliness I was left with when Father died is something you couldn't possibly understand.'

'What do you know' – he studied her from his chair – 'of my experience of loneliness?'

'Stop pretending, Francesco. You have an adoring little

144

wife to fill all voids. You have your cosy little nest of a home, where everything runs smoothly and according to schedule.'

'You're wrong.' He shook his head. 'It's not like that at all.'

'You were always the one to keep his back to the wall, to keep himself well protected from all attacks.'

'No. Camilla and I argue. We are like Mother and Father. Quarrels, scenes, bitterness. She wants someone different from me. She despises me for not earning enough.'

Alma lifted her head and stared at him. 'What do you mean?'

'I mean' – he gave her a weak smile – 'that you're wrong about me and Camilla. There's no cosy nest there. Far from it. I'm as much a failure in her eyes as I am in yours.'

'Francesco . . .'

'We quarrel constantly. When we are not screaming at each other the silence between us is worse.'

Alma moved to the table, sat down across from him.

'I can hardly believe it . . . you kept so silent about it. You were so in love with her when you first wrote to us about her, Mother and Father didn't have the heart to tell you of their doubts, of how upset they were to see you tying yourself to another country by marrying her. I remember how envious I was.'

She shook her head and reached out for his hand.

'It was like that at the beginning. I thought I'd done something I could be proud of: she was beautiful, elegant, a good family . . . but things changed – almost within the first year: so much can be turned over just like that.'

'Poor Francesco,' she whispered. 'What will happen now?'

145

'Nothing. Or rather I . . . I was thinking of coming back. For good.' He smiled at her exclamation of surprise. 'I . . . I've done quite well at work, they like me there. We have a subsidiary in Milan, and I know I could convince them to let me move there. You see . . . there is something more, something missing.' He stared down at his hands. 'I feel certain that coming back is the right thing for me . . .'

'I don't know, Francesco: what will it change, moving back?'

'This is where everything began, this is where everyone knows me, where I know the way things are. I've made my bid for independence . . . which seems to have brought me little satisfaction.'

'And Camilla – will she be happy here?'

'I don't know.' He sighed, looked away from her, out towards the darkness in the window. 'And I don't know that I could ever leave her: what would she do, alone, incapable as she is of facing the real world? And . . .' His voice sank to a whisper. 'I still love her, I suppose.'

Alma stood up, rummaged through a cupboard, took out a bottle of wine. 'Let's have a drink, shall we?' She placed the bottle on the table between them, then fetched two glasses and a corkscrew. 'Here. You open it.'

They sat and drank in silence, without offering a toast.

Through the window, Alma again caught sight of the August moon, a large ripe apricot. The night breeze carried distant laughter and the crackling sounds of the shooting alley and the old-fashioned strains of a melancholic folk dance rose towards the sky: the festa had begun. Alma smiled sadly. 'Once again we are missing our village festa.' She raised her glass to her brother. 'Father and I used to sit like this: a bottle of wine, and

146

we'd start predicting the world according to our dreams.'

'Father...' Francesco sipped his wine and looked away.

'I spent all my time going back and forth, from here to the studio. We used to discuss his deals – he was still always dabbling in some scheme, in some plan. We would often talk about you: "I know what he's doing right now," Father would say. "He's looking at the latest manuscript from some unknown author, and he's going to stick his neck out to get it published. And knowing my son, it will be a huge success." '

'Father...' Francesco whispered again.

'Or he would praise you for your courage: "How many people do you know who'd have the guts to set off on their own and start a whole new life far from their home and family?" He was so proud of you.'

'I never thought he'd be ... you'd be interested in my doings.' Francesco pushed a forefinger along the wooden scars of the table.

'Of course we were. And he most of all. He knew my life so well – I played it out right under his eyes: he never had to worry about me. But you – he always wanted to know that world of yours. He wanted me to help him map out the different moments of your life, so that he could feel he was there beside you.'

Francesco studied the table and his sister's small hand upon it. He raised his eyes to his sister's then looked beyond her, into the dark window. 'I'll come back ...' he began.

'Be careful, Francesco: returning to this' – her hand encompassed the high-ceilinged kitchen – 'what do you hope to find?'

From the piazza rose a great whistling sound and

suddenly the golden white sparks of fireworks filled the open window. Francesco smiled. 'The festa will go on without us.'

'We'll have to wait till next year. Then we'll definitely go, relive our youth ...' She gave him a happy smile. 'Next year ... next year will be a much much happier year, you'll see.'

19

The widow Lea fastened her suspender belt around her waist, then sat on her bed and began to roll up a stocking. She crossed her legs, pointing her toes, and slowly slowly pulled the nylon round her foot, then her calf, all the while admiring the curve of her leg. It was nice enough – she might be almost forty-five, but her legs were still as pretty as any young girl's.

Behind her, still drained from her lovemaking, lay the mayor, stocky body glistening with sweat amidst the white sheets that had been part of her dowry more than twenty years ago. 'Lea, Lea, Lea ...' Battistini crossed his arms behind his head and surveyed his mistress's body. 'I saw you dance last night, at the festa ... I could hardly contain myself – you made me go hot all over ...'

The widow smiled at the memory – and not only of this festa, but of all the others she'd danced at, summer upon summer, with partner after partner. Then she woke from her reverie and whipped the foot of the bed with the cotton skirt she'd let drop to the floor when Bettino had undressed her half an hour before. 'Get up, Bettino, Santa will be coming back from her rosary any time now.' She stepped into the skirt, took a deep breath and zipped up the tight black cotton.

'I want to stay a little longer ... I want to have a chat with my lovely Lea ...' From the bed the mayor whined his plea.

'I want I want I want,' the widow mocked as she repinned her long dark hair. 'You always want something. Why don't you ask me what I want? Eh?'

'Oh Lea, please, don't give me a hard time ... not you too...'

'I'll tell you what I want. I want my dear Bettino to buy me a nice present every now and then, so that I feel I'm not being used like some rag he can just wring dry ... I mean it, Bettino, I am fed up of giving and giving and never receiving even a token of your affection.' She spoke with a hairpin between her lips, and her arms arched over her head like a ballerina, as her fingers sought to twist a pretty coil.

'But you know how much I care about you ...' The mayor half-sat up amidst the sheets.

'Pretty speeches mean nothing. Your wife, who certainly doesn't entertain you half as much as I do, gets a nice house and nice clothes. I get nothing. You'd better remedy the situation, Bettino my friend.'

'Oh Lea, you are cruel!' But the mayor smiled at her reflection in the mirror on the dresser. 'But your wish is my command...'

The widow grinned at the man sitting up in her bed, white folds falling about his paunch.

'Well, now, if Bettino is going to be nice to his Lea,' the mayor whispered, 'what will she give him in return, eh?'

The widow approached the bed with the soft careful steps of a cat. 'Hmmm ...' she smiled and purred.

'I want ...' And Battistini took her warm white hand in his. 'I want Lea to force Santa to speak.'

150

'You idiot!' The widow Lea snatched her hand back. 'I've told you already, she won't talk, and I won't force her to do anything against her will.'

'But Lea ...' The mayor was whining, his voice as weak as a newborn lamb's. 'Lea, don't you understand that if she doesn't talk, the bishop won't believe us? Do you know that we sent a letter to Bishop Natti asking him to come here and meet Santa for himself, and he replied that there was no need for him to come, because he had heard about Santa's silence. "When the visionary regains her speech you may approach me once again" – that's what he said, Lea! And I can assure you he won't change his mind till your daughter changes hers.'

'I won't hassle her. She's unhappy enough as it is. It's quite plain to me that my daughter cannot bear this non-sense of yours about a shrine.' The widow slipped on her blouse, began to button it. 'I won't do it, Bettino. Don't waste your breath and my time on it because I won't nag my daughter for your sake.' She turned her back on him and her voice grew soft. 'Sometimes I see her looking so lost, so distant ... it breaks my heart that I can't reach her.' She rose and brushed down the folds of her tight skirt, keeping her back to him all the while. 'Who would have thought it – I, who never even wanted this child of mine ...' Suddenly she shot round, her index finger to her lips. 'Shshshsh, I hear her: she's back. Quick, quick, get dressed, before she comes up.'

With eyes as wide as the clock on Don Luigi's bell tower, the Mayor Battistini sprang naked out of bed, snatching first at his shirt, then at his trousers, whispering impre-cations all the while.

151

20

Alma was in the study, on the phone to Alberto. 'I'm so happy, so happy ... it went better than I ever thought ...' She was still slightly tipsy from the champagne that the gallery owner, Marisol, had offered at the private view. After the last guest had left the white-walled, perfectly appointed gallery, Francesco had driven them home from Torino. Miso Brusoni had followed, in his own car. The two men were finishing supper downstairs in the kitchen.

'I've heard quite a few people saying they're determined to commission you.' Alberto's voice struck her as incredibly distant. 'Rosso d'Arrighi, for one. Though I suppose he's got other aims in sitting for you ...'

'Oh Alberto, you keep thinking men are interested in me ...' She couldn't get cross, though, the exhilaration of her success still warmed her, like the champagne she'd drunk. Picture after picture had sold, and a critic from the *Gazzetta* had pinned her to the wall to ask her a thousand questions. She felt as if countless people had come up and handed her bouquets of flattering remarks ... she lit a cigarette, lay back with abandon on the sofa and closed her eyes, smiling at the memory of it all.

'That gruff fellow, too, that village notary talking to your brother ...'

'Who?' Alma smiled at her pretence.

'You know, the one who appeared last week at that disastrous lunch at Castel d'Oro ... he didn't stop staring at you all evening ...' Alberto's voice was testing her reaction, determining whether the danger he had scented had been averted.

'Don't be so silly,' she giggled. But she felt herself blush as she remembered Miso's dark eyes as she had moved about the room, conferring now with Marisol, now with a prospective customer. And when she had dared look in his direction, his eyes had met hers, filling her with confusion.

'I can assure you he has a thing about you. It was obvious to everyone – even Sofia d'Arrighi commented on it.' Alberto's voice was now piercing. 'He looked completely out of place. I suppose you like that sort of man, though, don't you? The salt of the earth type – obviously ill at ease in any surroundings that smack of sophistication ...' He gave her the opportunity to counter his remark but Alma avoided it, smiling all the while into the receiver at the thought of Miso downstairs. He had stood about when all the guests had left, talking with Francesco but following her with his gaze. And when Francesco had suggested they go back to San Lorenzo and eat a late supper together he had accepted with alacrity.

'Well, do you?' Alberto was losing patience.

'Do I what ... ?' she murmured, blowing perfect smoke rings into the air, refusing his jealousy any room in her thoughts.

'Do you fancy him? Are you toying with the idea ...'

'What idea, Alberto? I just can't understand what you're getting at.' But she was grinning broadly at her father's portrait.

'Stop playing games with me, Alma,' he barked, exasperated. 'It'll end in tears, mark my words. He can't handle someone like you ... leave him to his provincial little notary's world ...' Alberto's voice was menacing.

'My dearest Alberto, I do wish you'd rein in your imagination. A man – someone I have known all my life – comes to my private view and suddenly he's lusting after me and I am to keep away from a possible misalliance ... please ...' She laughed now, and from the kitchen Francesco called out to her, 'Are you coming for the grappa session?'

'I'd better go, my brother wants me to rejoin them ...' Too late she realized she had made a slip and steadied herself for his outburst.

'Them? So that burly villager came back with you?' His indignation spluttered over the line. 'God help us, Alma, if you start something with someone like that. It's just too ridiculous for words.'

'You mustn't worry. Think about the wonderful exhibition and how grateful I am to you for having helped me organize it all ... I am, you know, truly truly grateful.' She emphasized each word with a careful, slow articulation.

'I don't want your gratitude.'

'You're being a bore. Ring me tomorrow and we'll have lunch soon. I've got to join my brother now. Bye.' She hung up the telephone and turned to the mirror above the sofa. She knelt on the silk pillows, stared at her reflection in its gilt frame: quickly she combed her fingers through her hair, sucked in her cheeks, blew them out in expectation. Then she rushed downstairs to join her brother and Miso.

21

The two men had poured the grappa into three small glasses. The fire that Miso had made was scorching the bricks and the iron grate which had been used so often by Rina to grill the steaks they had loved. Francesco and Miso sat at the kitchen table, surrounded by remnants of salami, bread and tomatoes, by bottles of water and wine, by a row of blood oranges. They raised their grappa glasses to toast their youth.

'Ah, my sister rejoins us ...' Francesco pulled out a chair for Alma: she could see he was in a good mood, heightened by the wine. He had been delighted to have had Miso at the private view, and now here with them for supper: she sensed his relief at finding a flesh and blood interruption to their session of intimate revelations. She had felt him wearying of the new openness between them.

'Your brother's just been singing a hymn of praise to the women of the countryside. And he's right of course.' Miso gave her a wink. 'They've always filled me with awe – they boast the mysterious strength of your sex, with all the right priorities intact.'

'Right priorities meaning husband and children first?' Alma smiled as she sipped the harsh transparent liquid. To her right, the fire burned hot, the shadows of its flames seemingly advancing upon the table, her arm, her glass.

'Of course. And meaning, too, that they understand implicitly, innately, what it has taken me more than thirty-five years to comprehend: that it's not about struggling to become, longing to achieve, but rather just to be.'

'Carpe diem, amen.' She laughed and their eyes met across the table. She looked away, sinking her gaze in the grappa before her.

He took one of the blood oranges and began to peel it with his knife. Alma watched the peel swivel in orange snakes upon the table.

'Miso's right. True wisdom seems to course like blood through these women's veins . . . look at our friend Franca, for instance.' Francesco was warming to his topic, and his voice grew louder as he hurried through the words. 'She doesn't have to prove anything to anyone. She is content to be – to live each moment. She cares only about the here and now, doesn't worry about the endless possibility of tomorrow and the day after.'

'Oh please' – Alma rolled her eyes – 'I've heard it all before. What you call instinctive living is simply that poor Franca and women like her cannot afford to have any aims of their own – their lives have been swamped by the tyranny of children, husband and household duties.'

'Show me any woman from San Lorenzo and I'll show you a woman who is far more at ease, far more satisfied than any of those women in your gallery today.' Miso here smiled as he placed an orange segment in his mouth. 'Though I must say our village women are not half as attractive as that bevy of beauties you had gathered there.'

'The kind of woman you both find so praiseworthy has no thought for herself, no moment to indulge in reflection let alone self-examination, and is simply constantly answering the needs of those around her. Fine for some, but not for me.'

'But who is happier, as Miso pointed out? Let's be honest, Alma, the women – and the men too – in the countryside know that life is about learning to be satisfied.'

'You mean learning to compromise,' she snapped at them both.

'No. Satisfied.' Miso poured out two more glasses for her brother and himself. 'Satisfied because of the security of knowing every corner of your world, being at ease with every face and every feature of the landscape. And the blessed certainty of regular occurrences.'

'Heavens, what a boring life you've just described.' She gulped down her grappa, winced as it burned her throat. When she looked up, Miso was smiling at her.

'It really does strike you as a bore, doesn't it?' She felt ashamed by her words. His expression was at once amused and disappointed.

'Oh Alma, Alma ...' Francesco was laughing at her.

'But you can't seriously tell me you're happy to spend the rest of your life here?' She sounded exasperated.

'Why not? I'm content. That means waking up every morning without feeling anxious. It means reading the newspaper and shaking your head in disbelief at the nonsense people in the big bad world spout, and the follies they commit. It means feeling so linked to your community that, to coin a phrase, if you sneeze your neighbour catches a cold.'

'This no doubt explains why the villagers are marching like lemmings towards this mad, ridiculous idea of a shrine?' Alma felt the grappa heating her head, and the words shooting forth, unguarded.

'You're right. This is a sorry chapter in the annals of San Lorenzo. And it's driven a nail into the coffin of all my fond notions of collective rights and aims. You remember, Francesco, how when we decided that our aim was to rouse the villagers into a campaign – remember, we tried to make a fuss about that great teacher's wrongful imprisonment...'

'A campaign which proved a resounding failure, thwarted by an overwhelming sense of communal indifference. No one cared, no one moved a finger.' Francesco sipped his grappa.

'Well, now, I can assure you, I have learned that the masses can be galvanized into action – but only when they smell profit.' Miso shook his head over his disappointment. 'The villagers have become a posse of men and women who are champing at the bit, like dogs at a bone.' Francesco began coughing, he'd taken too ambitious a gulp of grappa. Miso slapped his friend's back and pursued his train of thought. 'The chief culprits behind this crime tried to get me to write a letter to the bishop for them – wanted him to come and see Santa for himself – as if, of course, an interview with Santa would be anything other than a monologue.'

'It really would be the limit, if they succeed with this madness of theirs!' Alma was laughing. 'How silly they'll look, if they ever achieve their replica of Lourdes.'

'Don't be condescending, Alma. Didn't you hear your friends at Lino's last week, ready to do exactly the same thing given half a chance? Snobs from Torino were just as likely to have cooked up this scheme as our good Battistini

158

was.' Miso's voice was angry. 'And anyway – isn't this just an amusing tale you can tell at a dinner party to prove how foolish provincial oafs can be?'

'Oh what nonsense!' Alma was feeling too drunk to deal with these accusations. 'As if San Lorenzo weren't our home! This is where we belong, Miso. Just as much as you.'

'You belong first and foremost to the well-nourished well-heeled world of the group you were with today. This village for you is a house set amidst a countryside that is a source of inspiration for your canvases; and for Francesco it is a treasure trove of memories. But for me, this is home. And for those villagers out there, it is home. We stand to lose a great deal if the scheme gets under way. Plastic figurines of Our Lady and plaster relics are just the beginning.'

Silence followed. Francesco, sensing that his sister had taken offence, broke in. 'What of my beloved Santa, then?'

'Ah well, Santa!' And Miso's eyes lit up with such warmth that Alma felt a surge of inexplicable jealousy. 'Santa is our untouchable icon, the girl next door, our little sister, a Madonna all rolled into one. Santa, of course, like the truly powerful, has retreated into splendid isolation. She won't let us down, Francesco my friend: she remains a little oasis of sanity and soul in all this mess.'

Francesco nodded, convinced. 'She was always like that, wasn't she. Remember how we used to talk about her to Gianni er Brutto...'

'Correction. How you used to drone on and on about her to poor Gianni...' Miso's voice teased.

'And Gianni used to say that while the rest of us stoop to examine our tiny footsteps and the insignificant distances we travel, Santa looks up and stretches herself beyond all this.'

'Here we start, with the delivery of our first saintly vision ...' And Miso crossed himself. 'What I so relish about your brother, Alma, is that you can rest assured that in his presence there will be some discussion, at some point, of the kingdom of God. I always suspected him of having a vocation, you know ...'

Francesco, relieved to see Miso's good humour restored, shook his head in mock misery. 'Do you see how Miso likes to make fun of me? Always giving my foundations a good shake – and then watches me come tumbling down.'

'Down to my level, Francesco. My neck gets stiff otherwise, looking up at you.'

Francesco wagged his finger. 'You mock, you mock ... But don't play the doubting Thomas with Santa. She's the real thing. And someone who has not lost her innocence is rare and wonderful.'

'Innocence pshaw.' Alma held up her glass for more grappa, thought better of it, and took some water instead. 'Innocence is just the inability to examine one's own instincts and desires.'

'It's not an inability – it's a choice. Santa has no interest in herself,' Francesco persisted.

'A type of humility the rest of us seem incapable of these days.' Miso winked at Alma.

'Oh, the two of you are impossible tonight. I'll have no more of it. And I'm slightly under the influence ...' She stood up, placed her hand on her brother's shoulder. 'I'm off ... good night, and thank you so much for coming all the way from London for the private view.' She stooped and kissed his forehead. 'Thank you, really.' She smiled at Miso but a sudden shyness kept her from kissing him good night.

'Have you had enough or shall we brave Vanna's bar?' Miso stood up.

'Oh why not, let's see what Vanna can offer us ...' Francesco stretched, rose, and the two men strode off into the village night.

22

'What cards! I'm going to beat you again!' the Mayor Battistini grinned. 'How many people do you know who are lucky in love, cards, money?'

The men were playing scopa in the piazza. The cards swapped hands – Neapolitan royalty, chalices, swords, sticks and Midas suns – faded prints of the Arabic heritage that had once held the reins of two kingdoms. Somewhere near Vanna's bar a group of youngsters sang in unison, while her son Grillo strummed his guitar with the sweetest languor he could muster.

Lights shone mellow inside the bar: Vanna stood behind the counter, adding up her bills and wondering how many supplies of oil, wine and bread her husband Claudio would need to get from the market at Castel d'Oro tomorrow morning. Claudio, dead cigarette in his lips, towel in hand, began stacking chairs. The men had been sitting out here for hours, playing cards and trying to predict what would happen with Santa and the shrine.

'After all that hot air, Bettino, all that fuss about your letter, Bishop Natti just doesn't want to know, does he?' The butcher Romeo shrugged his shoulders.

'Everyone could have done so well out of it . . .' Nuccio the baker shook his head over his cards.

162

'At what expense, though?' Gianni er Brutto ventured timidly from his corner. 'Our peace and quiet would go out of the window, and as for Santarella...'

'She looks as pale as a ghost already.' Claudio threw his cigarette butt into the basil pot outside the door. 'Thin and white and miserable.'

'It's time for bed ...' Don Luigi examined his watch, then pushed it back in the generous pocket of his cassock: it was, in truth, much later than his habitual bedtime.

'Go to bed and dream of your great shrine.' Rocco's singing voice cackled like a crow's.

Don Luigi sighed: no one ever understands your faithful servants, Dear Lord. He made as if to get up.

'Scopa!' Battistini, victorious grin across his face, slapped down his cards. Don Luigi fell back in his chair. The butcher Romeo issued a blasphemy that quickly brought the priest's hand to cross himself. 'What can I say, always lucky ...' Battistini gloated with self-satisfaction.

'Battistini, the kind Lord is letting you have a little victory before your future great defeats,' snickered Old Rocco.

'Shut your envious mouth!' The mayor raised his fist at Old Rocco. 'Men like you can't see further than the blackheads on their nose. I'm not working myself to the bone for me, you know. I'm doing it for all of us, and I hope to get this shrine up and running as fast as I can so that we'll all begin to benefit.'

From the shadows that surrounded Don Luigi's sacristy, Grillo and his friends sang some more: 'I'm going away, across the sea, with only an echo of your voice ...' Grillo's voice, low and sweet, floated above the piazza like some blackbird, while his eyes rested upon the baker's pretty daughter Veronica. Beside him, plain-faced Marta, Veronica's older sister, watched the young couple unnoticed.

'Listen to him.' Claudio's thumb pointed out his son beneath the tree. 'All he does is sing songs and mope because he can't go away. Youth!' And Claudio pushed the stack of chairs against the wall. 'What does he think he'll find, eh? You can cross the sea and the desert and in the end, every place is like your village.'

'Leave him be, a guitar does no harm, and it's pleasant every now and again to hear some songs ...' Gianni er Brutto closed his tired blue eyes and listened to the sweet music.

'A guitar doesn't bring in money, does it?' Claudio shook his head towards Grillo, whose profile had now moved closer still to Veronica's.

'Claudio, don't you remember?' The butcher Romeo set down his glass. 'You and I, didn't we dream of getting away ... you were depressed because you were being forced into a shotgun wedding' – here the men chuckled and Claudio made a rude gesture with his arms – 'and I ... I was angry about the Filomena business' – more chuckling from the rest – 'America, Australia, any far away place ...' The butcher Romeo forgot his defeat as he followed his memories.

'Yes, well ... we were saving money for the passage across the ocean ... from Genoa, on a huge ship: big dreams ...' Claudio pulled up a chair, took out a new cigarette, and lit it.

'In fact, the question is why we stayed, after all?' And the butcher Romeo shook his head with sorrow.

Nuccio the baker drained his glass of wine. 'God alone

knows what kept any of us here ...' He turned his white face from one to the other. 'The women are nothing special, the winters cold and the summers hot ...'

'Business is poor and life expensive,' added the marshal over the cards he was shuffling.

'People are unfriendly and lazy and that's only the ones we know well,' continued Claudio, while his son raised his voice in a plaintive cry – 'Let me sail away, let me pull up my anchor ... and I'll return your hero ...'

Gianni er Brutto hummed along with young Grillo's strumming.

'Well, I for one never wanted to leave.' The mayor lay back in his chair and crossed his legs. 'Never wanted to pull up the anchor and go off into the unknown.'

'Of course not, Battistini: better be a big fish in this puddle than a minnow in a lake, eh?' And Old Rocco burst into guffaws. But now he spotted the new arrivals. 'Well, well,' he croaked, 'what have we here? Brusoni and the Ferrati boy.'

'Francesco!' Don Luigi finally managed to rise from the tight embrace of the chair: he was fond of the youth, who, in contrast to his father and sister, had seemed so pious and serious in his younger days.

'Francesco! Miso!' Gianni er Brutto looked from one to the other, his face shiny with welcome. 'Look at the two of you, just like the old days!'

'Hello, Don Luigi. Gianni.' Francesco and Miso came to stand on either side of the elderly man. 'We're just sorting out the world – again, just like the old days!'

They smiled at Gianni, automatically exchanged hand-shakes and nods with the village men.

Battistini, who was making excited gestures in the

direction of the bar owner, now took over the situation. 'Sit down, sit down and have a glass of wine. Claudio, quick, let's impress young Ferrati with our fine wines. That old fox Franca tried to swallow all your lands in one big gulp didn't she? A terrible thing, that woman's determination. You'd better watch her or she'll grab the house next.'

'The house is not for sale.' Francesco smiled and looked round the men's faces: he felt out of place, sitting here in the light that streamed from the inn, surrounded by weather-beaten, work-worn faces he remembered from his youth. Did he really wish to come back here? Did he really think he'd ever fit in?

'Let's sit beside our old friend.' Miso ignored the chairs that Battistini had pulled out for the latest arrivals, and pulled out a seat next to Gianni er Brutto.

'Heard about the dreams of these ignorant folk?' Old Rocco, who had almost got up out of his chair, was pointing with his thumb at the cluster of men. 'As if the bishop in Torino had nothing better to do than to set up a shrine in our God-forsaken little village.'

Gianni er Brutto beamed up at Francesco and turned to Miso. 'And is he as successful as we always said he would be?'

Miso grinned. 'More.'

Francesco smiled. 'Look who's talking. Our friend the philosopher of the revolution has become a very wealthy man.'

Gianni laughed. 'Eh, you never can tell what card fate has up its sleeve.'

'Taste this, my good man, taste this!' And Battistini pushed a glass of wine towards Francesco. He poured another one and handed it to Miso, though his expression was markedly less friendly with the notary: the episode of the letter for Bishop Natti still rankled.

'You remember when we used to come to your court-yard and watch you fix everyone's things ...' Miso again ignored the mayor and crossed his arms behind his head and stared up at the stars.

'I loved having the two of you sitting there beside me, watching.'

'You warned us to come down to earth from our world of dreams.' Francesco raised his glass to Gianni er Brutto.

'Told us to settle for what was possible and not to break our heart on what was not.' Miso had joined Francesco in drinking to Gianni's health. The three men spoke in low voices, creating their own small nucleus on the fringe of the card game.

'Boys, boys, it does me a world of good just to see the two of you.' Gianni er Brutto, embarrassed by all the attention, rubbed his birthmark and looked down into his own empty glass.

'I still remember when you told me the story of God speaking to David as he walked in the countryside,' Francesco mused. 'And I went home to the garden and lay on the ground waiting for Him to speak to me, too ... I shut my eyes so tight, barely drew breath, and – nothing. Not a word. Not a sound. Not a whisper. And I had wanted so much to see, hear, Someone.'

'Eh, Francesco ... you were always in search of some-thing or Someone ...' Gianni er Brutto patted Francesco's knee.

'Tell us what's happening in the big world outside,

Dottore Ferrati.' The mayor could bear no longer his exclusion from the three men's talk. He pressed his arms against the table, as if to stake his own right to the revelations that would now spill forth. 'London's full of rain and Arabs, ain't it so?' Battistini showed the ignorant and provincial men round him how well versed he was with the world.

'Well ...' Francesco smiled, as awkward as when he'd first arrived in London and had to attempt English conversation.

'Come, come, with everything you've seen ... tell us.' Don Luigi rubbed his hands together.

'Do the men still wear those ridiculous hats?'

'Do you have to bring your umbrella everywhere you go?'

The questions were fired from left and right: Francesco watched Miso settle back in his chair, in silent amusement. He looked at the faces around him. Who were these people, and who was he to them? They floated before him, stepping out of a not so distant past, setting off faint echoes of memory that spread ripples like a good-luck coin dropped in a fountain.

Home – was this then home? Was this the place that filled his dreams, the village he longed to return to? His past lay hidden behind these men who wanted to treat him as a celebrity, when all he wanted was to feel that he had returned to the sameness of before.

'London – is nice enough. But this – this is best of all.' He told them what he knew they wished to hear.

'And nothing seems ever to change – even with the talk of the shrine ...' Old Rocco winked.

'My San Lorenzo is now a landscape of the mind,'

Francesco whispered. But only Miso heard, for the butcher had interrupted.

'Eh, you're right: while the rest of the world goes through big changes, look at us, always the same.' And the butcher Romeo seemed to wish for a denial from Francesco.

Don Luigi yawned behind his hand and broke away from the men. 'Too late for me already.' He left raising his hand to Francesco, and to the rest.

Rocco tugged at Gianni er Brutto's sleeve. 'You'd best come along, old man, I'll walk you home.' And the two men, after Gianni had extracted a promise of a letter from Francesco, made their slow and painful way home.

The piazza began to empty: Claudio cleared the tables of bottles, glasses, newspapers, ashtrays; he stacked the chairs against the wall, pushed the tables in a row beneath the overhanging roof, then joined Vanna in their bedroom upstairs.

The men began their goodbyes – a pat on the shoulder, a grumbled 'night', a slap on the back. The young people, their guitar-playing over, stood about, hands in pockets, fixing dates for tomorrow night. In the black air, tiny bats swooped down from the trees, the streetlights and Don Luigi's bell tower.

The Mayor Battistini remained in his chair. He stretched his big legs beneath the table, accidentally giving Miso's ankle a kick. He raised a hand in command when he spotted Grillo, guitar trailing behind him, as he made his way inside the inn. 'Before you go, boy, get us a bottle of wine . . . put it on my bill . . .' He waved his hand airily, as though this were his normal practice. Grillo raised an eyebrow, and disappeared into his parents' bar. 'Tonight

169

it's my treat.' The mayor cast a proud smile upon the two men.

Miso winked at Francesco, who answered: 'That's very kind.'

The three men watched in silence as Grillo placed a dark bottle at the centre of their table then disappeared into the inn. Francesco felt the warm air shroud him, heard voices rise within the bar.

Beside him, the other two had begun to talk, with the ease and jovial tones of men who don't take each other too seriously.

'I tell you ... it's a real pleasure to thrash out your ideas every now and then with people who understand what you are talking about.' Battistini sank his eyes into the wine before him. 'If only you knew, Dottore' – here he raised his eyes to Francesco once more – 'how I want to kick these ignorant lazy creatures every day, force some sense into them! I mean to say: who is working day and night to get the shrine off the ground? Me. Who will profit most when the pilgrims start coming? Them. So you would think they'd understand it is in their interest to help me, no? No. They don't. Just sit there and twiddle their thumbs. Or shrug their shoulders and play the fatalists, you know the type – "if He wishes, then so be it" ... what losers ...' Battistini shook his head and drank some more.

'A toast to San Lorenzo.' Miso raised his glass to Battistini.

'A toast to the shrine,' countered the mayor, 'and may it be built quickly, and bring a million pilgrims.' The mayor flung back another half-glass of wine.

Francesco sipped his wine and raised his eyes to Santa's

dark window. He wondered what she knew of these schemes. Above them, Claudio's voice could be heard, counting the day's earnings.

'I tell you, my dear Ferrati, you may have seen a lot of things in your travels, and I don't doubt you've done a lot ... but – and this may seem strange – I don't envy you one little bit.' Battistini shook his head with vigour. 'No, not one bit. You see' – he lowered his voice, approached his face to Miso's – 'if you move about you can't see anything through, can you? You don't get the sense of satisfaction of watching something you've built ...'

'You have a point there, Signor Mayor.' Miso grinned over his glass.

Francesco looked up at the minuscule lights of the stars and saw Camilla's pale face.

'Of course, to a man of the world like yourself, this shrine is not anything special.' Here the mayor paused and searched each face for signs of vehement disagreement; seeing none, he proceeded, slightly irritably: 'Of course, you two – you have seen much more important, much more amazing things. But be that as it may, this shrine is the most important thing to happen to San Lorenzo since the war brought the Americans and their dollars.' Here the mayor gave them both a smile. 'It should ensure me the mayor's seat for the next ten or fifteen years, as well. And a medal of some kind from the Region, I wouldn't be surprised.'

'Ah well, then it almost makes up for the ignorance you have to put up with, doesn't it?' Miso downed another gulp.

'My philosophy is this: everything looks good from the top, even this village and the thick-heads who live here.'

171

Here the mayor's corpulent figure leant back in the chair, and he stared out into the darkness where the hills rose unseen. 'My father, if he could see his son now ... do you know' – here the voice whispered – 'he was known as Matteo Who, because no one ever noticed him long enough to ask for his surname ... He was a shoemaker, about this tall' – the mayor raised his hand about a foot from the table – 'and poor as a church mouse. Our house was so cold, I used to make friends at school just to be able to play in a warm room ...' The mayor sighed, fell into a silence the two others didn't dare interrupt, then gave Francesco a wink. 'Well, I got out of poverty soon enough, you can imagine, worked so hard at school, I was head of the class three years running. Got a high school degree, worked a year at the mill in Susa, got myself a piece of land ... little by little, here I am. And who knows' – here the mayor gave a sly look at Francesco – 'where I shall end up?'

'But what of Santarella?' Francesco sat up, pouring more wine into the mayor's glass.

'Don't mention that girl to me, Dottore! The bane of my life, the sorrow of my days, that girl. Hasn't spoken a word for months and I'm beginning to think she's doing it out of spite against me ... against us all.' The mayor sighed and shook his head. 'To tell you the truth, I wouldn't be surprised if she were a bit' – here he tapped his temple – 'you know, dim-witted. Still, all that matters is that everyone is prepared to take the sightings seriously.'

'Are we to understand then that although the shrine is all your idea, you don't actually believe our Santa has seen the Madonna?' Miso couldn't keep the amusement from his voice.

172

Battistini burst out laughing. 'I'm a hardened old cynic. If I don't see, touch, smell or taste something – well, it's just not there for me. But if the Madonna is the only thing that will bring money to this village, well, then all I can say is that I believe the girl has seen Our Lady, a host of angels, and even St Joseph coming down on a cloud!'

The night air split as the sombre tolls of the church bell announced two. Battistini sat up, ran a fat-fingered hand through his hair and sighed: 'I'd best be off. My old woman gets anxious if her husband stays out too long ... Eh, it's easy for young men who are free of the ball and chains of matrimony ...'

The two friends sat in silence for a while: Battistini's exit had left a hefty void at the table, which they would have to fill with care. Left to their own devices, and their own company, they needed to adjust to the sudden intimacy.

'Well, well, well: our mayor's preoccupations leave me awe-struck – so far ranging and universal!' And Miso laughed, rocking on his chair's hind legs: 'Money, the Madonna, visionaries and opportunists, illusions of personal power and a holy pilgrimage site ... what more do you want? And a world neatly divided between winners and losers.' A note of bitterness had slipped in and Francesco shot him a quick look. 'And I'm not sure he hasn't consigned me to the box marked loser.' He gave a dry laugh but kept his eyes from his friend.

'He can't. You're successful. A notary, which means a fine upstanding citizen of the community, guardian of secrets as well as other people's money. You're a winner.' Francesco had kept his voice consciously light, as if they were joking, but he was wary of Miso's mood.

173

Confessions were not his friend's way, but melancholia was.

'Come come, Francesco. Do you remember what we said we'd do? You always knew you needed to get away – and you did. But think of me. I'd set my sights on becoming an academic, a leading light of the left-wing intelligentsia whose advice everyone from government officials to the humblest members of the working class would seek before making a move. But then I did poorly in every exam that came my way. God only knows what hounded me – my father's death, unhappy romances, I don't know what the cause was. But every dream of academe – phew' – he blew out – 'up in smoke.'

Francesco did not know how to respond. Above the two men Vanna was pleading with her husband to stop counting money and switch off their bedroom light. 'Miso ... Things have not exactly turned out the way I thought they would, either. And I'm in a country that is not my own, with a woman who understands me very little.' He downed the last wine. 'At least you've made a good solid life for yourself here.'

'Yes. Safe, secure, predictable. Not even a wife to alter my routine.' Miso's voice was flat.

'You never found anyone who ... ?' Francesco asked.

'No. No one whose presence, after a few months, I didn't find constricting.' He threw back his head to study the stars. 'So here I am, never in danger of climbing those dizzying heights of ambition old Gianni had warned us about. Which is why I look at someone like your sister and am filled with sheer awe – and terror, almost, terror at the thought of her falling from that high tightrope she persists in walking.'

'Alma ... a winner, would our mayor say?'

'Most definitely.' Miso laughed. 'I don't know what's got into me. I haven't talked this much since ... since those days we spent in Gianni's courtyard. It must be seeing you again – it makes me go right back ...'

'Yes.' Francesco studied the sky and the stars above. 'You know, I'm beginning to feel homesick. For the hills, and the vineyards. For the smell of tomatoes ripening. I miss the roosters' calls and the women in kerchiefs. And geraniums. I miss geraniums.' Francesco leaned back in his chair and breathed in deeply.

'Don't they have geraniums in England?' Miso's voice rose in disbelief.

'Not this red.' Francesco rolled down his shirt sleeves. 'What would you say if I told you I plan to come back to live here?'

'Come back ...? If you do, make sure you know what you will find.'

'I want an end to this restlessness. I want an end to the loneliness I feel when I can't share the desires and ambitions of the people I am surrounded by. I want ...' He laughed, head back. 'I'm not sure I even need to find what I want. But here at least I would be allowed to search for it. There – there I am pulled at tugged at pushed against all day.'

'Be careful, Francesco. Don't mistake a slippery stone for a safe step.'

Francesco didn't answer. They sat in silence. The last light in the inn had been switched off, and Miso's face was suddenly invisible. In the new darkness, Francesco rose. 'I'm ready for bed. Shall we go back?'

Miso raised himself by planting both palms upon the

table top and followed his friend. They made their way to the main road. Before they parted, Miso placed a hand on his friend's shoulder. 'After all this time – it's nice to talk again. It gets lonely, here, with only Gianni who always seems to understand...'

'London can be lonely too,' answered Francesco.

23

In the early morning, when the air is clear and still, you can see the Alps rise beyond the hills of Castel d'Oro. White and immense, they glow, seeming to belong to the sky rather than to the earth. The mountains form a new horizon for the intimate scenery of undulating fields, of village roofs and bell towers, of ripening vines and uncoiling river.

From the second-storey window, the air was so charged with sun that Alma felt she must lower her eyes to the orchard, where colours were muted by the shadows of leaves and branches. Apricot trees, persimmons, cherries, plums, figs, pears: the trees in the orchard echoed the intimacy of the hills and the fields, never growing to dazzling heights, their curving branches bowed low enough to be plucked clean of their offerings.

She stood at her easel, before the open window in Francesco's bedroom. It was a cool, sharp morning, a first declaration of autumn. From her brother's window she could see both hills and mountains, their contours blue against the white sky. Over the row of beeches that separated the vineyards that now belonged to Franca, the faintest moon shone. Everything beckoned – the roundly shaped fruits, the oval leaves, the zinnias that, ignoring

177

the ancient flower beds Mother had once cared for, now dotted the grass. A hundred memories lay bundled up within this garden, like so many piles of firewood left to dry for the winter.

A car now roared its way towards the village. She wondered if it carried mushroom-pickers, returning from their secret site with their booty. In San Lorenzo, the villagers waited eagerly for the first full moon after the last summer rains to mark the start of the mushroom season. Men and women rose at four in the morning, and stole to their car under cover of darkness, spades and boxes at the ready, trained dogs at their side, drove into the black hills, returning season after season to their favourite spot, whose location they guarded as jealously as family secrets. From the humid earth beneath the knotted roots of ancient trees, their dogs sniffed the pungent, telltale scents. The mushrooms – yellow, grey, red, brown in the golden glow shed by the flashlight – were carefully placed in crates or boxes. And then the competition was on: who had found what and how many? Who had got the best site of all? Who had enough to sell at the market at Castel d'Oro? Rivalries were fanned by exaggerated claims, jealousies stirred by mysterious smiles or all-knowing winks. For days, the piazza resounded with boasts and denials, claims and rebuttals. Why, the butcher Romeo and the baker Nuccio almost came to blows last September, because the baker accused the butcher of having trailed his car into the damp dawn, hoping to spy Nuccio's secret site. And weren't Vanna and her husband suspected of having bought their mushrooms from some farmer in Susa, because no one could believe that the couple – who'd never before had more than a half-empty crate to show for all their efforts – had found all those mushrooms on their own?

Alma imagined the village bickerings in front of Vanna's bar and returned with a smile to the canvas before her. She was working on a large landscape, a new commission that she had obtained through one of Marisol's clients. She was applying the blues and greens carefully, slowly, her eyes moving back and forth from the orchard to the canvas. She was smiling as she painted, and, suddenly conscious of her pleasure, she drew a deep breath: how complete, how serene she felt. Happiness, which until recently had shuffled and dragged its feet in approaching her, now suddenly pulled her at breakneck speed in its wake.

She had hardly returned to Torino this autumn: most of her commissions had come because of her paintings of San Lorenzo, and the success of the exhibition had fuelled her desire to work here, in the quiet days and nights of village life.

In the distance, the church bells tolled nine. When would he come? 'Honestly, Alma!' But she enjoyed chiding herself for listening out for his step on the gravel, and for rushing to the mirror when she heard his car drive up the cypress-lined path.

Every day, Miso dropped by. In the mornings, it was for coffee on his way to work. In the evenings, he came for a drink and to tell her some anecdote about village life, or about a client. Through him, she came to know a different San Lorenzo, one where the mayor was a greedy, grasping dictator, Gianni er Brutto a soft-spoken sage, Santa a mysterious pious presence, and young Grillo, whom she had spied behind the counter at the bar, a budding musician waiting for his lucky break.

Through the open window she suddenly heard a car crunching the gravel. He'd come! She rushed downstairs, then, halfway down the steps, she threw off her smock, tucked her shirt into her skirt, smoothed down her hair.

He stood there when she opened the door, and as always she took a few moments to articulate even a greeting.

'Hard at work, I see.' He was smiling as he pointed out the blue and yellow smears of oil paint on her hands.

Alma nodded and laughed. 'Of course. The private view's fired me to do more, and of course, better ...'

She stepped back into the kitchen and tried to be as unself-conscious as possible while she felt his brown soft eyes caress her body. He had never so much as touched her, and yet she felt as if she knew exactly what his touch would feel like. And she loved to watch him as he towered over her, a big, muscular man, who appeared so all-encompassing and yet was so self-contained that he never seemed to leave a trace of himself.

'Has that old widow Silvestri finally paid you?' he asked while she fixed the coffee. Inwardly she smiled, taking pleasure in his interest in her life.

'Yes, finally – though I had to speak very sternly to that son of hers – horrid creature.' She shook her head, exaggerating her annoyance to amuse him.

'You talked to Silvestri? Marco Silvestri?' He came round the table to stand by her, eyes wide. 'My God, the most powerful industrialist in the region, and you talked to him "very sternly"?! Alma, he's worth millions ...' He threw back his head and laughed. 'You'll never cease to amaze me ... are you never scared?'

'No,' she lied, shaking her head decidedly. The coffee gurgled on the stove, she took out the tiny cups, the sugar he loved. 'Anyway, I just explained that his mother owed me some money, and that I would appreciate it greatly if he could see that she paid me. That's all.' She handed him his cup.

'You've got more courage in one little finger ...' He rolled his eyes at her endeavours and sipped his coffee. 'Where are you painting?'

'In Francesco's room. A better view than from mine.'

'I like to find you at your easel: you look so engrossed, so different from the way you are in conversation, or in a room full of people.' She lowered her eyes to the cup of coffee before her, and blushed as she remembered how tense she always grew when he stood near her, how hard she had to concentrate lest her hand tremble as she dipped her brush in the oil paint.

'And what's the schedule today?' she asked him.

'Oh same as usual. I like my routine, you know ... I have a couple of people to see till lunch, then a nice bowl of spaghetti at my favourite table at Sandro's in Castel d'Oro, then a bit of paper work, drinks with the glamorous Signorina Ferrati if she wishes it, then a quick check of Vanna's bar, news on the television, dinner with my mother.' He finished his coffee. 'Excellent, best cup of coffee around – though I had best never tell my mamma that.'

Alma hid her disappointment by studying her cup: how could he endure such a well-regulated life, split in equal, digestible segments? The sheer routine of it, the small and insignificant occurrences that coloured his life and from which he drew such comfort and satisfaction,

181

filled her with dread. She suddenly recalled Alberto's words of warning and decided that as soon as the weather grew colder she'd retreat to her studio in Torino, and leave behind Miso and San Lorenzo. With the resolve firm in her mind, she flashed him a smile. 'I may be in Alessandria this evening, but give me a ring or drop by, because I am not sure ...' And she stood up and quickly took his cup and saucer from him, and began to wash up.

Miso looked slightly taken aback by her sudden burst of activity, but then he rose, pushed back in his chair. 'I'll come by just in case you're in and you want an aperitivo with an exhausted notary.' He turned at the door and winked. 'Work hard.'

Alma felt angry and confused and rushed upstairs. She picked up her smock from the banister where it still hung, and dragged it on the steps behind her. It took her almost an hour before she could concentrate once again on her landscape.

'Signorina!' She heard Grillo's cheerful voice. Alma drew to the window but before she could answer she saw the call had not been for her: Grillo, astride his bicycle, stood before the tiny frail figure of the Signorina Teresa.

The signorina, dressed in lavender, was making her slow way back to her house, a shopping net in one hand. Alma could not hear the exchange now between the two figures but she saw the Signorina Teresa hand over – after a coy shake of the white head, to show a make-believe deliberation – her shopping net to the young boy on his bicycle. They moved slowly down the road towards the signorina's house, the signorina's stride suddenly alert and almost jaunty, Grillo's bicycle zig-zagging slowly, so that the signorina could keep up with him.

Through the branches of the hazelnut trees, Alma could follow their progress only intermittently as the two figures now came into view, only then to be hidden by the green leaves shimmering in the September sun. She could hear the signorina's unintelligible, happy talk, could see her tiny hand go up to check her lovely white hair that she combed up into a French knot every morning, and fixed in place with three tortoiseshell combs. She could see Grillo patiently nodding, pedalling slowly, trying to keep his bicycle from swerving under the weight of the shopping net that he'd added to his case of bottled water. Of course, the signorina could send her daily, Madda, to do her shopping for her. But then, she would be depriving herself of the conversations in Nuccio's bakery, where the warm scent of bread seemed to stir the village women's appetite for gossip; or in the widow Lea's shop, where behind the counter stood the lovely, silent visionary, who seemed unaware of the hints and innuendoes about her and the shrine that floated among the women as they bent to choose the best red peppers in the crate, weigh in their hands a cluster of purple grapes, pick carefully amidst the figs whose seams had split to reveal their pink flesh.

Alma's heart tightened at the sight of the dainty little lavender figure who, as they arrived at the great red gates of her property, placed a hand upon Grillo's shoulder to thank him for his kindness. Acts of generosity such as this one had grown so rare in the signorina's life that she savoured each one fully, concentrating on them as much as she would on the ivory beads of the rosary she had brought back from Santiago de Compostela all those years ago. Alma watched the signorina go through her gates, close them softly behind her, make her way slowly down her white gravel path, carrying once again her burden of shopping and loneliness. Within minutes, the kitchen window opened, and Alma heard the sweet strains of a Mozart piano concerto.

Alma pulled away from her window sill. Quickly she turned on the radio and switched the channels until a frothy light-hearted song filled her room. And in a loud voice that dispelled the silence of her room and drowned out the soft Mozart from the signorina's open window, Alma joined in the cheerful refrain.

24

They were walking along the river bank. Like a moat, the river protected the east side of the village, separating it from the wheat fields beyond, from the undulating stretch of hills, from the long plot of the birches. The water, as it swayed from right to left, touched the land that had once belonged to the Ferratis and was now Franca's.

Miso had spent his afternoon tasting the new wines in the cellars run by the provincial co-operative. 'It's the best way to start the season,' he'd explained, as he came into the kitchen to drag her out for a walk. He'd been animated, slightly drunk, and had waltzed her round the kitchen table when at first she'd refused to leave her easel. 'Come along, Signorina Ferrati, we'll go for a nice walk and I'll show you the real San Lorenzo.'

Every hill, every field, every bend in the river seemed to hold moments of his youth. He pointed out each landmark with pride, as if she had never set foot in this corner of the world. At times they would come to the same patch of land and Alma would recognize it, try to claim it for her own – but his memory would overcome hers. So that these ancient vineyards which had once been her family's, and which reminded her of the long al fresco lunches to sample the newest wines which Father had organized with Bernardino and Alberto della Rocca, brought Miso back to the first grape harvest he'd ever worked on, together with a group of village boys. The great expanse of wheat fields, which had been explained to her as the boundaries of her forefathers' land, to be studied during every seasonal change for signs of bounty or barrenness, were for Miso the site of a thousand couplings, part of village folklore. And the woods beyond, which for Alma had been uncharted territory, where she would venture almost with trepidation, to walk her thoughts, like a pack of hounds, through the mossy undergrowth, were famous, Miso explained, as the place where Santa's first sighting had occurred.

'Our sacred Santa: where is she now I wonder?' Alma asked.

'You can see her, every now and then, walking through the village on the way to church. Or helping her mother behind the counter. But she still won't speak.'

'I wish I could see her – I'm sure that a look at the holy girl would do this sinner some good.' She smiled.

'I see that when it comes to making the leap of faith, as they call it, your feet are as leaden as my own.'

'Hmmm . . .' The sun was touching the crest of the hills now, and the breeze had grown cool. They had come to the edge of the woods, and Miso held back a branch so that she could walk untouched onto a narrow path. 'It is of course rather difficult for me to come to terms with holy speak, visionaries and miraculous occurrences. Personally' – her voice dropped – 'I would like nothing more than to be visited by the Mother of God. I'd even settle for my Guardian Angel. Anything, really, to bring me back to that certainty of childhood.'

'It's not for me, all that. What good have believers ever done the rest of us? Many of the great wars have been brought about by religion but very few of the great changes. Aquinas talked a great deal about free will, but few pious people I know have deployed their will in the service of others.'

'Such a cynic ...' She smiled at him. They had reached a clearing, now, a spot that seemed as if under the spell cast by the light and silence that filled it. Alma suddenly remembered: this had been her goal during those long solitary walks during which she had pondered her future. She pulled Miso's hands. 'Come, come.'

He laughed, and allowed her to lead him to the very centre of the clearing. The breeze stirred the leaves around them, as if awakened by the movement of the sun towards the hills.

'Let's just stand here.' Alma stood quite still, face turned up towards the trees that touched the sky. 'For me, this was always the centre of the earth.' She smiled at Miso.

'Tell me what you see, then, in the centre of the earth?' His hand pulled a blade of grass that he brought to his lips.

'Hmmm ...' Alma squinted up at the sky. 'It's warm, it's soft and full of light. There are all the people I love: my parents, my brother ...'

'You haven't loved many people.' Miso was standing behind her, trailing the blade of grass across her shoulder.

Alma closed her eyes. The scent of grass rose around her. Was it true? Yes, perhaps he was right: her life had only room for a very few. She had given little time or energy to the discovery of others, and had dreaded yielding any part of herself. Her days had been taken up with

187

the attainment of her goals: the paintings, an exhibition, some form of critical recognition ... but sometimes she wondered, was this enough? What was it Francesco had said – 'I'd rather see you fat and happy by the stove with a couple of children ...'?

Miso's voice returned, to break into her thoughts: 'Tell me what else there is, in the centre of the earth?'

'A house, a river, green hills like these. The sun always shines and everything is calm and serene.'

Miso grinned at her. 'It's too dull a scene, don't pretend it would suit you. I can see you banging on the doors within minutes, begging to be let out.'

'You're wrong ...' Alma began, head shaking.

'No. If what you always wanted was a quiet, cosy little place, you wouldn't be living alone in Torino, you wouldn't be painting. You'd be married to a man who gives you one of the family jewels for your engagement, and a fur coat on your first anniversary. You'd have thick ankles and a thick waist from childbirth and a bored face that gives you away to every man who bothers to look at you, from the postman to the butcher ...' He gave her a big grin. 'No, you haven't conformed. You are a free spirit, one of life's true adventurers.'

'I wouldn't be so sure. This past year I achieved so much I'd wanted to achieve ... and all in all I wasn't too happy. A true adventurer should be made of stronger stuff.'

'The past year can't have been easy for you.'

Alma shot him a quick look. 'No. No it was not.'

'But you survived. And alone. You don't know how few people can live with their own company. I simply can't understand the others: I refuse to see life as a game of musical chairs, where the object is not to be caught out alone.' Miso here threw back his head and gave a short laugh. 'The future ... you can be excited about that.' Again the blade of grass traced her shoulder. 'My old friend Gianni er Brutto used to tell me: live each day as though it were a village festa. Plenty of good wine, sweetened with songs, a few fun rides and maybe even a prize or two.'

The leaves above them shivered and rustled as the breeze grew bolder with the waning of the sunlight. The form of the moon appeared, distant and white, waiting for the sun to slip away among the hills.

'San Lorenzo is so beautiful, isn't it ...' Alma whispered: 'It's so peaceful, so soothing to feel at home.'

The breeze suddenly dropped and all around them a hush fell, as if everything – leaves, grasses, clustered fruit, slim branches – that had previously stirred, trembled, rustled, now had filled with torpor. In this new stillness the light too seemed softer, and fell in lazy folds, allowing cool dark shade to gain ever greater patches of ground and trees.

Suddenly a figure stood at the edge of the clearing, radiant as a vision. They remained immobile as Santa drew closer, head slightly bowed. In her hands Alma saw the rosary beads shine.

'Santa,' Miso whispered. The white figure looked up, but she continued to walk with slow silent footsteps, bright against the trees. She skirted the clearing, but she hardly seemed to move: it was as if the air were carrying her forth, lifting her above the grasses, leading her away from them.

Miso and Alma stood still, silent lest she vanish. But

within moments she had gone, hidden by the trees.

'She is beautiful,' Alma whispered, as if the apparition demanded awe-filled silence in its wake. 'She hasn't changed at all since Francesco used to be in love with her.'

'She seems untouched by everything – time, the conniving schemes of the mayor and his mates ...' Miso shook his head. 'God alone knows what the future has in store for someone so unprepared for real life.'

Alma watched the orange light of sunset creep beneath the branches, and remembered the same soft glow in the kitchen when, at the end of summer, the pinecones burned in the fireplace. 'We had best go back...'

They retraced their steps in silence.

Months had passed since Bishop Natti had refused to come and investigate the silent visionary of San Lorenzo. While the ground froze, and the days grew short and sunless, the mayor and his allies hung about the bar looking despondent and drained of the energy they had gleaned from their common vision of a shrine. Their disappointment was so palpable, so keen, that even Old Rocco had shaken his head and told Gianni er Brutto that this time he'd desist from 'pulling that idiot's leg'.

'I just don't know what stone we haven't turned, at this point: we have written him a letter of invitation, we made sure that the *Gazzetta* covered the story and took those lovely photographs of Santarella walking into the church, trying to slip into her mother's shop – yesyesyes, and then we even sent him two crates of that fine Barolo from my vineyards ... Tell me what else there is for us to do to convince Bishop Natti?' And the mayor twirled an empty wine glass between rough fingers.

'If only he'd left us some room for hope ...' sighed Don Luigi.

'If only Santarella would speak!' The marshal tapped the floor with his cane. At the mention of the visionary, though, the mayor's face took on such a painful expression that neither the marshal nor Don Luigi dared probe further.

'If only I had influence with someone in Rome ...' murmured Don Luigi.

'Eh, Rome ...' began the mayor. And then, slapping the table before him so hard that Claudio shot him an anxious look from the counter: 'But of course! I've got it! We must send someone to Rome. Forget the small fry like that imbecile Bishop Natti' (here Don Luigi looked pained and crossed himself at what surely amounted to a blasphemy), 'what we need is an important figure in Rome to back us. We need to impress the key people, not some provincial prelate! We'll send an emissary with a specially worded plea!'

The mayor's mention of an emissary eclipsed the disappointment about possible delays to the building of the shrine: from that moment, every man in the village thought himself the perfect ambassador for San Lorenzo. Excitement buzzed, as noisy and indiscriminate as flies in a stable, from house to house, over the news that someone would be chosen to carry forth the delicate mission. Only the women, excluded by their gender from the role of ambassador-to-the-Curia, kept their heads in the ensuing chaos, each one privately reviewing her husband's past and wondering how he could possibly consider himself worthy of such spiritual distinction.

Over the billiard table, over the evening games of scopa, while the black sky strewed snow as if it were seeds, and the window panes in the bar were curtained by the cold weather, the men of San Lorenzo argued over and sifted through the candidates for the job.

'We need a man who can speak well, a man who knows

how to make the right impression,' said Romeo the butcher, as he downed another sip of grappa and studied his hand.

'Well, he can't be a shopkeeper: it's too obvious that he would stand to gain from the building of the shrine,' growled the Marshal Ciuffi from his chair near the counter.

'Someone who stands to gain from this enterprise is the only hope we have,' argued the baker Nuccio, awaiting his turn to pick up a card. 'Who is more convincing than the man who sees what a mint he can make out of the pilgrims?'

'We need a holy man, one who will impress the bishops with his humility and faith, and who will show them that this village still believes in miracles.' These words, uttered by Don Luigi, cast a silence over the group of players. Humility and faith? A holy man? The villagers looked at one another, lit their cigarettes, considered this new angle of the issue before them: who, among them, had led a blameless life? And they thought over their past deeds – which proved difficult; and then reviewed their neighbours', which proved easy.

The sins of all the villagers were now examined: it was learnt that Claudio, Vanna's husband, had been forced to buy poor Checchina's silence when she had been pregnant five years ago; that the butcher Romeo's brother was spending his third month in prison in Ovada, for having received stolen goods; and that Nuccio the baker beat his wife every night.

For weeks, for months, the people of San Lorenzo aired forgotten grievances and uncovered old secrets, so that the winter showers fell upon besmirched reputations that had been dragged through the streets and the piazza.

It was Don Luigi who put an end to the stone-casting of his parishioners. One morning, during one of their habitual conferences, he informed his two allies of the appearance of a new contender: 'Vincenzo. Vincenzo is our man – a bit simple, I'll grant you, but a good, God-fearing farmer. And, more important, he has a cousin who is in Divinity School in Rome, and his wife used to go to school with Bishop Natti's niece ... yes, Vincenzo is just the man for this mission.'

'Do you really think so, Father?' Marshal Ciuffi tugged at his moustaches: in truth, he had rather hoped that he himself would be chosen for the task.

'Vincenzo,' explained Don Luigi carefully, 'has an honest manner. He looks as good as bread, and as simple. What better envoy could we hope for? Remember that the men of the cloth have a suspicious nature – anything that smells of speculation would not go down well.'

'Well, then, we've decided – Vincenzo it is!' the mayor shouted enthusiastically. He had no wish to procrastinate further.

Vincenzo, pious farmer and father of nine, was summoned by the triumvirate to the mayor's office, where he was informed of the great task that lay ahead.

'What an honour! What an honour, Signor Mayor ...' wheezed the farmer, his long face and trembling nostrils much like a rabbit's. 'If you knew what happiness ...'

'Save your breath for your mission.' The mayor punctured the poor man's balloon of fervent exclamations. 'And for God's sake, don't stand trembling like that when you visit the bishops in their palace.'

When the mayor had placed the thick cream-coloured

envelope into the frightened farmer's hands, Don Luigi blew out a long sigh of hope and anxiety, and raised his hand above his humble head, beginning the sign of the cross. But Battistini interrupted him: 'But you haven't got a car!'

'I don't, your excellency, I don't.' The poor man shook his head and turned up his palms for all to see that they were empty.

'Well, you'll have to borrow ... let me see.' The mayor thought a moment – he was not going to lend his own pride and joy to this snivelling cretin before him. 'You'll borrow the butcher's car, his Fiat ... I'm sure he'll be more than happy to assist us in this matter.'

'Yes, your excellency.' The lips quivered, the eyes darted from side to side.

'Well then.' The mayor rubbed his hands together in sudden good humour. 'You have to go to Rome, find the key bishops, hand over our message and get their reply.'

And so it was that, one week later, with an ancient cardboard case in one hand, and a great plastic bag full of homemade pies and focacce in the other, Vincenzo stepped into the butcher Romeo's car early in the morning, a few days before the feast of St Nicholas. More than half the village filled the piazza to see him off: they waved and cheered and forgot in their excitement all disappointment about the triumvirate's choice of ambassador. Only the butcher Romeo seemed less than ecstatic at the sight of the little Fiat that set off and disappeared from view.

26

Alma sat in the study, by the fire, darning the cardigan she had torn inadvertently on the doorhandle. As she bent over the wool she'd found in Mother's sewing basket, she thought of Miso. Alberto had been right: they were too different. His concept of the world seemed to begin and end here among these hills and vineyards. Everything beyond struck him as uncharted waters where sirens lurked, ready to lure him into a deep, dangerous world. And she suspected he saw her as just such a siren: she amused him, attracted him, of that she had no doubt. But she sensed that he was alarmed by her, saw her as a danger. Beneath that strong sunbrowned exterior, he was timid, and above all, he seemed wary of placing a foot wrong. His sense of balance was precarious, and, she felt certain, only recently achieved.

'No,' she said out loud, shaking her head over the cardigan, it would not do.

The pine tree's branches brushed against the window pane, pushing their wet needles against the glass. A perfect autumn had given way to a wet cold winter, and she had withdrawn inside the house to continue her painting. Every weekend she pledged to return to her studio flat in Torino. But she never packed her bags, and when the woodcutter's cart had rolled into the gateway to see if she wanted to order any logs, she immediately said yes.

The wind outside was swelling, pulling and pushing the poor trees in the garden, imperious, hard-hearted, threatening.

Her thoughts returned to Miso. He spoke of their lives as separate and contrasting – hers trapped in the social and artsy currents of a Torino she did not recognize from his description; his, unfolding in smooth rich quiet waves here in San Lorenzo. Their meeting point, this village, was a landscape he claimed as his own and where, he implied, she could only consider herself a visitor. Her house and generations of ancestors might belong to San Lorenzo, but she, Alma, with her dreams and her expectations, she could never remain within the confines of this village. She felt as if in separating himself from her world and its inhabitants, he were rejecting it for its transient appeal, its hollow claims to happiness; and this rejection, in her vision of him, raised him high above her: he was capable of leading a life of simplicity and of integrity, where she ... She caught her breath: Miso stood before her, smiling, conscious of having caught her unawares.

'The door was on the latch, so I came in.' Beneath his gaze she blushed, threw down her cardigan, picked it up once again, tossed her head lightly and failed to regain composure.

'This is a first: I don't think I've ever seen you doing anything even remotely domestic.' He grinned, squatting beside her, the better to study her needlework. 'My mother couldn't do it better herself.' He held the wool to his eyes for a fake examination.

Alma moved away from him on the sofa. 'Don't tease,'

she pouted, as she struggled to gain hold of her light-hearted persona.

'You make a very fetching picture sitting here darning. Very old-fashioned. Very heart-warming.' But as he sat beside her on the sofa she felt he was as tense as she was.

This is madness. He's wrong for you, you for him. We must put a stop to these meetings.

'We really should put a stop to these meetings of ours, you know.' She would not look at him as she spoke.

'What do you mean?' His voice was quiet, emotionless.

He's not what you want. He wouldn't be happy in your life, and you would tire of his.

'I mean that this is not going anywhere, Miso.'

He stiffened on the sofa beside her, but did not speak.

You need someone different, someone . . .

'We can't afford to play around like teenagers, neither one of us. We both know we want very different things out of life . . .' She kept her eyes resolutely lowered.

'Ah . . .' He did not move. 'I see.'

'So I think we should stop seeing each other. It's winter now, I can stay away in Torino for a while . . .'

His hands took her face, brought it close to his. 'Don't say another word.'

She raised her eyes. 'Miso . . .' she implored, but she no longer knew what she was asking him for. When he kissed her, she felt as if she had abandoned all claim to herself. Neither spoke, and it seemed as if hours had gone by before they were making love on her bed, watched by the Madonna and Child from their faded tapestry.

27

Inside Vanna's bar, mulling over their coffee cups, Old
Rocco and Gianni er Brutto caught the sun that shone
through the window pane. Vanna was drying last night's
glasses, Claudio was hidden by the pink pages of the
Gazzetta dello Sport and in a corner, looking laconic and
sounding lugubrious, Grillo strummed a song he'd
recently made up for the baker's daughter.

An air of expectancy filled the bar: today was the day
San Lorenzo's emissary Vincenzo was supposed to come
back, bearing news of the bishops in Rome. Old Rocco
stirred a third spoonful of sugar into his thick coffee. 'So
today's the Day of Judgement: will the people of San
Lorenzo continue to play the fools and pursue the cock-
eyed scheme dreamed up by the mayor, or will the
bishops take the matter out of their hands and put the
whole spectacle where it belongs – in the bin?'

'We can rest assured, Rocco: the clerics in Rome will
not be mocked by the likes of Battistini.' And Gianni er
Brutto caressed his birthmark.

A blast of ice-cold air now froze the old men and both
uttered obscenities as the former postmistress, Pina, came
in for her morning gossip with Vanna. Snow flakes carried
by the wind followed her into the bar, and the tiny

postmistress stamped about to free herself of the white powder on her coat, boots, hat and scarf.

'Eh, Vanna.' Pina approached the counter, behind which Vanna gave her a nod. 'Eh, Vanna ...' And Pina unbuttoned her coat, removed her scarf, took off her little felt hat and crossed her arms upon the counter. 'The goings-on in this village ... poor Carla Brusoni has not seen that son of hers for weeks now – he's always holed up in the Ferratis' house with the signorina ... She's told me she's worried sick because the signorina doesn't cook him dinner, and he's looking a shadow of his former self...'

'I shouldn't think Miso's losing weight because Alma Ferrati isn't cooking for him ...' Claudio looked over his pink pages of sport. 'They've got better things to do in that house ...' And he sighed with envy.

'Please, Claudio!' But Vanna was laughing. 'I wonder where all of Miso's big ideas about the rich and the snobs have gone now, eh?' And she set the glass she'd dried on its head against the mirrored wall behind her. 'Do you remember, Claudio, when we used to go around with him when he was still a student ... all the nonsense he'd spout about the unjust this and the unfair that ... and now look at him, spending every minute of the day with a woman born with a silver spoon in her mouth.'

'And who wouldn't spend every minute of the day with a woman who looks like that, eh?' And Old Rocco laughed and tapped the cup before him with his spoon.

'He's a good man, Miso,' Gianni defended his friend. 'Takes care of his mother, does a good job, leads a quiet life. He had a lot of ideals in his youth, and he liked to dream up ways this world of ours could become a better place to live in. And what's wrong with that? He used to have a thousand ideas about how he could help people . . .'

'And what a lot he's done for them in all these years!' And Claudio snorted his disapproval.

'And he's difficult and moody,' Pina the former post-mistress put in for good measure.

The doors opened again, and this time it was Miso himself, blowing on his gloveless hands, stamping the snow off his boots.

'Well, well, speak of the devil,' muttered Old Rocco with a grin.

'What's that?' Miso made his way to the counter. 'A coffee, Vanna please.'

'Oh, nothing.' And Old Rocco here put on an air of elaborate innocence. 'Just saying that you look so thin, my boy.'

'Hush, Rocco.' And Gianni raised his hand in greeting. 'Miso my boy, all these men are envious of your good fortune . . .' He smiled but Miso's frown erased the smile immediately.

'Trust the lot of you to have nothing better to do than to talk about others.' Miso gave Vanna a cool look as he took the espresso from her hands.

'Oh, get off your high horse, Miso,' Vanna teased, wiping her hands on her apron and giving the big man a friendly grin. 'You do as you please, but there's no harm in our discussing it.'

Miso didn't answer, but his face remained set. Vanna caught Pina's look and rolled her eyes.

Outside, the corriera tooted as it stopped at the corner of the piazza. And, as was true each time that the rattling blue bus pulled up in San Lorenzo (at seven in the

201

morning, then at eleven, then at four), the shopkeepers stopped their chatting, the men pulled their bicycles to a halt, the women looked out of their windows: who was going, who was coming?

'Saved by the corriera!' And Old Rocco laughed and rose. He and Gianni made their way to the door and stood against the pane, noses pressed, the better to see.

The corriera's doors opened with a great creak. 'Look at this!' Rocco shouted, excited, gesticulating to those inside to come to the door: 'It's our messenger! It's Vincenzo!'

'Why's Vincenzo there, I thought they'd lent him Romeo's car?' And Claudio ran up to the door to see for himself.

Old Rocco was right. There, beside the corriera, crumpled and wrinkled into a bundle of fatigue, San Lorenzo's envoy to the bishops raised a faint hand in salute.

Now from the other side of the piazza the men saw the mayor, Don Luigi and the marshal approach the corriera. The three men surrounded their messenger, only to pull him in the direction of the bar.

'What in heaven's name is this?' The triumvirate burst through the door, dragging the empty-handed specimen with them. 'What's he done, the fool?' The mayor was apoplectic.

It didn't take a gypsy to read poor Vincenzo's face: misery and worry spread over his down-turned mouth, over his pavement-fixed eyes.

'Tell us what happened in Rome!' the mayor was shouting.

Their messenger was huffing and puffing, sadly lacking Mercury's winged heels.

'Oh dear Jesus, what can I say, Signor Mayor, what can I say except that I will never recover from the horror of this journey ... Blessed Mary ...' And Vincenzo shook like the corriera, over each bump of a word.

The spectacle before them was irresistible, and Vanna, Claudio, the former postmistress and even Miso drew close to listen to poor Vincenzo's ordeal.

'Here, here, let the man sit down.' Don Luigi, voice and hands atremble, tried to pull up a chair for the hapless ambassador.

'Well, I got to Rome. It took me a while, just to get used to the place ... and what with one thing and another ...' Vincenzo pulled out a dirty handkerchief from his pocket and began to wipe his brow. 'It took me ages to find a decent pensione ...'

'For Christ's sake, Vincenzo: pull yourself together and spare us these details. Tell us what the bishops said!' Battistini's threatening red face came towards Vincenzo's.

But Vincenzo coughed, sat down, shook his head and gasped for water. 'Vanna, get the man a glass of water!' Battistini spat out his order like a general on his last stand.

Vanna fetched the water, and practically poured it into Vincenzo's mouth. After a long swallow Vincenzo began to drive more smoothly down the lane of his adventures, although, every now and then, as a particularly gruesome memory soared before his eyes, he grimaced with the panic of a rusty driver. 'There I was, in the middle of a strange city ... one bishop says no, he can't see me the first day then no, says another one, he can't see me either, I tell you frankly, I never thought they'd hear me out.' A gulp of water. 'Then, finally ...' And the audience held its breath.

'Get to the point!' The mayor's face burned with fury.

'Get to the point, Signor Ambassador!' croaked Old Rocco, laughing.

'As I was saying, finally one bishop calls me in. A great, huge palace' – here the little man's arms opened wide – 'the likes of which you've never seen. Huge marble staircases, chandeliers and paintings from floor to ceiling ... He calls me in, a polite man, calm and refined ... he knew my uncle ...'

'Don't make me lose my patience, Vincenzo!' The mayor raised a tightly clenched fist.

'Well, after a chat, after he spoke highly of our village, after he praised what he had heard of Santarella – after all this, he began to explain why we can't have the shrine.'

'The bishop said no?' And the Marshal Ciuffi nearly speared the poor rabbit with his cane.

'The bishop said no.' And Vincenzo, his duty done, fell back upon his chair like a sack of flour.

The mayor erupted: 'He said "no" then? He said no and you didn't argue? You didn't ask to speak to another bishop, even an archbishop?'

The doors burst open and in rushed the butcher Romeo, coatless, hatless, blood-stained apron flapping before him. 'Where is my car?' he shouted, and had to be restrained by Claudio.

'Yes, where is Romeo's car?' The mayor was spitting now, but Vincenzo didn't dare take out his handkerchief to wipe his chin.

'That's the worst of it all: there I was, in the middle of the night – last night, that is – and I hear noises from my room ... I hear shouts: a fight, I think, and I put on the light and lean out of the window, and what do you think

I see?' He turned from one face to the next, eyes wide. 'I see three hoodlums, big as houses, break into Romeo's car!' The shock this statement produced brought a triumphant smile to Vincenzo's face. 'Yes I tell you: big men, three of them, breaking into your car, carving it with their knives like a cheese ... I call out, I shout, but in that God-forsaken city, do you think anyone comes to help? No one, nothing. No police anywhere, not even a carabiniere, and that crook of a pensione owner had made himself scarce...'

'So where's the car?' And Romeo grabbed the chair upon which Vincenzo quaked.

'It's ... still there, I've got the address of the pensione, everything, but how could I have driven it today, eh, there's no steering wheel, no wheels...'

'This is too good to be true: we lose a shrine and a Fiat all in one go!' Miso burst out laughing and Old Rocco cackled.

'Damnation. Damn it all,' said the mayor, covering his face with his hands. He collapsed in a chair, the marshal at his side. Don Luigi mopped his brow with his kerchief, speechless.

Vincenzo finished his glass.

'Get him out of my sight!' Battistini screamed.

Vincenzo opened his mouth, but thought better of it, and, with a last reproachful look at those who had subjected him to such a nightmare, scampered off home.

'Ahiahaihai.' Don Luigi, sitting next to the mayor, shook his head. 'And all we were trying to do was offer Our Lady a token of respect, build her a shrine where we could worship Her ... I should have gone myself, Bettino, I should have gone myself...'

'What a defeat, what a defeat!' The marshal bowed his head beneath the weight of failure.

The mayor's face was set, his jaw clenched. 'Let's go, men, let's go talk things over.' And, without so much as a look in the direction of his mockers, he led the other two out of Vanna's bar. Behind him, Miso and Claudio fell about laughing.

'Eh, I remember when Mussolini had the motto "Only God can bend the fascist will" painted all over the school's wall ... But we didn't need divine intervention here: it just took Vincenzo and a long-skirted bishop to bend our mayor's will in two ...' Old Rocco took hold of the faded pack of cards and, with a grin at his old comrade, began to deal.

28

It was snowing in San Lorenzo, and the grey skies of dawn held only the faintest light. Alma lay in bed, her head upon Miso's chest. She could hear his heart beat beneath her ear. She watched him: eyes shut, lips parted. The chest rose and fell in slow, calm motion. She did not know if he was asleep, but she didn't want to talk to him now. She wanted to feel him against her and remember the words and gestures of the Miso who filled her memory.

For the past month, they had been constantly together. She wouldn't let him stay at his mother's, not even for one night. 'She'll come to hate you, if you keep her son away every night, and return him in the morning wrung out like some rag, dark circles under the eyes,' he had joked. But every night he yielded, and stayed with her.

She loved to bring him coffee in the morning, before he returned to his mother's home to change for the day. She asked a thousand questions about which clients he had appointments with, which contracts he'd have to draw up. And then, when he had gone, and she tried to work at her easel, she'd apply her oils with a distracted hand while he stood before her, now preparing a contract for Franca Felici, now registering Nuccio the baker's latest van, bending over his desk, or standing by the door, shaking someone's hand as he saw them out the door.

Miso coughed, half-opened his eyes, smiled upon seeing her. 'Do you expect me to sleep with you lying on my chest?' He turned on his side, embraced her so that she fitted snug against the curve of his body.

'Hmmmm ...' Alma smiled. She smiled at the feel of his warm skin, the affection in his touch. She closed her eyes. Flesh. She wanted to paint his naked flesh and fill her canvas with its warm tones, its dark smoothness shadowed by the curves of ribs, hips, belly. She wanted to place him against the green and blue landscapes, reclining in the grass, gazing up at the heavens with those eyes that softened when they lit upon her, yet still held something back.

'I want you to tell me what you are thinking,' she'd whisper as they lay back on the pillows, and she felt the calm sweetness that filled her after their lovemaking.

'I want I want I want – how easy it's obviously been for you to get what you want.' And he never answered.

She longed, impatient, breathless, for his touch every time they met. In their lovemaking, she felt as if she plunged herself into a warm dark sea where the only life was his, where the waters bleached her of all intellect, leaving intact only her senses.

She loved to hear him describe his long-held interest in her: 'An obsession, that's what you were for me,' he told her as they lay in bed and he caressed her hair. 'I remember sitting in the piazza, in the summer, everyone lolling about on their motorcycles, sitting in their cars listening to old cassettes, debating what we were going to do ... and then you'd come, sometimes with Francesco, sometimes on your own, and the minute you arrived, everything became exciting, everyone shook off their torpor . . . And God, you always looked so good. I didn't know you could feel so lustful about anyone . . .' He laughed at the memory. And she drew great pleasure from the unspoken truth: that she had been unaware of him.

'I remember one evening I was bicycling down the road towards Susa. There was one period – more than one summer, I hate to admit – when I always looked over the hedge, tried to peer into this house. I liked to try and see you moving about inside, in the windows that were lit up. And one evening I saw you: you were getting ready to go out, I saw you brushing your hair, trying it up, twisting it this way, and you pirouetted in front of a huge mirror as you did this . . . I felt slightly ashamed that I kept watching, looking in. I remember that catching you like that, unawares, made me feel very close to you . . .' And he pulled her into his arms, embraced her tight.

He had a thousand stories about her in their youth, but she never recognized herself in the Alma he created. She felt nothing in common with this dazzling, elusive, elegant creature, and at times she worried lest her true self would pale into insignificance. But she had little time for concern, for every moment seemed taken up with him: she felt as if her life now alternated between exulting in his presence, and his pleasure in her company, and waiting for his return.

'Are you happy?' she would whisper before they fell asleep, back to back.

'Yes.' And he would reach out with his hand to pat her thigh.

29

For Shrove Tuesday, Alberto had rung with a peace offering: would she come to Torino for a dinner dance he and Bernardino were giving – 'with your notary, of course: my clemency knows no bounds...'

Alma, touched by Alberto's generous capitulation, had immediately accepted. She hadn't been back to Torino since her affair with Miso had started, and after two months of quiet, she longed to go somewhere loud, people-filled, light-dazzling.

But Miso was reluctant – as she had known he would be. He was always teasing her about 'those aristocrats you see' and her 'social butterfly existence'. She tried to reply with half-hearted remonstrances about how, in truth, she had attended very few parties in Torino, mostly if they offered an opportunity to promote her work. 'I do paint, you know, though in your eyes that may seem a courtier's job ... I can't just sit about and have endless teas with society hostesses...'

'Of course, of course, the painting's kept you from sinking into their well-upholstered armchairs – never to rise again.'

She never quite knew whether he took her painting seriously, or whether he saw it as a part she had decided to play at the moment, for want of a better role.

'Couldn't we stay here? Vanna always organizes something at the bar for carnevale. And Grillo said he's going to lay on an incredible display of fireworks,' he went on. 'Anyway you know those people – Alberto and the like – I always feel uncomfortable with them . . .'

Alma insisted. Miso held out. Alma begged. Miso yielded. But on the Tuesday morning, Alma woke up with high fever and swollen glands. 'I can't bear it. God's on your side,' she sniffled behind her tissue.

He laughed. And expressed his obvious relief at not having to go to Torino in a hundred attentive gestures. He cooked her chicken broth, fixed her endless tisanes, brought her every newspaper, moved the radio into her room. His kindness made her laugh. 'You like me best when I'm deflated, powerless and ill.'

'At least you're finally still.'

'This is not the way we were supposed to spend the carnevale . . . I can't bear it . . . just look at me!' she moaned.

'Don't be silly: a red nose and runny eyes lend you a certain je ne sais quoi.' He laughed, gave her a pat, lay down beside her, newspaper in hand. 'Go to sleep and you'll feel better.'

They lay next to one another throughout the afternoon. Alma, slipping in and out of sleep, swam in memories: a five a.m. mushroom-hunt undertaken with Francesco and Father, after which Father instead of driving them to school had brought them to a café in Alessandria where they'd had hot chocolate; a bout of influenza she had had when a little girl, which Mother had turned into a delightful experience by allowing her to wear her own silk nightshirt; a midnight swim in the river, with

211

Francesco and a schoolmate of his ... Lovely, forgotten episodes floated towards her, as heart-warming and unexpected as a stranger's chivalrous gesture.

She was woken by a fountain of golden specks that cascaded through the persimmon tree. She saw Miso standing at the window. He was staring out, smoking, holding his cigarette out of the window that he'd left ajar. Miso. He was, he told her, a creature of habit. And she could see that in routine he found the structure he spoke of as essential to his contentment. Every day was the same. In the morning, he drank the coffee she brought him, then went home to change and read the papers with his mother. He liked to work through the day, at a white, neat, glass-and-chrome office in an old building in Acqui. In the past, the evenings had been spent watching television and reading the newspapers after supper with his mother. Every now and then, he went to Vanna's bar 'for the odd drink, to find some male company, for a change'.

'You need to be shaken out of this torpor,' she teased.

'I like to do things in a certain way. I'm very content with this life of mine, thank you very much.' And then, when she pouted that he loved his routine more than her, he'd laugh: 'Dear God, woman! I've changed my whole life since I've been with you!'

She knew that she did not fit into this neat scheme and yet she could not believe that he would wish to cling to its numbing regularity.

'Grillo's pulled it off: it's spectacular.' He had seen that she was awake.

'You mustn't stay in, Miso, go and join them, I'll be all right.'

'What? And leave my little invalid? Of course not.' He

212

put out the cigarette and came towards the bed.

'I kept dreaming about my childhood ...' She pulled his hand, to make him sit beside her.

'That's why you looked so beatific. Shall I pour you a glass of the Barolo my client sent me? Great stuff.' She shook her head. He left her side, poured a glass from the bottle on the dresser, returned with a smile.

In the window coloured fragments of light exploded.

'Some fireworks display,' Alma murmured, grateful that they could watch it from here rather than from Vanna's bar, where she always felt an object of curiosity, and he always donned the aloof air she now knew was his protection in all social occasions.

'Grillo's outdone himself. Bright young man, you know. Big ambition to become a singer. And who knows, he may just make it. Perhaps he won't hit a dead end and have to turn back.'

She heard the bitterness and quickly, before he could withdraw, she asked: 'When did you hit the dead end?'

He cast her a probing look. But she could see that her sudden vulnerability as she lay there, weak and in his care, had dulled the habitual combative spirit with which he reacted to any prying.

'When I did poorly at exams. Mind you' – he gulped the wine – 'the results were nothing to be ashamed of. They just weren't top marks. And the top marks are what you need to enter the hallowed halls of academe. And top marks were what I always thought I could get, what my professors had always thought I could pull off. I swear to you, I knew more than any of those others who excelled – but I don't know ...' He was holding the wine glass with both hands, contemplating its red. 'Every time I sat before

213

the exam papers it was as if shutters had been drawn, and I had to search in the darkness for what I knew was there. By the time my eyes had adjusted, and I could find what I was looking for, time was up.'

'Why academia?' she whispered, watching his profile. The dark eyes shut, for a moment, then opened again.

'I wanted to belong to that élite that makes for progress. I wanted to have an impact, change the things that since I was so high seemed to me false, unfair. I wanted to learn the great general theories, to harness them to the service of those particulars I lived with. I didn't want to spend the rest of my life being the little boy who spots the emperor's naked body and cries out for all to hear. It didn't seem enough, suddenly, to notice. I wanted to understand the whys, the pressures, the rules. And then I would have come up with my own blueprint for the perfect society. Someone once said that there were two human imperatives: fairness and security. At least I have found the latter. Here, burying myself in this village life.' He turned to her now, but his eyes were distant. 'Strange, it's not so long ago – seven, eight years now. Yet it seems like a whole lifetime away.'

An explosion resounded through the room. Once again, an enormous shower of gold fell upon the trees outside the window. Miso whistled, rose and moved to the window, empty glass in hand. 'It's a marvellous show. I'm so glad for Grillo. It meant a lot to him, tonight's success.'

But when he returned to her, Alma saw that his eyes were full of tears. She took his hand and kissed it.

30

'Eh, Alma, you're ruining my poor boy's health. Can't you take time out from the love games and cook him something? Or just come here, the two of you, and I'll fix you a proper meal.' Carla Brusoni gave Alma a wink as she ladled out her bean soup. Alma blushed but did not reply, trying to curb her resentment of the instant familiarity Miso's mother had adopted from their first meeting. Her gaze rested briefly upon the small, sinewy, brown figure before her. 'Eh Alma, I gave him to you bursting with health, big, brown and strong ... and look at what you've reduced him to!'

Miso laughed affectionately and Alma relented, smiling an admission of guilt. 'All right, Carla,' – she tasted the soup with a great show of relish – 'but you'd better share some of your wonderful recipes with me then!'

'You'll get on beautifully, you'll see,' Miso had confidently predicted, his arm wrapped round her shoulders as they had made their way to the square modern villa for the first time. 'You're exactly alike, strong, optimistic and with boundless energy,' he'd said, squeezing her closer to him, so that she could hardly continue walking, laden as she was with the flowers and pastries that she'd insisted on bringing to her hostess. 'And whenever the conversation flags, just ask about my father. She worshipped him, because she was a poor farmer's daughter and he a notary who believed in justice and talked of empowerment and rights and duties ... He was a local councillor for a while, and she drank in his every word and so did I of course. She saw him as a champion of good against evil, as the inspiration behind so much ...' His voice was sweet with affection.

The conversation never did flag with Carla Brusoni. 'Eh, I could write a book about all the strange things that happen to me, and all the people I meet,' she told them as she led them to the kitchen table ('No fuss, Alma, you're family') – and promptly shared her views on everything from the mayor's greed to the village shrine as she served them huge helpings of polenta and rabbit sauce.

'My poor Clemente, may he rest in peace, he always warned us, didn't he Miso, about Bettino Battistini. The man doesn't have any friends, and who can trust a man who struts about and gives himself fancy airs but has to sit alone whenever he sets foot in Vanna's bar? Eh, my Clemente was right, as always. Look at the nonsense the mayor's now got us into! And as for his mistress, that Lea – pshaw!' And Carla Brusoni wrinkled her nose with all the dislike that a plain woman feels for a beauty. 'No wonder that child of hers has to speak to Our Lady – her own mother's never been there to comfort and care for her!' And here Carla Brusoni stood beside Miso, and lowered her face to his, so that her features struck Alma as a simian replica of her lover's. 'Unlike me, Alma, unlike me: I never had him out of my sight. He sat on my hip everywhere I went, my little bundle of love.' And she

216

ruffled Miso's black hair and despite his protestations Alma could see he was happy.

Tonight, as always in this home, Alma felt as if she were penned into a tight dark cage from which only time could deliver her. She hated the dark, pretentious house of theirs, with its smell of floorwax, its incessant television, the plastic flowers in a copper vase in the kitchen. She hated the massive cut-glass chandelier, the red velvet sofa and armchairs with their lace arm rests, the brass-framed mirror that hung above the chest of drawers with its photographs of Miso. She hated the way Carla wore a housewife's smock, and padded about in felt slippers ('They polish the floor as I walk') and, after each meal, cupped her hand around a toothpick which she inserted into her mouth. She hated the talk of class that Carla liked to unfurl, like some protesting marcher's banner, while studying her face for reaction.

'I never met your parents, you know,' Carla said, voice accusing, eyes shiny with malice. 'Never so much as exchanged a word with them. We used to see your Pa's friends bursting through the village with big shiny cars, giving themselves airs and graces. My husband, bless him, made enough money to keep us in comfort' – with a gesture she indicated the room and the ceiling above their head – 'but we have remained simple people.' Alma felt as if she were a little girl, playing with Francesco on the black and white tiles of the drawing-room floor: the game consisted of not stepping on the black tiles and Alma remembered how deceptively simple it was, when you began, to be cautious and careful not to set a foot wrong, but how with each new step it grew more difficult not to lose your balance and slip onto the black.

217

'And how is the painting going, then, Alma?' Carla was back at the stove now, removing from the oven the apple tart she had baked that morning. 'I told my son that he should have you paint his portrait, but you know how modest he is.'

'Yes, well . . .' Alma murmured.

'And the house, how's the crumbling pile?' Carla Brusoni laughed jovially. 'You know, when your pa died, we were all wondering how long you and your brother would keep it for . . .'

'For ever, thank you very much,' Alma snapped, eyes flashing. 'In fact, my brother wants to come back to live here, you know. He's trying to organize his work so that he could be based in Milan.'

'How extraordinary.' Carla Brusoni's eyebrows shot up. 'But what in the world will a city sophisticate do here . . . he doesn't belong here does he?' And before either Miso or Alma could reply, 'And in the end, I suppose, nor do you.'

'This is my home.' Alma spoke softly softly, lest her tone betray her dislike.

'Well, whatever you think.' Carla Brusoni shrugged. 'And what about Easter, the two of you will eat here won't you, so I can do my spring lamb with rosemary . . . I know you're not a cook, you like to paint, but I can tell you, my dear Alma, men prefer food in their stomach to a pretty picture they hang on the wall.'

Miso now mounted a half-hearted defence of her: 'Alma's painting is very good. Highly praised.'

But Alma had seen the way he looked at her when she took to her easel during the weekends, when he was about the house: he donned a quizzical expression, as if she were pouring herself into clothes that were too tight or too young for her. It was as if Alma at the easel didn't quite fit the image he had of her. He never asked her about the commissions, never enquired about the work-in-progress. She said nothing, but determined that she would no longer give him unrestricted access to herself: she would cordon off areas of her emotional life.

'Oh, I don't doubt it. But you should paint the cast of characters we have here in San Lorenzo – all that misery, ignorance and squalor to sink one's teeth into!'

'My mother's idea of art is rather politicized I fear, Alma.'

'Then you'd be disappointed by my work. Not an ounce of social conscience.'

'Well, it would be difficult to have a social conscience in your position: I mean why would you want to change anything, sitting where you are? You've got it all, the cards are stacked in your favour.'

In vain, Alma protested that she had only a modest income, that she did not mingle with an exclusive circle of wealthy aristocrats, that she hardly ever saw her family friends any longer. Carla would not be deflected, and Miso joined in the teasing. Alma watched him: he, whose voice was always quiet and careful, as if wary of inter-ruptions or contradictions, here took on the bluster of the man certain of support.

'What makes you always talk of the world in terms of us against them?' she burst out that night, when they were home in her bedroom.

'Experience.'

'Who is "them", Miso?' she asked, exasperated, as she

219

flung her skirt on the faded pink chintz of the stool by her dresser.

'All those whose money and family have removed them from the concerns of the man on the street. Anybody like your friend Rosso who feels entitled to mock or toy with others' destinies.'

'And in this world view why do I belong to them? Why must you put me in a box, why must I be categorized and labelled?'

He grinned as he took off his shirt and folded it neatly on the back of the chair by the window. 'The better to contain you perhaps. Otherwise, you should take a look at yourself – you rush everywhere, after everything. Last week a landscape, this week a portrait, and you're never satisfied, never tranquil. Hell, I thought painting was a serene occupation – you make it seem a nail-biting, hair-raising experience. Can't you take it all less seriously?'

'It's not a pastime, Miso. It's my life.'

'Scale down these ambitions.'

'Why must I think small when I want big?'

'Can't you see that you're exhausting yourself?'

'But there's so much I still want to see, feel ...'

He laughed and took her in his arms. He kissed her. 'You speak as though there were an infinite well of pleasure for us to draw from ... but is this really your experience?'

'Yes.' She closed her eyes and repeated fervently, 'Oh yes.'

31

It was night and tiny bats flapped in the black air, encircling the streetlights. Alma and Miso were taking an aimless after-dinner stroll along the main road. Miso had draped his arm around her shoulders, so that Alma was concentrating on adjusting her gait to his.

They walked in silence: she was apprehensive about a commissioned portrait, and still felt resentful at his airy dismissal of her worries: 'Oh please, Alma, you should stop agonizing so ... it's just another portrait, and you've done enough by now to know you can always pull it off.' She hadn't said anything more about it, but she had slipped his comments into that secret drawer of her mind where she now arranged, in neat rows, the disappointments between them: his constant mocking of her 'socialite' friends from Torino; his lack of interest in her work; his complaints about her lack of domesticity.

The spring air was cool, and snow still crowned the more distant hills. They strolled down the slope towards Susa, and Alma listened to the crickets and to the faint talk of the village men who were playing a game of bocce. Moderating her pace to Miso's slower one, watching him out of the corner of her eye, she felt she had donned some stranger's clothes, mannerisms and speech. How little of herself she recognized in the woman strolling beside Miso. She had stepped into the womanly tradition of trying to please. That tradition, which had moulded her mother, and so many other women she had studied, was taking hold of her, leading her to total immersion in Miso's world. She was trying to predict his needs, to forecast his moods, to reach his conclusions before he did. She wanted to please him: and she watched him so carefully, listened to his words and silences so anxiously, that she felt she had no energy left for herself.

Over the hedge, beneath the white moons of the street-lights, the village men cast their bocce onto the sand.

The butcher Romeo, whom this exertion threatened to reduce to a sweaty gelatinous mess, was recovering from an unexpectedly good throw: a centimetre closer to the target ball than anyone else had come.

Grillo, who was squatting in the sand to measure the distance, gave a thumbs-up sign. 'Well done! It will be difficult to beat this one!'

'Well done, Romeo: for once you've made your fat work for you.' And Rocco, who in this light seemed to have shrunk to a tiny olive, clapped with mirth. 'And look at that, you've attracted an audience. The Signorina Ferrati and her squire, our notary.' And with his head he nodded in the direction of the hedge, over whose fronds they could see Alma and Miso slowly approach them.

Nuccio the baker was rolling back his sleeves. He winked at the old men who sat on the bench beneath the light. 'Do you think if I come closest the signorina would grace me with a smile?'

'Shshshsh.' Gianni er Brutto drew an index finger to his lips and shook his head. 'Don't be so silly.'

But the butcher shrugged. 'They're carrying on right under our noses, they can't expect us not to pass comment.' His voice seemed to rise from the very depths of his bitterness at his own sexual inadequacy.

'Have you seen him dragging his feet about? She's kept him on the boil so long, he's reduced to nothing like my old wife's broth.' Old Rocco puckered his thin lips and spat.

Grillo guffawed loudly: he was new to the jokes of his father's friends, for this spring marked his initiation into the rite of the village bocce game. Every now and then, he looked to his father for a cue.

Claudio, who had earned his wife's ire by escaping from the bar tonight, nodded. 'She may like to paint, but I suspect she's partial to a bit of a romp while the oils dry on the canvas.' Here everyone chuckled and heads turned in unison to spy on the couple who walked on, oblivious, beyond the hedge.

'It won't last long, mark my words.'

'Oh shut up, Rocco.' Gianni was indignant now. 'Why shouldn't it? They are happy enough, just look at them. All this talk spoils everything...'

Nuccio the baker laughed. 'Old Gianni keeps lecturing us, but he doesn't understand that we can't help scandal-mongering, when there's so little else to do. Except this.' And here he caressed the wooden ball in his hands, took aim, brought his arm back, then cast the ball underhand, so that it formed a slight arc before it sank into the sand a hair's breadth away from the butcher Romeo's. Now he turned to the old men on the bench. 'Oil and water don't mix, Gianni, we all know that.'

'They're from different worlds,' the butcher grumbled,

223

as he took out a huge red kerchief to mop his brow.

Claudio lit a cigarette and nodded. 'I know Miso. He's pretending to be something he's not, just because she – and the whole family – has always dazzled him. But soon enough he won't be able to put up with the way she carries on – the painting, the parties in Torino, never standing still long enough to be a wife and mother of the kind we grew up with ... And she'll get bored without her friends in their flashy cars and their cocktails every night.' He drew a long puff from his cigarette, satisfied that his analysis had been correct.

'Do you see,' Nuccio the baker smirked, 'how nervous she looks when she sets foot in your bar?'

'You'd think we were going to eat her.' The butcher made a grimace.

'Well, I wouldn't mind a nibble.' At Claudio's words the men roared with laughter.

Alma and Miso heard the laughter as they drew closer to the hedge. They could see the white beams that lit up the bocce field, and hear the wooden clapping sound of the balls as they hit and moved one another. Men's voices rose into a cheering crescendo, sank into a drawn-out moan, the one pushing out the other like the wooden balls upon the sand.

'Let's watch them a bit, shall we?'

Miso looked down at her, eyes uncertain: he was always diffident when he asked her to partake of his world, whether it be a grappa at Vanna's bar or a meal at his mother's. She followed him as he made his way round the hedge onto the field. Two old men (she recognized the birthmarked Gianni er Brutto whom her brother had admired) sat on the bench, while the others stood about, polishing their balls as if with their caresses they could perfect their throws.

'Want to have a go, Brusoni?' Nuccio the baker held up the hand that gloved a ball.

'Why not, Miso used to be a good shot before he took to his books and ledgers.' Claudio grinned as he approached the couple. 'Please sit here,' he said to Alma, through lips that clamped a cigarette. With a gesture of exaggerated ceremony he dusted off a corner of the bench upon which Old Rocco and Gianni were perched like lustreless birds. 'Come on, Brusoni, show us whether you're still capable of a decent throw.'

'Thank you, Claudio.' But Alma inwardly cringed at Claudio's manner. His half-mocking, half-flirtatious approach was the same one every village man had adopted towards her ever since, as a teenager, she had ridden on the back of their motorcycles to join them for a pizza in Acqui or an ice cream in Susa. They had shared enough memories, she and Claudio, and Nuccio, and Romeo, to have erased the deference mixed with a touch of contempt the villagers reserved for complete strangers. But their paths had always been so different that no one in the village could approach her as one of their own. And Alma, for her part, never felt completely at ease with these men who saw the legacy she had inherited superimposed upon her. 'They stare at me as if I were an exhibit,' she complained to Miso after a rare excursion to Vanna's bar. 'Don't be so silly,' Miso had laughed, 'they just enjoy attractive women in their midst. And don't forget, you're involved with one of them.' And she could see that he was pleased with himself, and enjoyed the knowledge that his winning over Alma Ferrati was the subject of village talk.

Before Miso, she had had increasingly little contact with the villagers; now, she felt more conscious of them, as if in their expectations and condemnations she could find clues to the man beside her.

Her eyes sought Miso's. But he was studying the sandy aisle upon which sat the bocce. He had relegated her to the sidelines, she could see, while he was bent on impressing the men he had grown up with. Alma watched Miso select a wooden ball, watched him feel the weight of the sphere in his grasp, watched the concentration freeze his features into a frown. She kept her eyes on him, while feeling the gaze of a dozen pair of eyes brush her own figure with the critical appreciation of a painter. But young Grillo, who stood a few paces away, now gave her a wide smile, and Alma felt suddenly reassured.

Miso stretched himself tall, took a step forward, threw the ball underhand. Its thud as it landed and dislodged the butcher's was greeted with applause and whistling from everyone but Romeo.

'Well done, Miso, well done!' Gianni er Brutto cheered.

'Bravo!' Alma clapped and smiled at Gianni beside her.

'Eh, some men have all the luck!' Old Rocco spat onto the grass beside him, then slid a sly look at Alma sitting on the other side of Gianni. 'I'm not sure he deserves all the bounty fortune has laid at his feet.'

Alma laughed.

Miso was trading jokes with Nuccio the baker and Claudio, their backs turned to the bench. As Alma watched the comradely shoulder-slapping, the dusting off of past victories, and fearful failures, she felt him so distant that she suddenly wanted to drag him home and lock him in an embrace.

'He's still the best of the lot,' Gianni murmured beside her.

'He's a great shot.' She nodded enthusiastically.

'Any news from Francesco ... he promised he'd write to me, but not a word ...'

'He's a terrible correspondent. All I have gleaned from the handful of letters he did manage to send is that the work is – as usual – going well, and that Camilla seems in better health ... And of course he'll be back here in August ... as always.'

'Do you think he will come back for good, as he plans?' Gianni stroked his birthmark with a pensive hand. 'I can't quite see why he thinks coming back to San Lorenzo would make him happier ...'

'I don't know, Gianni: in the last letter his mood seems changed, and instead of writing endlessly about his longing for these hills, the vineyards and the quiet – he wrote about London in a completely different way, as if he'd invested more in his life there, and had grown fond of its figures, its colours, its moods ... like suddenly discovering a great liking for a painting that has been hanging on your walls for years and that you'd always thought you were indifferent to ...'

The players had moved to a corner of the field now, talking in loud voices, gesticulating wildly as they threw imaginary balls onto the pitch.

'Miso was always the best.' Grillo stood beside her, hands in pockets.

'And you, do you play?' She beamed at the curly-headed youth.

'A bit. Just started, actually. Beats drying glasses behind

227

the counter and counting bottles of Martini and Strega ...' He blew out a sigh.

'Miso tells me you have quite different plans for your future?'

Grillo shone with pride: to think that Alma Ferrati should take an interest in him, to know that she had discussed his plans with Miso ... he practically spluttered the first few words: 'Well, yes, I want to sing. Become a proper cantautore, write my own songs and give concerts up and down the country ...' He ran a hand through his curls. 'I've already started to write a few things, you know ...'

'Good for you. Any chance of your playing at the festa? They always have those drones from Castellazzo – perhaps this year you could take their place?' Alma watched as the group of men continued to trade jokes and past escapades, ignoring everyone else.

'If only!' Grillo's eyes shone. 'It would be a great break. I doubt though that the mayor will let me.' Here he lowered his voice. 'He's such an ass.'

'From the mouth of babes the truth spills forth,' Old Rocco cackled and slapped his skinny knee. 'Claudio, your son's got brains as well as a nightingale's voice.'

'Leave my son alone, Old Rocco. He's got enough nonsense in that head of his ... eh, children, children, whoever said they were a blessing didn't have any ...' Claudio called out over his shoulder from the tight little circle of men. But as he spoke, he cast his son such a look, that no one, least of all Grillo, was deceived.

'Won't you have a go, signorina?' Grillo had placed a timid hand on the bench behind her.

'Oh, I couldn't possibly, Grillo, this is a man's game isn't it?' she laughed up at him.

Grillo crouched beside her: 'I'll show you how, don't worry, give it a shot...'

Alma stole a look at the men who stood about Miso. Then she stood up, dusted off her skirt, laughing at his beseeching expression: 'If I hit anyone, and maim them for life, let it be upon your head.' But she followed him onto the field. Grillo chose a wooden ball for her, carefully wrapped her hands upon it – 'Here, hold it firmly like this' – and drew back her arm, in slow-motion repetitions, to show her the feel of the throw. Beside him, Alma concentrated on repeating everything he did. Finally, she cast the ball: it arched high into the black air, making a swishing noise that sounded like the concerted whistling of a group. With a great wooden clap it hit the butcher's ball, pushing poor Romeo's ball even further from its original position.

'That was great!' Grillo clapped.

'Great!' Alma echoed beside him, laughing.

'Ah look at that, Miso, your woman's playing a man's game now!' Old Rocco threw out from his bench.

'May the Good Lord preserve us!' The butcher Romeo left the men and strode up to the ball Alma had displaced. The butcher shook his head mournfully, drew out his kerchief and blew his nose with the vehemence of a curse. 'God save us from these women,' he muttered, disconsolate.

Miso laughed as he came up to Alma. 'Come along, Alma, let me take you away before you make too much trouble.' He placed his hand upon her shoulder, grinning over her head at Grillo. 'She's a natural, isn't she?'

'A natural,' Grillo confirmed, nodding vigorously.

'Let's go.' Miso led her away from the men who cast long envious looks in their wake.

'It won't last, mark my words.' And the butcher Romeo shook his head. 'You can't mix two different worlds.'

32

'Shshshsh! Stefano, keep your voice down ...' Alma pressed her index finger to her lips as she turned the key in the kitchen door. 'Shshshsh, I don't want to wake Mi— anyone up.'

Rosso d'Arrighi's son, Stefano, stood right behind her as she closed the door. 'Ah, the mystery man, of course,' he whispered into her hair. 'My father had warned me when I asked who you were.' She could smell the alcohol on his breath. They had both drunk quite a lot at his father's party tonight, and she had had to ask him for a ride home because she didn't dare drive back all that way. It was two o'clock in the morning and she felt guilty at the thought of Miso sleeping in her bedroom.

'Be good and let me find the switch.' She giggled as both their hands patted the wall and then found the switch at the same time. With the light on, she pulled out a chair for him to sit on.

'Will you please please make me a coffee?' he whispered, smiling. She looked at his happy, sun-bronzed face, at the blue eyes that held no secrets and thought him adorable. And how he had danced with her! For at least two hours, they had twirled and jumped and had cleared the floor, sending Alberto into a black mood. But Alma

231

had loved it: she hadn't danced like that for ages – indeed, hadn't been to a party since the autumn and the start of her relationship with Miso.

'You were wonderful tonight – I've never seen anyone dance so well . . .' His blue gaze caressed her.

'Oh, but I've never had the perfect partner until tonight,' she laughed and tapped his hand lightly, flirting. 'You must promise me you'll be my regular dance partner from now on . . .'

'You must promise me you'll leave your mystery man then.' He frowned as he spoke, trying to appear serious.

Alma looked at his flushed, earnest face. Really, how old was this young boy – twenty-two, twenty-three at most? 'Shshsh, not another word like that out of you, young man . . .' But she had to hold her hand to her mouth, she was laughing so.

She hadn't told Miso about Rosso d'Arrighi's party. She had rushed off, in the afternoon, and had left him a note saying she was meeting a prospective client and sitter. 'Alma plus one' the embossed card had read. She'd immediately rung Rosso to say she'd be coming on her own: 'My "plus one" is a shy bear of a man who'd much rather stay at home and read the newspapers,' she'd laughingly explained. But in truth she had wanted to go by herself, to step back, just for a night, into her old social world, with its wealthy, disreputable, dishonest, charming men and women. A world Miso professed to hate, a world peopled with 'them'. She hadn't wanted to bring him along, lest his mocking eyes follow her round the room, and his self-conscious manner spoil her fun. She wanted to float and be fêted – and with Miso beside her, neither would be possible.

Now she opened the refrigerator door and withdrew a carton of orange juice. Stefano d'Arrighi followed her every movement with adoring eyes. She smiled down at the sweet young face that Rosso's son raised to the light. 'I can't make you coffee, Stefano, but just drink this and you'll feel better.' She proffered the carton of orange juice.

Stefano smiled and obediently gulped down the orange juice she served him. 'Alma ...' he whispered. But she wasn't listening: there, on the refrigerator, sat the invitation: she hadn't brought it along because she knew where Rosso and Sofia lived. But why had she left it behind? More important, what if Miso had found it, and seen where she had really been?

'Couldn't I bring you back with me to Torino? We danced so well together ...?' Stefano's hand was on her arm. Alma shook him off. Then, seeing the hurt in his eyes, she pecked him on his forehead. 'You'd better go now, sweet thing.'

She pulled him up with both hands, then pushed him on his way. She shut the door behind him and switched off the light while she heard him start the car. She took the first steps up the staircase, took off her shoes, ran lightly up, the cold stone sending shivers up her spine. In the darkness she let herself into the bedroom. She could make out Miso's form, stretched on its side, upon the bed. She unzipped her dress and gave a sharp cry of alarm when he suddenly lit the lamp.

'You scared me!' she accused him before he could accuse her. She drew closer to the bed, gave him a quick false smile, and continued to undress, her movements clumsy.

'Why did you go to Torino?'

233

'Oh . . . you remember Marisol's prized client the Countess something or other . . . she wanted to meet up for another talk before she finally sits for me . . . she's paranoid that I don't understand her enough to do her justice . . .' The lie came out perfectly formed.

'Really?' He sat up now, and stared at her as she undressed. Alma kept her eyes upon her stockings as she slipped them off. Naked, she slid into the bed. She reached for him beneath the sheet but his hand pushed hers away. 'You didn't by any chance fit in Rosso's party as well?'

Alma felt fear, like nausea, rise to her mouth. 'Miso . . .'

'I don't know how you found the party when you left the invitation in the kitchen.' His voice held no emotion and he wouldn't look at her.

Alma sighed: 'Miso, I'm sorry. I just knew you wouldn't like it, it was the kind of thing you hate . . .'

'So you decided for me that I wouldn't come. Thank you.'

'Miso, please!' Again he pushed her away as she reached out to touch him. She sat up, cupped his chin with her hand and turned his face towards her. 'You wouldn't have enjoyed it, you know that.'

'You mean you were embarrassed to have me with you.' He slowly replaced her hand upon the sheet and lay down, his back to her.

'How can you say that?'

'It's true isn't it? The country bumpkin, the uncouth man from the provinces . . . Alma's ball and chain . . .' His voice came quiet from over his shoulder.

'Miso, please, listen . . .'

'No. You listen.' He turned onto his back, stared out, away from her. 'I'm only here tonight because I wanted to see whether you'd tell me the truth. Which you didn't.'

'Miso, how can you be so unfair? You never tire of telling me how you loathe my snobby friends in Torino, how you dislike those uppity airs they have, how you can't share their view on life ... But every now and then I might perhaps want to see them ...'

'You haven't answered me. Why did you lie to me about tonight?'

Alma drew a deep breath. 'All right. Yes, I wanted to keep it from you. I didn't want a scene. I don't want to go back to my old life in Torino – but I don't want to bury myself in this village life, either ...'

'I don't remember asking you to bury yourself in village life. A quiet regular existence is only fit for second-class citizens like myself. Who could ever ask the amazing Alma Ferrati to lead a life that was anything but exciting and dramatic?'

'Oh stop this. You'll end up spoiling everything with your bitterness, you'll turn everything as sour as yourself ...'

'You don't have the faintest idea about me, do you?'

'Oh yes, I do. All too well. You've been paralysed by your disappointments and you refuse to venture outside the confines of your familiar little world of Mamma's kitchen and that white box of an office of yours, and Vanna's bar. Here you can play the big fish in the little pond, here in San Lorenzo you look damn good ...'

'Alma ...' His voice almost pleaded.

'No comparison between you and the butcher, you and the mayor ... who could fail to be filled with admiration for Miso Brusoni in a village of half a dozen farmers and shopkeepers?'

'Alma!'

'You've settled for the compromises. You've...'

'Stop it, Alma.'

'I won't. And I won't stop stretching for the very best either. I don't want to end up like you!' She burst into tears. Beside her, Miso lay completely still. She couldn't hear his breathing through her sobs. She embraced him. 'Miso, Miso, I'm sorry ...' she wept against him, her forehead on his chest. He didn't move. 'Miso, forgive me ... please ...' She wept uncontrollably. He turned off the lights and lay back, his arms crossed behind his head. Her body pressed against his flank, Alma wept until the first sun came up. When he awoke, before six, he dressed in silence, then came round to her side of the bed and placed his hand on her shoulder. 'Alma, I'm going now. What you said last night – I'm not going to be able to live like this. I don't think I can carry on. I'm sorry.' He left the room. She heard him walk slowly down the stairs, then heard the kitchen door slam.

33

It was summer. The hottest, according to the *Gazzetta d'Alessandria*, since the war. The village men sat before Vanna's bar and predicted in gloomy voices that there would be a devastating drought. Beneath the tireless sun, men on tractors and women in their gardens spoke in hushed tones about the ruin this would bring to the farmers. Everyone watched the clouds that appeared, insubstantial as fanciful daydreams, against the hazy sky. They watched, and hoped or prayed for rain.

In her garden, beneath the persimmon, Alma stared at the half-finished portrait of a society lady before her. Its sitter was clamouring for it: but it was too hot for Donna Patrizia to come and sit outside – 'oh much too hot, I couldn't possibly, Alma dear' – and Alma was to finish it without any further sittings. Alma had placed Donna Patrizia on a chaise longue in the garden, with the house as backdrop. She lay languidly, her plump figure draped upon the striped cotton, dressed in red, faded from a luminous to a tired beauty, and Alma now stared at the curvaceous figure and at the pink and grey brushstrokes of the unfinished background.

It was only midday, but she was already tired, and cross. Cross with herself because she had not finished this commission on time; because she had not been painting as she ought to be; but above all, cross because she had chimed in with the chorus of generations of women who sought their men's approval above all else. His expectations, his desires. Yet, as she studied the unfinished lines, the smudged contours and empty corners, she knew her loss was palpable. Her canvas showed her what she feared: she had lost Miso, and was in danger of losing herself, as well.

Miso ... Two months had passed since they had separated, but still his memory inhabited every corner of her life. She took up her brush, and without any enthusiasm began once again to apply the blue that would shade Donna Patrizia's indolent figure.

All around her, the day beckoned. The crickets' chorus came loud from the dry grass. Through the persimmon's bright foliage she could see the orchard trees, their twisted branches laden with fruit. A bird wound its way through the branches, appearing, then disappearing among the green, as if an unseen, quick hand were pushing a needle through a colourful tapestry. Alma set down her brush on the easel and breathed in the hot clear air, the heavy scent of the earth. Her gaze rested lovingly upon this, the stretch of land she knew best, her corner of the world.

Suddenly, amidst the curves of the fruit trees, she saw a pale figure move. Santarella. Her eyes widened: the girl walked slowly, her gait slightly lifting the white folds of her dress, the mantle of her long black hair. Alma stood quite still, as if her own slightest movement would frighten away the apparition. Santa continued to move forth, her luminous figure glowing beyond the trees, bright against the sky. Alma listened to the silence that had stolen upon the orchard. In this new stillness, the sun seemed to grow so dazzling, that Alma brought up her hand to shield her eyes, as if the radiance could blind her. Now the young girl came to a clearing: she did not move, her figure ablaze against the backdrop of trees. Alma watched as Santa bent her head in the white light, clasping her hands before her.

Alma watched the young woman pray. Her eyes filled with tears at the beauty of the bowed head, the pale figure that stood so still in the sun. She stood at her easel, and joined her hands like Santarella before her. She joined her hands and waited, eyes closed, for the words of prayer to come to her. She had learned, with Mother standing beside her bed, an endless litany of prayer: for 'your dear ones', for the guardian angel, for the sick, for the dead. Prayer had come easily then, while she studied her mother's profile, lips moving, eyes downcast. Prayer had proved as comforting as when at dusk Mother ordered Rina to close the gates, thus separating Francesco and Alma from the village children who still played in the road. In those days, the certainty of faith had seemed palpable to Alma, and evil and good as distinct as the black and white tiles on the marble floor. Alma locked her fingers tightly, and tried to intone the prayers of her childhood. But they had grown as faint as the text in Mother's ancient prayerbooks.

Alma raised her head: the sun was in her eyes now, blinding her. She moved her head to recapture the vision of Santa. But the bright figure had vanished and only sunlight filled the clearing. She turned back to her easel, and found a thin, dark-haired man standing reluctantly at the entrance to her home.

239

'The Signorina Ferrati?' the man asked, peering at her with an uncertain air.

Alma set down her brush, and pulled off her smock. 'That's me,' she answered and made her way to him. 'May I help you?' She smiled at his obvious discomfiture. The man's hand shot out, white and clammy, and shook her own proffered hand. His hair, which was parted in the middle, hung lank and black. His bulging grey eyes met hers but quickly shifted away, to gaze at the orchard and the fields beyond.

'So this is San Lorenzo.' His voice was strained, embarrassed. 'I heard so much about this house and property from your father.' He quickly crossed himself, but in a hurried meaningless way that spoke of habit rather than conviction.

'You're a friend of my father's?' Alma's voice betrayed her disbelief. 'I'm sorry, would you like to come in?' She pushed the door so that it opened and he followed her into the dark entrance.

'Please, please, don't let me be in your way, I know it's lunchtime, but I thought it would take far longer to get here from Genoa.' He tagged along at her heels like a nervous hound out on his first shoot.

She showed him into the drawing room, where all lay in shadow because she'd kept the shutters drawn since the heat wave had begun. 'Please sit down.' She smiled, trying to calm him: his pale face seemed to have grown even paler, and with his right hand he combed his hair behind his ears. He couldn't sit still, his hands now nervously pushing at his hair, now sinking into the pockets of his cream-coloured trousers, now holding onto the lapels of his jacket.

'My name's Simone Pacco – but everyone knows me as Pacco.' Alma nodded. She couldn't help smiling: how could this man, so painfully nervous, so ill at ease, possibly have had anything in common with Marcantonio Ferrati? And she wondered at her father's ability to make friends with anyone, anywhere, as he searched for amusement and adventure. She wouldn't be surprised to learn that behind his back, Marcantonio had poked a great deal of fun at poor Pacco. Indeed, she could almost see her father mimicking the nervous hand, the bulging eyes, could hear him adopt the nervous voice of the man before her.

'It's so hot ... would you like something cold or a coffee?'

'Oh, a coffee would be wonderful. I hardly slept a wink these last few nights ...' He was up again, striding up to the mantelpiece then back again to the sofa. 'You're very kind. I hope I'm not intruding.' He sat down upon the sofa, but immediately sprang up again to follow Alma into the kitchen. 'Please, let me assist you ...'

'How did you get to know my father?' she asked while she made the coffee.

'We were involved in a real estate development together.' The man was leaning back against the wooden kitchen table. 'May I?' he asked, as if he did not dare to take off his jacket without her permission.

She nodded, but the eyes she fixed upon him now were serious. 'What development was this, exactly?'

'It was a great piece of land on the outskirts of Genoa.' He pulled off his jacket and revealed two great patches of perspiration beneath the arms of his shirt. 'We were going to build a block of flats on it. We needed money though.

Your father didn't have any and as for me – well, I never seemed to be able to hold onto money, somehow. But the idea was so good, you know, we really could smell a great deal ...' Beside the stove, Alma felt the stealthy hand of dread approach her. 'So your father said we would just have to find someone who would lend us the money. I had no doubt he could – he was the most charming, persuasive man I've ever met.' Here the pale grey eyes filled with tears as they settled for a moment upon Alma. She tried to smile, but fear had seized her heart and as she filled their coffee cups she saw her hands tremble.

Pacco sat down now at the kitchen table, his hands fluttering about the sugar bowl. 'So he went to borrow money from some "connections" who put him in touch with someone they knew ... In the end, as I knew he would, he came up with the goods. We had the money for the down payment, we bought the land, started building the block of flats.' He was gulping his coffee from its tiny espresso cup while she watched, immobile. 'The problem was, the construction group we hired – they were thieves, good-for-nothings who had no business selling their services. The foundations were wrong from the start ... we were halfway through building the block when suddenly part of the foundations gave way. Money down the tube, and the construction crew were clamouring to be paid ... nasty moment, I assure you.' Alma saw beads of perspiration shine upon his forehead. 'Even your father, who could talk a bedouin into buying sand in the middle of the Sahara, wasn't able to convince them that they should forfeit their pay ... and I can tell you, we didn't want to get in their bad books.' A black strand of hair fell forward. Pacco pulled it behind his ears and gave a weak smile. 'Anyway, suddenly we had to repay the loan and had made no money from our investment.'

In her chair, Alma held the edge of the table as if she feared falling.

'Things were looking bad – even Marcantonio looked worried – when suddenly' – he clicked his fingers in the air – 'our dubious lender was thrown in jail for some bad deals he had pulled.' Pacco's high voice rose in laughter now. 'Well, you know full well how quick your father was to find the silver lining in any cloud ...'

'Yes.' Alma's voice was flat.

' "We've been saved!" he was laughing and laughing, "we don't need to pay him back now that he's behind bars ..." ' Pacco drew a heavy sigh as he spooned out the sugar from the bottom of his little cup. 'So we didn't. The loan shark went behind bars and we didn't breathe a word. But ...' He replaced cup on saucer. 'But he's out now. And he knows where to find me, signorina. And I have as little money now as I had then.'

Alma felt as if she were sliding down the muddy bank of the river, into waters that had turned a fearful black. She tried to speak but what she uttered was a sob that brought panic into Pacco's grey eyes. 'Signorina, signorina, it's all right, calm down ...'

'I don't believe you ... I can't believe you,' she murmured.

'I'm sorry to upset you so, signorina ... but of course I have all the paper work, of course I brought it along, to show you.' And his hand slipped into his jacket pocket, and emerged again with sheets of folded paper. She stared blankly at them, looked on speechless as Pacco unfolded them upon the table before her. 'Yes, you see, look here, it's all a bit faded and the ink seems to have run here, but can you recognize Marcantonio's signature here?'

Alma was still reeling. She said nothing.

'I haven't come to ask you to pay my half!' And he shook his head, sending his lanky hair across his face. 'I've just come for your father's half.'

'How much?' Alma heard herself ask, voice strangled.

'Four hundred million.' He pulled out a large handkerchief from the same pocket that had held the contract he had shown her, and patted his forehead dry.

'Four hundred million,' she repeated. She looked up at the ceiling, at the great window through which her garden lay still in the dazzling light. She felt her heart beat so slowly that she thought she would die. 'Four hundred – that's about how much this is worth ...' She made a gesture to encompass the house and garden outside. 'No, no, no,' she shook her head. 'It can't be true!' Her eyes bored into him, as if hoping for a denial. But Pacco sat silent.

Alma hid her face in her hands. 'How much time do we have?' she asked.

'As long as I can assure our friend that he will get the money, I would have thought even he could wait till the autumn.' Pacco's voice seemed to reach her from a great distance. Alma brought down her hands, crossed her arms upon the table, allowed the tears to stream down her face. 'Please let me have a word with my brother. He's in London.'

'I know, your father was always telling me about the two of you, he was terribly proud ...' Pacco sighed.

'I'll ring you. Leave me your number, address ...' She stood up now, her hand holding onto the back of her chair to steady herself. 'You'll hear from me soon.'

Pacco held out his clammy hands as if to embrace her, but then picked up the papers that rustled on the table, replaced them in his jacket pocket and gave a little cough of embarrassment. 'I'm sorry, signorina, sorry to give you a shock.'

Alma held up her hand as if to stem his weak professions of sympathy. She showed him to the kitchen door because she didn't think she could walk to the entrance without falling down. She watched his thin cream-suited figure make its way through the gates. She sat down on the kitchen steps, buried her head in her lap and wept till she had no tears left, and her grief had hardened like cement to encase her heart.

34

It had been Pina, the former postmistress, who tipped off the village about the Ferrati house being put up for sale.

'I was there, in Alessandria, at the *Chronicle* offices, waiting to renew my subscription.' Perched on her bicycle, one foot down to act as brake, black eyes shiny as hard little pebbles smoothed by water, Pina stood in the middle of the piazza and regaled Vanna and the Signorina Teresa with her discovery. 'And all of a sudden who do I see striding boldly up to the advertisement counter?' – here Pina almost dropped her bicycle with excitement – 'The Signorina Ferrati! For sale! I saw the ad she was placing with these very eyes. For sale! Who would ever have thought it! The Ferratis sinking so low ...' Here she shook her head with false compassion. Then she turned to the Signorina Teresa who, as the Ferratis' neighbour and only social equal, was expected to feel the greatest sympathy for their losses. 'A sad end, isn't it, Signorina Teresa, for Marcantonio's heirs to be reduced to this!'

'The dear Lord has not been kind to the Ferratis.' The signorina shook her white head with sadness, and at her side her shopping net, through which two pears and a paper-wrapped cheese could be seen, hung mournfully. Her tiny frail figure, in her mauve dress, seemed to bend a little further, as if to carry not only the burden of her own lonely spinsterhood but also her neighbours' misfortune. 'Those poor young things,' she ventured meekly. 'Without their parents, without their home . . .'

'Yes, poor things.' Vanna felt suddenly ashamed at the thrill the announcement of the sale had given her. 'Money, it seems, is not everything.' And Vanna shook her head.

The former postmistress was disappointed at the reception of her news. 'Well, you needn't feel too sorry for them – after all, they know how to look after themselves, the one in London, the other latching onto Carla Brusoni's son . . . and in truth, everyone's been predicting this for years . . . Didn't Franca Felici say that Marcantonio's debts were bound to catch up with him sooner or later?'

That evening, over the oilcloths set for dinner, the women informed their husbands of the forthcoming sale. What news! How the mighty fell! In the piazza, over games of scopa, at the counter in Vanna's bar, the men of San Lorenzo crowed over the crumbling of an estate that, throughout their lifetime (and that of their fathers and grandfathers before them), had shaped their notion of wealth, breeding, and social ambition.

'Study hard and do your homework, and who knows that you might not one day own a house as big as the Ferratis'?' 'Count your pennies and maybe you'll save enough to have a home like the Ferratis'.'

The Ferratis' house: it was as much part of village lore as the partisan's statue in the middle of the piazza; as the nighttime departure of the butcher Romeo's wife and the dawn arrival of the widow Lea with little Santarella in one arm. Everyone seemed to know about the ceilings

247

where naked cherubs floated, the chandeliers from Venice, that hung from the ceiling like frozen rain, the ceramic tiles from Naples and the carpets from Arabia.

How many memories and myths, individual and collective, centred round the great home at the end of the village! There was the mysterious disappearance of the luscious village girl who had served as maidservant there before the First World War. There was the sad tale of the architect from Verona who had died on the same day that the house, his masterpiece, was completed. There was the man who, suspected of having been the lover of one of the Ferrati ladies, was found in a bathtub of blood during a ball. And wasn't there a ghost, too, among the ancient porcelain basins and the worn leather cases in the attic? And hadn't a child once tumbled into the well at the corner of the garden?

During two world wars, through the great TB epidemic, during the countless droughts, and the rare floodings of the Bormida, the Ferrati house had stood, impregnable, a silent witness to the fickleness of fortunes and the tortured ways of men. And now, after two hundred years of being admired with looks whose appreciation was tinged with envy, now the great house was theirs for the taking. For many of the villagers, it was as if a splendid but haughty virgin had finally been seduced and abandoned: they approached greedily, with an ironic wink, and only a residue of respect.

Everyone knew, of course, that there could be only three real contenders for the purchase of the Ferrati home: only Franca, the mayor and the butcher could ever come up with the money needed to buy the ancient house. And though everyone cast predictions and forecast bids, the rest of the village men felt like spectators at a game of bocce.

It was only when the auction of the contents of the house was announced ('Almost everything is going to be sold!' Pina the former postmistress had cried with delight as the 'Auction' notices were posted up on the walls that lined the main road) that every man and woman in San Lorenzo felt involved in the Ferrati downfall: for, if only a few could aspire to buy the house, a great many could hope to buy a ladle, a hatbox or a chair.

The shrine was all but forgotten as the people of San Lorenzo replaced the vision of Our Lady gracing their hill with that of the Ferrati porcelain gracing their mantelpiece. Everyone began their calculations: budgets were reviewed, bookkeeping pored over, accounts corrected. Wives argued with husbands and family members quarrelled as everyone ventured to estimate what could be bought for how much. Who could resist the temptation to buy a few relics of the Ferrati estate? Even Old Rocco, habitually as difficult to stir as a pile of wet grass to take fire, had allowed himself to slip into the overflowing excitement: 'That house,' he told Gianni er Brutto, speaking loud enough for the Marshal Ciuffi to hear him, 'my dear friend, is the only shrine our village will ever have – and I want a memento from it.'

35

'Oh, Francesco!' His sister threw her arms around him. Francesco stood at the kitchen door, case in one hand while with the other he embraced Alma.

'Shshsh, Alma, it will be all right ...' He set down the case, hugged her while she wept, inconsolable, her forehead pressed against his chest.

'Our home, Francesco, our home!' Her sobs resounded in the high-ceilinged room like the pebbles they had thrown in the well at the end of the garden. He stroked her head. 'Don't cry so, Alma, we'll get through this somehow.' But still she stood, sobbing against him. 'Who are we without it? What do I have left?' The words were hardly intelligible, smudged by her weeping.

The sun entered through the door he had left open behind him and whitewashed a wide streak upon the kitchen table, floor, fireplace. A trio of bees flew in and out, buzzing now by the plates and glasses she had set on the table, now by the unkempt rose bushes that stretched outside the window.

They'd talked on the telephone almost every day since she had rung to tell him about Pacco's visit. For days on end he had spent time, talking with Barbini, with Aunt Lucia, trying to unravel their father's business in Genoa, trying to pinpoint the loan, and from whom it had been obtained. He'd hoped against hope, in those dark nights, that Pacco had lied or at least exaggerated, and that the loan was not recognized by law. But in the end, Pacco had been proved correct: together, Father and Pacco owed 800 million to a businessman described by Barbini as 'dubious'. There was nothing to do: they'd have to pay up. They'd have to sell the house, auction its belongings.

When Barbini had rung him with the final news, Francesco had been unable to reply. His eyes had burned, his heart had beat so loudly, he thought Camilla would hear it in the next room. His home – gone. He'd never be able to come back to a place he could call his own, to a village that for centuries had known his family, to a world whose features he knew at every stage of the day. They had lost San Lorenzo for ever. He had sat, immobile, in his study, and had heard voices – his father, his mother, Rina, Alma as a little girl, the people of San Lorenzo – call out to him.

'I'm sorry ... come in, come in.' She drew away from him, sat down at the table. 'I ... I just don't know what I would have done if I hadn't known you were coming ... the man from the auction house was here all of yesterday to catalogue everything, to get every item ready ... you should have seen him sizing up our belongings ...' She was drying her eyes with the back of her hands. He set down his case by the stove, not wishing to leave her even to go upstairs to his bedroom. 'Surprisingly enough Aunt Lucia's been a real help – loves organizing anything, even when it's the sale of her own family legacy ...' She half-smiled. She took out a handkerchief from her skirt pocket and blew her nose. 'I'm sorry, I haven't been strong about this ...'

251

'You don't have to be strong. I'm here now. Let me take care of this.' His voice sounded so confident, he was taken aback by it. But Alma merely smiled at him through the tears that continued to stream down her face. 'Thank you. I feel better just having you here.' As she sat he went to the refrigerator, took out a bottle of water and poured some into the glass before her, then filled a glass for himself. She drank, obedient, then pushed towards him a brown folder.

'You must have a look at these bids, Francesco: they're bound to ask us when they come for the auction ... the butcher, the mayor and of course the indomitable Franca ...'

'Yes.' Francesco took the folder. Inside there were three white envelopes, each one, in different handwriting, with his name on it. Slowly, he opened each envelope, took out the bids, laid them out, side by side, on the table before him.

' "Please let me know what competitors offer you, and I shall, I am certain, match their price." Our friend Franca won't take no for an answer.' He folded Franca's letter, replaced it in its envelope. He read now the other two bids: the butcher's was even more flowery than the one he'd written when he'd tried to purchase the lands. With words like 'honour', 'cherish' and 'treasure' repeated throughout, it was as if he were writing a second marriage proposal, more than a decade after his first one had landed him in his disastrous brief union to Filomena. The mayor's was a terse offer delivered in a few typed sentences. He was ready to go to 350 million for the house – but asked to be told of Franca Felici's offer: 'Let's have an auction for the house as well, I'm ready to outbid the woman Felici.'

'We should look kindly upon Franca: her determination to inherit the Ferrati estate will enable us to push up the price.' Alma's voice sounded suddenly bitter.

'The mayor's bluffing, of course, but you're right: we'll use him to get at least 400 out of Franca. Barbini said the house is worth at the most 380 – but he thinks the likes of Franca and Battistini might well pay more.'

Alma now rose. 'I bought some salami and cheese. I didn't want to cook, but we'd better eat something, I suppose.' She set about taking out the paper-wrapped food, placing it on the table. She was slow in her movements, and the energy he always saw shine from her, had gone. Francesco studied his sister's face, her lowered eyes, the still mouth: did she feel betrayed by their father, or did she view the speculations, the risk-taking as yet another expression (out of bounds, frowned upon, but somehow acceptable in a man like Marcantonio) of their father's search for greater adventures?

'I have sorted out a few things for you to look at ... What two people can collect in a lifetime!' She sliced the bread. 'Mother's books filled with dried flowers – remember, from our walks with her – and a million and one little bookmarks some nuns must have sent her, with saints' lifestories and prayers ... not to mention her sewing kits, sewing boxes, scraps of lace from that altar cloth she sewed. And Father's chest of drawers, filled with, of all things, handkerchiefs – who'd ever have guessed he had collected so many? It breaks my heart to part with anything, anything they even touched.'

They sat across from one another and tried to eat. Alma looked out of the window at the vineyards, the fig trees, the dry grass that lay immobile in the silent sun. In the

253

distance, the hills rose blue, speckled with villages against the hazy sky. 'We've had a heat wave. Weeks on end without a drop of rain and this temperature ... the farmers are despairing.' She turned to her brother and murmured, 'Do you remember Rina, how suspicious she was of the gypsies. And do you remember what she gave as her reason: "Who knows what they could do these creatures, they have no home to lose, no neighbours who will tell their tale, nowhere to run to and hide." That's us Francesco, gypsies now. Nowhere to run to when we need to hide from those prying eyes out there.' Her eyes fell upon her plate. 'Who are we without it?'

'We'll pull through, don't despair.' He ate slowly, his eyes on her. He'd never felt her need him before.

'What of your plans to come back?'

'I've unmade them.' Francesco sipped his water, and remembered this morning, when Camilla had hung about his room, trying to convince him she should come along. 'No. I'd best go by myself. I need to concentrate on Alma. We need to take care of the auction, the sale. I'll be a few days.' She had slipped into the fearful expression that she had worn ever since she had realized he planned to go back to San Lorenzo. 'You will come back won't you?' Camilla asked in her small girl's voice, body quivering as she stood at the foot of his bed while he packed. 'I'll come back. You know that.' She had bowed her head and wept. He'd never talked to Camilla about his plan to return to San Lorenzo. Yet she had known. And suddenly he'd seen her fear, her great black eyes watching him as if at any moment he would break the news. His heart had ached for her as she said nothing but waited and watched, the terror visible. And over the months he had uncovered, as he pulled slowly and carefully at her need for him, that she loved him still.

'And Miso?' He was tentative, and paused, allowing his listener time to choose her answer.

Alma shrugged, fled his glance by looking for her packet of cigarettes. When she was by the stove, lighting a cigarette, she answered him without turning around: 'I ... Miso ... With Miso it will never work. He wants a nice woman whose quiet life revolves around his, not a self-centred painter who thinks every day is a gauntlet cast down to provoke her into action.'

Alma drew to the window. She smoked as she stared at the garden, dry and still, beneath the unflinching sun. She had once counted all the trees in their garden – eighteen in all. Six cypress trees, evenly spaced, a tall copiously weeping willow by the well, two walnut trees, two hazel-nut trees, one persimmon and six pines. The overhead sunlight robbed every tree of its mystery at this hour, bleached the tall grasses where as children they had hidden from Mother's and Rina's watchful gaze. To their children's eyes, the garden had seemed immense, tall enough to reach the skies, as wide as the horizon. Now it seemed an intimate extension of their home, where their past hung like ripening fruit. In those days, they had ever been conscious, in their games, their wanderings, of Mother and Rina; and had always known that certain corners of the garden were out of bounds – the well ('Don't you know that a little boy once fell in there, a hundred years ago?' Rina's scolding would reach them) the vine-yards ('Don't you go getting in the way of the men there, they're spraying it with copperdust') the gates ('Stop hanging onto those bars, you'll look like animals in a cage when the villagers go by'). Now the entire space was theirs, but only for a few more days. She turned back to her brother.

'And now, what will you do?' Francesco was watching her.

'Oh . . .' She combed a hand through her hair. 'I'll return to Torino. Maybe get a proper flat – the studio will seem cramped, if I can't come here on weekends. And there is the painting. I have more commissions than I can carry out, so I know I won't starve . . .' She shivered as she stared out of the window. She cocked her head: 'Listen to the crickets,' she whispered. 'When we were little, I used to think that the stars made this sound – during the day I was rushing about so much I never noticed the crickets, I only finally heard them at night, when the stars were in place.' She raised her eyes heavenward.

Francesco smiled. 'The music of the stars . . . you could only hear that in San Lorenzo . . .'

And now Aunt Lucia's immense car began its habitual argument with the gates. Alma's expression froze, then she pushed out her chin and strode out into the hot sun.

'There she is. My niece, Alma, Signor Bertinelli.' Aunt Lucia emerged from the car, undid the silk scarf round her head, began to remove her driving gloves as she cast a wounded look at her niece. 'Alma wouldn't let her aunt come and give her a hand with the sorting . . .'

Moustachioed, diminutive, Signor Bertinelli descended majestically from the car, and bowed over Alma's hand. 'We shall try our best, signorina, to fetch the highest prices for you. Leave it all to us, we'll take care of everything, you may rest assured.' The words slipped out, smooth, and well-polished from use – they had been repeated a thousand times to elderly widows, spinsters, lonely old bachelors. The blue eyes gleamed: 'Let us proceed then. A look at what you have assembled.'

They entered the kitchen, but within seconds Signor Bertinelli pushed past Francesco's muted welcome and made his way to the drawing room, pale eyes quick and sharp, slipping from surface to surface, from price to price, from estimate to estimate.

He appraised the Empire sofa covered in its faded silk, studied the gold-leafed mirror and the twin sconces that flanked it, the chandelier and the paintings. On every item there was a small white sticker, sporting a number, and Signor Bertinelli clucked his approval. A few pieces from the bedrooms – chairs, prie-dieux, two hand-painted screens – had been brought downstairs. 'Open those shutters, signorina, we want everyone to have a good look at our things ... let there be light!' He swanned about the room as if he were the host of an important drinks party. 'Hmmmm, yes ...' He touched with a flitting hand the back of a porcelain amphora. 'That should fetch us a pretty price ...'

Alma stood close to Francesco. He wrapped his arm round her shoulders. 'Don't worry,' he whispered. 'Don't worry.'

And she felt a great surge of love for her brother: it was the two of them against the outsiders.

36

Leading the first arrivals was Pina the former post-mistress, small and dark and tightly coiled upon herself, a grin of anticipation upon her round face; a string bag hung from her bony wrist, the same one that Alma had seen when they'd met in the village shops. ('She looks like she's just buying some fruit ...' Alma whispered to her brother. 'Did you expect her to come with a cart?' Francesco shook his head.)

Brother and sister had prepared themselves for the onslaught. Standing together at the door they greeted the village men and women who came – many for the first time – to their home. Like an ill-assorted pilgrimage, old women, old men, middle-aged housewives, robust sun-burnt farmers, flour-complexioned shopkeepers, children – it seemed as if everyone in San Lorenzo were coming to the Ferrati auction, bent on paying homage to a once-hallowed place. Even the terrible heat, that had scorched so many fields and threatened to ruin so many crops, could not keep the people of San Lorenzo away. And as the villagers came up to the young Ferratis in their entrance doorway, their approach was one in which the wary deference afforded the scions of the grandest family mingled with a touch of satisfaction at the toppling of the mighty. Francesco and Alma watched, voices quiet. They never strayed too far one from the other.

'Oooooh, what grand things – I never knew . . .' Nuccio the baker had come with his daughters, pretty Veronica and plain-faced Marta.

'Look at these lovely curtains!' Young Veronica, who only last night had been kissed for the very first time by Grillo, held up the red silk to her face in the mirror.

'Eh no, my dear Vanna, money is not everything.' Pina the former postmistress peered at one of the Florentine candelabras that Marcantonio had brought his new bride more than thirty years before.

'But it certainly smooths the bumpy rides,' Vanna said with feeling.

'I'd set that down – it costs more than you can afford, I'll warrant,' the marshal, eyes and medals gleaming, couldn't resist warning men and women as he passed them by.

The villagers began their viewing in earnest now: sleeves were rolled up, spectacles placed upon noses, gloves (many of the women had donned their Sunday best) were removed. A hundred candlesticks, vases and porcelain cups were raised up to the light, a hundred more were brought down to eye level. And as they exclaimed over the treasures before them, and exchanged estimates on their value, the villagers privately wondered who would walk away with what.

In the drawing room, chairs and armchairs stood in tidy rows, each one sporting a small white sticker with its lot number. The tables and three sofas were pushed against the walls. All shutters had been pushed open by the indefatigable Signor Bertinelli, whose shrill voice

259

resounded throughout the room: 'Don't touch! Take care!'
He moved about the villagers with the ease of a seasoned
performer. In the dining room, there were rows upon rows
of folding chairs, brought in by the auctioneers for their
audience. The great dining-room table sat beneath two
windows, a heap of multicoloured tablecloths, linens and
curtains upon it.

The butcher Romeo arrived. He was red-faced and
sweaty by the time he set foot in the Ferratis' entrance –
still deprived of his beloved Fiat, which according to the
police in Rome had 'simply vanished', he had been forced
to walk from his house at the other end of the village ...
and walking did not seem to agree with the large man
('He seems incapable of physical exertions of any kind,'
Old Rocco liked to say with a wink, reminding his cronies
of the poor butcher's fatal flaw) – the butcher looked as
large and red as the carcasses that hung behind his shop
counter. But now that he was here, and had taken a few
moments to adjust his breathing, loosen his collar, wipe
the perspiration from his brow and upper lip, how he
enjoyed himself! How he sniffed at the leatherbound
volumes, how he caressed the damask curtains piled in a
soft mound upon the table ... 'Mine, this could be mine
...' he whispered.

By ten o'clock a number of strangers stepped through
the door – people from Alessandria, who had seen the
advertisement in the *Chronicle*; villagers from the surrounding hills, who had come more out of curiosity than
out of greed – they had passed the great grey house time
and again, on their way home or to their fields. A handful
of old family friends appeared, suddenly shy and
nervous: they didn't know what they could do for the

young Ferratis, how they should act, in this house where in the old days they had eaten and drunk and laughed. Among them, Alma spotted Bernardino della Rocca: she immediately looked away.

She looked for her brother and saw him standing silent, expressionless, as a woman accidentally shoved him, and her small husband stepped on his foot in their hurry to study the chairs in the drawing room. She felt suddenly as if she could see herself and Francesco from a great height – they had shrunk, she and her brother, reduced to insignificance by grief and loss. She turned towards a new group who were making their way into the drawing room, and caught her breath: for a moment, she had been convinced that Miso was among them – that he had decided, despite everything he'd said, to come and stand beside her. But she'd been mistaken – and now sighed: he had kept away after all, just as he'd told her: 'I am sorry. I wish I could be of help ...' His voice had remained expressionless over the telephone.

'Ah well, we aren't the first as you feared, my dear.' Here came the Mayor Battistini, making his way through the browsers. 'Come along, Anna, we are serious about this, so we'd better get to know what's on offer.' With his cuckolded wife at his heels, Battistini pushed his way towards sofas, armchairs, porcelain sets and crystal chandeliers.

'Bettino ...' Anna Battistini would meekly implore as her husband with great exclamations sat on the sofa, punched the stuffing of a chair, turned over a stool – leaving his imprint it seemed on everything in the drawing room.

'Oh, oh, here she comes, Franca Felici, looking like

261

she means business.' Old Rocco was rubbing his hands together, glee lighting his face.

Franca had, indeed, arrived: up to the Dottore Ferrati she came, with loud remonstrances of respect and affection; around the table of porcelain cups and plates she strutted; before each and every piece of furniture she stood, big arms folded as she lost herself in calculations and countercalculations; and a few steps behind her, ever respectful of their matriarch, her brood of sons and daughters picked through everything their mother had discarded, examined everything that had caught her eye.

From the moment Franca stepped into the Ferrati house, curiosity and expectations were raised: what would Franca buy? Would she buy the most, as always, this insatiable Felici woman? How would the mayor and the butcher take to the competition?

'Looking as full of good health as ever, my dear Franca.' The mayor held a china candelabra in his hands.

'Holding up quite well, thank you, Signor Mayor. Hmmm ...' The woman approached, her eyes fixed upon the china candelabra. 'I think I quite like this piece ...' The big brown fingers that had weeded, pulled up potatoes, milked cows' teats, now lay soft upon the painted china columns. 'Yes I like this.'

'I've spotted it already, Franca.' The Mayor pulled the candelabra away from the odious woman's hold.

'But, my dear Battistini' – Franca placed her fists upon her hips and laughed so that her gold tooth glittered like one of the diamonds of the chandelier above her – 'whoever bids highest will get it – it's not a matter of who saw what first ...' And with this threat in the air between them, Franca grinned and made her way to see the coal scuttle that stood in the drawing room.

'Alma, my dear, do you have a second? It's about my brother ...' It was Bernardino della Rocca, trying to make himself heard above the shouting of the mayor. Alma saw him trying to approach her, politely sidestepping now Pina the postmistress, now Nuccio the baker.

'I'm sorry, Bernardino – this is not really a good moment ...' And Alma smiled down at Veronica beside her, pretending great interest in the silk curtain that the girl was caressing. 'Yes,' she answered a question that Veronica had not posed, 'this is from Venice ... Forgive me, Bernardino, I've just promised my young friend here that I'll show her where the other half of this curtain is ...' And quickly Alma took Veronica's arm in her hand and led the wide-eyed girl through the crowd.

In the drawing room, the auction was about to begin: at his lectern Signor Bertinelli was polishing his spectacles, a half-smile already on his face. He knew he could do well out of this auction, he could already sense excitement and anticipation stewing among the people here. And there had been a few very nice pieces – the French Directoire chairs, the Art Nouveau candelabra. Not that they would be appreciated by the greater part of today's audience – nothing but country bumpkins who'd come to enjoy the demise of a wealthy family – but he'd spotted Marianni, the dealer from Torino, and Lucentino, the dealer from Acqui, mingling among the crowd.

Signor Bertinelli smoothed down his moustache, cleared his throat, allowed his cool blue eyes to study the audience for a minute, and pounded the lectern with his gavel.

'Let's start then shall we? First lot: a set of twenty-four Venetian fluted glasses, a silver-plated fruit bowl and six Limoges figurines . . . we shall start the bidding at 300,000. 300,000, do I hear 350,000, yes, what about 400,000, then for these treasures of – yes, we have 400, what about 450 . . .' The words and numbers came fast, quickly rolling like dice in a tumbler, like a cashier's register at a shop, like the spinning of a roulette wheel, urging the audience to catch the fever to buy more, own more, have the most.

No one cast a look in the direction of Francesco and Alma Ferrati as they stood completely still by the drawing-room doors, looking like sad footmen out of uniform.

Alma listened to the galloping rounds of bids and the tears filled her eyes. She felt as naked as if she were at the doctor's – everything was exposed, being examined for flaws, for weaknesses, for durability. Did these people, with their thoughts of bargains, value and prices, did these people think at all about the Ferratis who had purchased, inherited, used and loved these things?

She felt someone's stare, and looked up to find Carla Brusoni. She realized that tears were sliding down her cheeks and quickly wiped her face, pretending that she had not recognized Miso's mother. 'Will I, can I survive?' she asked herself, feeling the little eyes upon her, burning with curiosity. She moved off, fearing the woman's approach. The entrance hall was full of people. She walked slowly, away from the house and its people. She walked and thought of nothing, half-closing her eyes in the extraordinary heat about her. She listened to the lulling crickets' song. The orchard spread rich and green to the left, the pergola where clusters of grapes hung unripe and small to the right.

She walked, distancing herself from the cries and exclamations, the questions and appraisals. The sun was strong, it must be midday. She suddenly spotted, beneath the spreading laden arms of a fir, a woman's seated figure. Someone, it seemed, had also come away from the din of the auction. As she drew nearer, Alma recognized Rosa, one of Franca's large daughters-in-law. The young woman's dark head was bent slightly towards her shoulder, and Alma now distinguished an infant in the curve of her embrace: Rosa was giving the baby her breast. The sweet stillness of the two interlaced figures, the maternal roundness of bent head and protective arms, the complete abandon with which the child lay back in the warm cradle of his mother's embrace, stirred in Alma an immediate response – a yearning so strong that she had to cross her arms as if to give herself strength. The two, mother and child, formed a perfect circle seated beneath the tree's widespread branches.

She did not approach, lest she disturb mother and child, but stood silently watching, and felt as if her own eyes – woman's eyes, painter's eyes – were as hungry for this spectacle as Rosa's son for his mother's milk.

The auction went on until late afternoon, when the sunset brought forth shadows and the villagers brought home their new acquisitions. Two vans and three cars were needed to carry to the Felici home the objects that Franca had bought.

37

'It will rain.' Francesco pointed up at the sky where clouds seemed to stalk an elusive, invisible victim. He and Alma were wandering around their garden. Franca Felici and her booty had left almost an hour ago, but still they would not venture back into the house newly stripped by the auction.

They walked aimlessly, Francesco a few paces in front of his sister, making way for her by pushing back a branch when it hung before them, warning her against an unexpected root, or a hole. The air hung heavy about them, with the sun already hiding from the approaching storm.

'Franca asked me about the sale. I told her the mayor's prepared to beat her proposal. But you should have seen her – she just laughed and laughed. "I'll offer you 420 – payable immediately. Just tell him that and you'll see that bloated braggart deflate faster than if a pin had pricked him." ' Francesco cast her a swift look. 'And it was true: you should have seen Battistini's face when I told him the price Franca was prepared to go to ... ! That is more than we could have ever hoped for ... I think by next week we shall have everything settled and the contracts signed.'

Alma's expression was as empty as their house. 'Yes ...' she murmured.

'I want you to come to London for a while. Let me and Camilla look after you.'

'We'll see . . .'

Rain began to fall. Swollen, deliberate drops that burst upon their heads, upon the foliage, upon the parched ground. Slow, fat drops fell, haphazard, almost unintentional, leaving behind them a snail's glistening trail. But within minutes, the rain quickened its pace, rushing now towards the ground, humming so loudly that only the crackle of thunder could be heard above it.

'Come, Alma!' Francesco pulled his sister from beneath the branches of an ancient apple tree, ran with her hand in his towards the house. The rain poured down, as harsh as blazing sunlight, and the dry grass beneath them seemed to sizzle with it. Above them the white lightning broke through the sky again and again. Thunder resounded in the distant hills like a doomsday prophet with his terrifying portent. They rushed, wet and shivering beneath the garden foliage, burst into the kitchen.

'Quick, quick, take this.' Alma seemed suddenly to have woken from the state of stupor he had found her in this morning: she rushed to him with a drying up cloth and he saw her run to the guests' bathroom next door, reappearing with two towels. They dried their hair, their arms, their legs. Alma laughed: 'Well, they were all praying for rain, and the Good Lord answered.' And then with a half-smile at him: 'He didn't listen to my prayers though, and I am sure they were as heart-felt.'

They continued to dry themselves while the shutters beat against the house, pushed by the wind that the storm had brought to life. Alma held her head down, tousled her hair with now her hand now the towel. She stood up.

'We'd better drink something to warm ourselves.' She cast the towel on the back of the chair, took a bottle of wine from the case beneath the credenza, looked about for the corkscrew. She opened the bottle expertly, and poured two glasses. They sat in silence, at the kitchen table that Nuccio the baker would bring away – 'when you've sold the house, signorina, not a moment before, we don't want you eating on the floor after all . . .'

'The worst is, there is simply nothing we can do, is there, except grieve?' Francesco gulped his wine.

'No. I'm not sure even Father could have talked his way out of this mess. He took one gamble too many . . .' Her voice was low, detached. 'When that man, Pacco, came to tell me about the debt, I was so angry, so disappointed. I kept addressing Father as though he were standing beside me, hurling abuse at him, asking him why why why he had left us in such straits. And then it came to me: he would have seen it as a new challenge, as a new obstacle to overcome. He would have immediately rushed about, trying to borrow from a hundred sources to pay back the debt – patching up the gaping hole. But we can't do the same. You and I don't belong to that world where you can trade with nothing but words and hopes and talk of tomorrow.'

'No, I suppose we don't.'

'And he knew we didn't. He wouldn't have expected us to fix this – he would have expected to do it all himself.' She cocked her head. 'Listen to the rain . . . the village will have something to celebrate the night of the festa . . .'

'Of course, the festa. Friday night, isn't it? We must go.'

'No . . .' Alma shook her head. 'I couldn't bear to have them look on us with pity.'

'We must, Alma. Our last festa.'

'The festa ...' she murmured, both hands around her glass. 'How can everything go on? I don't understand ... why isn't everyone standing still, dressed in mourning, choked with emotion. I thought the whole world would come to a standstill. Instead ... It's like the walnut tree that was uprooted when we were little – do you remember that storm – the worst in decades ... I felt it was so deeply embedded in the soil, that the earth would tremble, and the hole would be so huge that the garden would cave in. But not at all. There was a gaping hole there where it had stood, but almost immediately, we chopped the trunk and the branches for firewood.' She shook her head. 'I don't want to dispose of our grief so readily. I can't, any more. I tried so hard when Mother, then Father, died ... when Miso left ... Now there is nothing left. No strength – it's gone ...' She bowed her head.

'You'll survive, Alma. Even this. We both will.' And the firmness and confidence in his voice surprised them both, and she raised her face and half-smiled. 'Will we?'

38

The Mayor Battistini tapped at the widow Lea's back door and waited in the darkness for his mistress to throw down her keys. God, how he wished that she would entrust him with a spare set – just to avoid his heart-in-throat wait in the dark shadows that divided her house from that of Pina the former postmistress. He sighed as he rummaged in the black grass for the jingling bundle that had missed his nose by a hair's breadth. Still, once again he was safe: everyone thought him with his wife and his wife thought him in the piazza – a man has to lie when he wants it both ways.

He found the widow undressed, in bed, hair streaming down her white shoulders. He took off his clothes without a word, switched off the bedside lamp, then lay very still.

'Well, what's wrong?' The widow's lazy voice breathed upon his chest. 'Is it the auction? You're upset because you didn't get everything you wanted?'

'I could have killed that Franca. She's a man in drag, I swear it. God, what I would have given to beat those prices of hers ...' The mayor sighed.

'Well, aren't you going to ask me to close my eyes and hold out my hands?' The widow's tone was mocking.

'Oh Lea, please! I had my wife at my heels the whole

time. I couldn't have bought you something under her nose, now could I?'

The mayor tried to caress the round shoulder, but his hand was pushed away.

'You're as mean with me as you're unfaithful to her.' She shook her head in disdain.

The mayor punched the mattress beside him. 'Lea, please, things are difficult enough without you doing this ... Now, there's something important I want to tell you. No one knows, so – lips sealed. Bishop Natti's written to me. Contrary to all expectations he wants to come after all.'

'Here? To San Lorenzo?'

'Yes. Now, Lea, you do understand that if that ... that daughter of yours remains silent ... the bishop won't be impressed, will he?'

'Bettino ...' the widow began, a threatening note in her voice.

'If she'd just open her mouth, the bishop won't hold out ... they need a miracle as much as we do.'

The widow sighed beside her lover. He could see her white oval face, the dark shining eyes. 'Damn it, Lea, let me talk to her if you won't.'

The widow's body withdrew from his. 'Don't start again,' she snapped. 'I won't have her harassed. She's miserable, she's so pale I'm worried sick. I've never seen her so unhappy.'

The mayor sat up and ran a hand through his hair. 'How do you know she's miserable when she hasn't spoken for over a year? She's probably having a cosy little chat with Our Lady, laughing behind our backs.'

'Oh, don't be a fool. She's my daughter, I know her. She's my own flesh and blood.'

Battistini cursed, remembered the girl sleeping next door, and buried his mouth in his hands. 'God! I could wring her neck – nothing but a nuisance, like a pebble in my shoe ... first she starts foaming at the mouth about some vision or other, so that everyone gets excited, then – then the silence of a tomb.'

The widow Lea switched on the light and sat up in bed. 'Shut up.' She threw him a cold look. 'I'm not going to have my child suffer for your benefit. If she doesn't talk, she doesn't talk. If it doesn't suit you, more's the pity.' The widow took her heavy black hair in one hand, swept it over her left shoulder.

'Come, Lea, don't pull that face ... think what it would mean ...' The mayor used his coaxing voice and tried to draw her towards him.

'It won't make any difference in my life, will it, whether the pilgrims come or not. You'll make the millions, and your wife and your son will enjoy them with you.'

The mayor sighed. 'Well, if that's the way you see things – obviously you're just a selfish woman. If you don't understand that the more money there is to go around, the more everyone will benefit, well then ...' Again his hand reached for her, but the widow pushed it away.

'You've never lifted a finger to help me and my girl, Bettino. Never.'

'Jesus Christ, Lea, what am I to do? Get a divorce? What kind of a father would I be, eh?'

'Well, there we are, you see.' The widow spoke in her calm sensuous voice. 'You are a good father, and I am a good mother. You won't divorce your wife, and I won't let anyone bully my little girl. Now get dressed and go

272

home.' With that, the widow switched off the light.

'Lea, Lea, don't be angry ...' The mayor snuggled against her. 'I didn't know she meant so much to you ...'

'She is the only thing I have, isn't she? No husband, a home that's made up of two little squalid rooms, a grocery shop ... at least I've got Santa. And she's only got me. I have to stand beside her. Too bad about your schemes.'

Battistini waited a moment in silence, then began to caress the widow's soft hip. Fingernails dug into his wrist. 'Damn you!' And the mayor rolled out of bed.

He bent down to search for his socks, slowly felt the cold tiles with his hands, found one rolled up sock, then hit his head against the iron post at the corner of the bed. 'Damn you!' he burst out again.

From the bed the widow giggled. 'Seek, seek and let's see what you will find ...' she whispered in the dark.

Battistini now moved on hands and knees to a pile he could discern at the foot of the bed: ah, at least he'd found his shirt and undershirt. He dragged the sleeves onto his arms, half-closed the buttons which would require revision beneath the streetlamp before he reached home, and now searched for his trousers. To hell with this darkness, to hell with Lea for mocking. His hand felt something, and then there was light.

'Aha, what are you stealing from a poor widow?' The widow's eyes widened with mirth and her hand covered her mouth: Battistini looked down and saw the suspenders and stockings dangling from his hand. 'What a picture you make, Bettino ...' And the widow giggled again.

Battistini straightened up from the ignominious position, scowling. 'Stop laughing, Lea: if it weren't for that poor innocent next door I'd have you over my knee this minute.' But he spied his trousers, pounced upon them like a lion, slipped them on and scowled at his mistress. 'All right, you've had your fun. Now get the girl to talk. I'm going.'

He strode off, heavy feet upon the creaking stairs, and heard her giggles all the way down. He was tired, they hadn't made love, and Anna was certainly still up, waiting for him while she read her prayer book. Whoever said a man's life was easy?

39

The caravans that bore the festa's entertainments approached slowly, from the hills of Susa and Castel d'Oro. They rolled, in single file, up steep climbs and down smooth slopes, now appearing now disappearing, their painted tops shiny among the green of the farmers' fields.

It was Grillo who first spotted them: 'They're here! The gypsies are here!' he shouted from the doorway of his parents' bar. In the piazza, the children took up his call, repeating it as they zigzagged with their bicycles through the streets. 'Gypsies! The gypsies are here!'

The caravans parked themselves around the piazza, spilling onto the main road. Out came the men and women who, each year, set up the Ferris wheel, tombola, shooting alley, wheel of fortune, sweets stall in the hill villages. For two, three days, the people of the caravans took over a village, led it through the rites of annual festivities, served it the bright, warm nights of games and dances, then disappeared to erect somewhere else their tribute to another patron saint.

Custom dictated that the men of San Lorenzo lend the gypsies a hand to lay the wooden boards of the dance floor: every year, at the arrival of the caravans, the village men – with a great deal of cheerful competitive spirit, with much swaggering and loud blasphemies beneath the weight of the boards – helped to cover the piazza with the wooden planks.

'Papa, are you coming to lend a hand?' Grillo popped his head into the darkened bar, then without waiting for his father, rolled up his sleeves and made his way to the centre of the piazza, where a cluster of village men and children were already carrying planks and tools. Nuccio the baker teased the butcher Romeo for his slow pace, and the Marshal Ciuffi, too old to lend a hand, tapped his cane against the pavement like a general passing his troops for inspection.

'Oh my, oh my!' A piercing cry as the former post-mistress Pina rushed through the piazza on her bicycle, coming to a screeching halt before the marshal. 'Marshal, you never told us! You never breathed a word!'

The marshal remained silent and feigned ignorance.

'Marshal, you and the mayor and Don Luigi never told us that the bishop's coming! Bishop Natti coming to San Lorenzo for our festa!' The former postmistress practically squawked in excitement and her little leg trembled as she stretched it down to place her foot firmly on the pavement.

'Bishop Natti! Here!' Above the piazza, from her second-storey window, Vanna was drawing in her husband's shirt for tonight. She hung out over her sill: 'Is it true?!'

'Bishop Natti is coming to see if Santa's had a vision! He's coming to see whether we can have a shrine! Don Luigi's Rosina just told me!' The former postmistress was triumphant in the glory of her discovery.

Nuccio the baker came up to the marshal. 'Is this true, marshal? Is the bishop coming to pay us a visit?'

The marshal cleared his throat self-importantly. 'Yes. The bishop wants to see the place for himself. After our arduous campaign, he's yielded and decided to see whether our village truly houses a saint...'

He wasn't allowed to continue. 'The bishop's coming! The bishop's coming!' The chorus was as loud as that of the birds who, in October, line the electricity cables along the road, waiting to fly off together to the south. 'Bishop Natti's coming! He'll be here for the festa!' The excitement infected the gypsies as well, so that they too were joyfully repeating Bishop Natti's name, turning it into an ecclesiastical mantra.

'Well, well, so the bishop's coming to see for himself the way the ground lies ...' Claudio crossed his arms, cigarette clamped in one corner of his mouth.

'Santa!' It was Nuccio the baker, arm raised and finger pointing towards the widow Lea's windows. 'Santa is at her window!' His call was taken up by excited buzzing, and from the shops, from the bar, villagers poured out onto the piazza.

'Ahhhhhh ...' Low and expectant, a moan escaped the group: above them, framed by the window, a figure in white could be discerned. Santa stood above them, pale face shining, serene.

'Santarella!' Vanna called out from her window.

Below her, Pina the former postmistress stood transfixed. The figure at the window remained motionless, silent. She seemed as self-contained as if the sun that lit her had spread a film about her, sealing Santa from those beneath her.

'Why won't you talk, Santa?' And the butcher scowled up at the silent visionary in the same way that he approached his poultry victims.

'Won't you speak to Bishop Natti when he comes?' Nuccio the baker asked from his shop door. 'Can't you help us out?' From the sidelines, the gypsies had stopped their work and were staring up at the white figure.

Santa stood immobile at her window, brilliant in the morning light.

'Santa, do something, say something!' And Claudio threw his cigarette onto the ground and stubbed it out with an angry heel.

But Santa merely looked on, silent, unmoving, and her figure grew so brilliant in the sunlight that the villagers had to bring up their hands to shield their eyes.

Now the widow Lea appeared beside her daughter, and for a moment the two women seemed to stand in close alliance against the villagers below. Then the widow's hand reached for Santa, and the women withdrew into the dark room.

An angry murmur spread among the up-turned faces. The men and women of San Lorenzo remained in the piazza, imprecations salting their speech, condemnations of Santa and 'that wicked mother of hers' floating up to the widow's windows.

'She'd better speak when the bishop asks her to.' The butcher Romeo made a rude gesture beneath the widow's sill.

'She'd better not let us down. We can't lose this opportunity, with the bishop here and ready to bless the whole enterprise ...' And Nuccio the baker withdrew into his bakery, where he began anew to draw up lists of new machinery, new equipment that would be needed to feed the multitudes.

Talk of the shrine, that for so many months had subsided, giving way to the auction and then the sale of the Ferrati house, to Franca Felici's fearful ambitions, to the mayor's frustrated ambitions, erupted once more. Collective aspirations were dusted off, and once again the men and women of San Lorenzo spoke with one voice and felt with one heart. The shrine was a dream that might just take place!

The villagers only began to melt away when the morning sun stood directly above them. The gypsies returned to their work, watched over by the old men from their bench, and assisted by Grillo and his friends.

'Jesus, even if she doesn't talk, even if there's no shrine, it doesn't mean the end of everything!' Grillo muttered to himself as he hammered down a plank of the dance floor.

'The boy is right,' put in Gianni er Brutto from his chair at the card table: for the first time in over six years, he had won at scopa, and he was celebrating with an early aperitivo with Old Rocco. 'The festa will go on, everyone will dance . . . Why wreck a tradition?'

Old Rocco looked into the pale gold of his aperitivo. 'It's all we have.'

'Anyway, it's something to look forward to.' Gianni raised his glass.

'Something to look forward to?' Claudio shook his head. 'When destiny's dealt you a losing hand, the future seems nothing but a longer time in which to feel pain.'

Old Rocco lay back in his chair and squinted at the young men who squatted, nails and hammers in hand, over the board. 'What do we have to look forward to, tell me that?'

'Beh, Rocco ...' Gianni stroked his chin with a pensive hand. 'The mushrooms will be out in a few weeks ... that's always good fun...'

'What do you mean?' Old Rocco shot back. 'We're too old to go off looking for mushrooms, waking at dawn, walking up those steep paths in the icy cold!'

'We can't go looking for them but we can still eat them – soft enough even for our teeth!' Gianni grinned.

Claudio stood in his doorway and watched his son and the young men around him nailing down plank after plank. He shook his head. 'Let's hope that fate will be kinder to them.'

As if drawn to the piazza by his words, Morgana, the clairvoyant who each year set up her caravan between the candy floss of the sweets stall and the explosions of the shooting alley, approached the group.

'Ask Morgana! Go ahead and ask her!' cackled Old Rocco from his seat. 'Come on, Gianni, let's see what kind of future the good wench sees for you ...' And the Sicilian slapped the table before him and beckoned the ample-bosomed clairvoyant.

'Oh please, Rocco ...' Gianni er Brutto, shy of all the attention, embarrassed by his friend's laughter and the cluster of gypsies who now approached the card table, tried to shoo away Morgana. But the lady stood her ground: and mistaking Gianni's protest for lack of funds, she generously waved her hand. 'Nonsense: this palm-reading is free, my gift to you ...'

With a great flourish of her black and red cotton skirts, and a tinkling of her gold half-moon earrings, Morgana sat herself beside the old men and snatched Gianni's skinny hand. The black head bent over the well-creased palm, the long curls fell over the thin wrist, the warm breath (sweetened each morning with three basil leaves) tickled the trembling fingers. 'Oooooh,' she murmured. 'Aaaaahhhhhh ...' she continued. And then, pushing Gianni's hand away, she turned with a radiant smile to the villagers around them: 'In his hand I see many more years to come ... I see a quiet life with friendly faces ... I see a happy decade ... and there are village roofs there, too, it must mean that the next ten years will be very prosperous ones!'

Morgana grinned at them all, rose from her chair. 'A lucky man!' She disappeared with a great flourish of her skirt, and the villagers dispersed. At the card table Gianni er Brutto smiled at the thought of his forthcoming years.

40

The hour of the siesta lay, thick with drowsiness, heavy with heat, upon the village. Shutters were drawn, roads and the piazza stood empty. Even the poultry in the courtyards and the roaming dogs respected the afternoon silence. Only the laundry (fresh shirts and dresses for tonight's festa) flapped and waved from a balcony here and there.

The widow Lea lay in her petticoat upon her huge bed. With an arm bent over her forehead, the widow stared at her daughter as she looked out of the window. Beyond Santa's pale profile, the metal skeleton of the Ferris wheel shone bright, its tiny carts painted red and green.

The widow slid her right foot up and down on the coverlet, as she bent then extended her knee: but she drew no comfort from the pretty curve of her leg and a sigh now escaped her. If only life depended on your looks ... ever since she'd been so high, she had made them turn in the streets, made one man after another promise her diamonds as big as a tomato, a house as huge as the Ferratis', and God alone knew what else. But where had it led her? She had married in the end that poor Matteo, may the Lord bless his soul: she had felt a yearning to protect that young, blue-eyed boy, with his innocence and the weakness of a newborn kitten. But within a few months, he had taken up and died after a drive in his tractor on a cold October day, when she was expecting their child.

The widow's gaze returned to Santarella. Silent, completely still, her daughter looked towards she knew not what. How difficult it had been for her to love this daughter of hers. Lea had been so very young ... and always, it had seemed, running, rushing from one supplier to the next, from one client to the other.

'Oh Santa!' The widow listened in wonder at her own heart's anxious call. When had it begun, this love that filled her with pain at her daughter's silence? When had the strong yearning to protect her child's happiness taken root? The widow Lea shook her head in awe at the mystery of it all: Santa now filled her life, as necessary as breathing and eating. Santa had taken hold of her heart with the unconsciously greedy fingers of a child grasping for its mother's milk.

'Santa,' she murmured, half-sitting up in bed. 'Santarella, shall we go away from San Lorenzo – would you like your mamma to bring you away from here? It wouldn't be so difficult you know, we could sell the shop, the house. And it wouldn't be difficult to leave San Lorenzo behind – what do we have here? No land, no friends...'

Santa's pale eyes turned to her mother, and for a moment the widow saw an incredibly sweet smile light up her daughter's face.

'Santarella ...' she murmured, her heart full of love.

Alma lay on her bed and looked up, meeting the serene

gaze of the Madonna and Child who smiled from the tapestry. The afternoon heat glazed the walls of her bedroom, whitewashed the red tile floor by the window. She had left the shutters wide open, the window ajar. The garden below was abuzz and glowed with light, but beyond the hedge and the trees, the village was quiet, asleep in the hour of the siesta.

She felt restless in the warmth, and thoughts of Miso now always followed her to this bed. Miso ... but she wouldn't allow the thoughts to unravel, and sat up against her pillows, the better to see the green world of the garden.

The last days in San Lorenzo ... she felt the tears well. Every night, in her dreams, sad partings took place, leaving her to wake up feeling tired and anxious. With the sale of the house she would operate in a vacuum, much like a mime: she'd have to pretend that surrounding her was her beloved stage set – objects, rooms, a garden with associations that spilt forth memory upon memory. In truth, she would stand alone.

Silence filled her house. She rose, dressed, went downstairs into the kitchen. But again Miso's voice followed her here. 'Alma ... why are you so difficult? Why can't you be like the other women I know, the women I'm used to ...?' A thousand times he'd asked her: 'Can't you be like the women I grew up with?'

She looked about her, at the familiar kitchen that stood silent, still half-claimed by shadows. How different this kitchen had been when Mother and Rina led their lives here, with their wholesome housewife ways.

She thought of the clean, warm smell of baking mingled with the dry pungent scents of onions, garlic, herbs that hung, head down, in plaits by the sink. The gleam of copper and aluminium; the soft glow of gas beneath the heavy iron pots; the regular noises that like a clock broke the silence: dicing, scrubbing, paring, slicing, pounding, kneading. Like the centre of the earth, the kitchen was always warm and in constant motion, layer upon layer of womanly activity humming within.

Alma admitted to herself that she had never belonged to that world. The women in the kitchen were soft-featured, soft-spoken like her mother; or broad, earthy matrons like Franca Felici. They were bent on their duties for the pleasure of others: they worried about Grandfather's indigestion, about Grandmother's false teeth, about Father's acid stomach, about the children's lack of appetite. The women in the kitchen allowed their emotions to bubble quietly away like soup in the cauldron, with the lid left slightly askew to evaporate some of the excess juice.

In this kitchen she had sat and watched her mother and Rina as they cooked and spoke, washed and laughed at the sink or stove. Rina toasted their bread and warmed their milk, and brought Father's coffee up to his bedroom: but her place was always by Mother. They would strain tomatoes or roll out dough and argue over recipes in loving tones. And when Mother would allow it – or when she was out of the room – Rina would tear apart each villager's reputation with the same ease with which she tore open bean pods. 'Ah no, signora,' she would defend herself against Mother's half-hearted scoldings. 'I'm not telling you this because I want to gossip. I am telling you what these miserable creatures did so that you can see how wicked men and women are. Especially,' she stressed, snapping off a bean's head with such vehemence that the children blinked, 'men.' First and foremost among guilty men was her husband, the drunk, good-for-nothing Pinin. 'A slithering snake, my dear signora, a low-lying, weak-bellied reptile who every time I turn my back slinks out to the bar and downs six grappas ...' Guilty, too, were the villagers, about whom she knew every thought and every move. How Rina could talk! It was as if every villager's reputation were thrown in the tomato strainer and then churned by her brown, vigorous arm. Before Alma's wide and hungry eyes, Rina re-enacted a hundred incidents, a thousand tales of village life: the widow Lea's siren wiles, the butcher Romeo's impotence, Sicilian Rocco's naughty daughter who had to have a shotgun wedding with a Northerner ... 'In a village as small as this one, my treasures, the houses are so close together that you know what your neighbour's doing before he does it.'

In this kitchen Alma witnessed the acts of domestic magic that keep a child entranced: the upturned glasses that, newly rinsed, moved by themselves on the countertop; the amaretto wrappers that could fly to the ceiling when Rina lit them with a match; the crystal glasses that produced delicate notes when you rubbed their rim with a finger ...

'Why couldn't you be more like the women I am used to ...' Miso'd said. Had she grown up to be like these women in the kitchen, with their domesticity and their selfless responses, she would have been part of the pattern that was familiar to him. She would have had the measured steps to fit the regular cadences of his world, and the generous instincts to place his needs above her own.

A door banged shut within the house. Francesco? But silence returned. The room glowed with mellow light and Alma rose and approached the window. She leant out, studied the luminous shapes below. 'San Lorenzo,' she whispered, 'San Lorenzo.' She went out into the garden.

'Alma.' It was Miso. He was smoking, standing beneath the persimmon tree.

'Hello.' She didn't look at him, but at the flat green leaves that hung from the persimmon.

'I wanted to come by after the auction, to see how you were – but ...' He stopped, took a few steps away from the tree.

The silence between them hung heavy, sun-drenched.

'Is Franca buying ...'

'I don't really want to talk about it.' She wanted to weep, now, for the house, for their rupture, for the forth-coming sale, for her return to Torino and its lonely life amidst canvases and casual acquaintances.

She made as if to stride past him back into the house, but he grabbed her arm. He turned her to face him, and placed both hands on her shoulders. 'Alma, I'm sorry. I'm so sorry – about everything. I – don't know why it is that when we care about someone we immediately want to change them. I wanted you to be slower, softer, to want less, move less ... Alma, you made me feel drained ... I had built my life here, and you came and disrupted it, and demanded yet more.'

She didn't speak, and kept her head bent to keep from his gaze the tears.

'In the end, it was as if we were guests in each other's house. We never felt at home with one another. Alma ...'

287

His hands dropped from her shoulders. 'Alma, you're the most extraordinary woman . . .'

'Extraordinary? Is that good?' she whispered.

'Yes. Very good.' He pressed his lips against her forehead.

She looked up. With his index finger he dried the tear that had slipped down her cheek. She gave a half-smile then turned and walked away.

'Promise me one thing,' he called out to her.

'What?' She didn't turn.

'That you will dance with me tonight.'

'Yes.' But before he could reply, she was inside the house, and had closed the door behind her.

41

Francesco had fallen into a deep dark slumber after lunch. For what seemed like hours, he had sat beside his father and mother down in the garden, counting the fireflies while Father read out the bits of news (someone's bankruptcy, a robbery, the opening of a new factory) that interested him. He had awoken when Don Luigi's bells sounded four, and he felt panic-struck at the thought of having missed two hours of his time in San Lorenzo. Soon, the village, like his parents, would be relegated to his dreams.

He searched the house for Alma – and then, recognizing Miso's voice in the garden, decided to leave them and go for a walk.

Was it a rapprochement? Had Miso come to claim Alma once again? He doubted it. The two had struck him as an improbable couple when she had revealed the affair over the telephone. Alma would continue to pull and pull, while Miso would try to hold firm – until, for fear of losing his balance, he would push her away. But he wasn't worried about Alma, she would soon find someone else: despite the loss of this house, despite the break with Miso, his sister would soon throb again with passion for life.

He had come to the piazza now: it had been converted

into a dancing arena, with tables surrounding polished floorboards and a small, raised dais towards the back. The Ferris wheel's seats were cradled by the breeze like so many airborne cribs rocked by an invisible hand. Francesco spotted Gianni er Brutto and Old Rocco beside the entrance to Vanna's bar. He made his way to them. Beaming, Gianni half-rose from his chair. 'Hello,' he added soberly, 'the auction, the sale ... I am so sorry.' On his right, Old Rocco was loudly snoring.

'Yes. My last festa. And one of my last days here ...' Francesco's eyes pricked with tears.

'Don't speak as if you'd lost everything. You know better than that.' Gianni's limpid eyes sought his. Old Rocco snorted in his sleep, opened one black, unseeing eye, closed it, and relapsed into his dreamless sleep.

'Gianni ...' Francesco sighed. 'I wanted to achieve so much ... I feel as if I've wasted my time. What do I have to show for it?'

Gianni shook his head. 'Did you see the young man who's just left me? Young Grillo, Claudio and Vanna's boy. He wants above everything to become a cantautore – a songwriter and singer who will tour the world with his guitar and his compositions. He's just sat there for an hour, telling me how he's going to force the mayor to give him a slot tonight during the entertainment ... Grillo reminds me so much of you and Miso at his age: always talking about reaching for something grand, somewhere way above your heads, hoisting yourself up on some dangerous ledge the better to reach high – but meanwhile, here' – he tapped his heart – 'at home, you've built nothing. You've got nothing solid you can stand on. With no point of departure where did you hope to arrive?'

'I don't know ... for so long I thought all I needed was to come back here and all would be much simpler ... there's no time to sort things out anywhere else. It's as if here you can wait till the sand settles back on the river bed, and the water becomes clear again.'

'You would have found out soon enough, Francesco, that San Lorenzo is the same as anywhere else. Do you think we sit about and talk of God, fate, faith and the meaning of coincidences? Of course not: whether the roof is leaking, whether the drought will be harsh next summer, whether the cows are looking poorly ... With so much to worry about, when would you have the time to think about anything else? Only old loners like myself – those of us who have no one to worry about, who've been left alone all their lives' – here he brought a hand to his birthmark – 'only those like me have the time to sit and study the great jigsaw puzzle...'

Beside them, Old Rocco spluttered but continued to sleep.

'Well – I'll never know what it would have been like to come back ... even before we knew we had to sell the house, I had realized coming back would have meant leaving Camilla. I could never have done it. So, like you, I'm spending all my time mending and fixing and patching things up.'

'It's a nice occupation. Gives a man a sense of purpose. You become necessary.'

'Perhaps. I have your blessing then?'

'My blessing? Yes – I suppose we all need blessings. Isn't that the role of older people?'

'I wonder if I'll ever come back here ... ever see you again...?'

291

'You won't need to, you know. San Lorenzo is well lodged inside there.' He pointed to Francesco's chest.

Somewhere, a shutter banged and Old Rocco sat up, snorting and coughing. 'Damn you, you old bag of bones! Waking me up like that! Are you mad to give a man such a fright?!'

Francesco and Gianni laughed. 'Well, I'll leave you then ... till tonight.'

'Till the festa.'

Francesco took the main road, followed it to the path that led to the river. He walked and walked, thinking of nothing but the earth beneath his strides and the sun that was glowing softer, as if melting like sugar in the warm waters of the river.

Francesco walked at the edge of the shadowless green waters and listened. A thousand soft noises made up the silence of the countryside, so that you could walk and remain heedless of the concert that rose from the earth and the air. But if you did listen, you could hear one note and then another, gentle in its singleness, joyful, and strong in its harmony within the chorus. Crickets, birds, the rush of the river, the breeze that swung from the trees: he heard each call.

He strolled beneath the sun that now lay heavy as a winter coat upon his shoulders, and thought of the years that lay ahead. He saw Camilla: he should have rung her by now, told her of his safe arrival and imminent return. How distant she seemed – the delicate face, the childish body, nothing seemed to fit here among the bold-coloured, fecund, ripe earth.

And now, with the auction, the sale of the house, this

refuge, this place that he had persisted in calling home, would be no longer his. San Lorenzo: he had always seen it as the fit backdrop for the beginning, and for the end, of life. No more. 'Everyone has a place,' Gianni had said. Was this his? In moving away from these hills and vineyards, from the land of his forefathers, had Francesco unwittingly trampled upon the signs that marked his path? He wondered what advice Father would have proffered. But he knew that Father would have shaken his head and exclaimed: 'Why do you feel you need others' advice?' Here he would have lit a cigarette with an impatient hand, frowning at his son the while. 'You have everything, everything! A good career, a beautiful wife, enough money to support her – what more does a man need?'

The heat glazed the water, the grasses, the leaves that hung limp from the trees. The sounds of the countryside droned louder, as if the late afternoon sun had brought a fever upon the fields. Francesco felt his body grow drowsy, his limbs soft and boneless beneath the sun.

Suddenly, before him, a white figure appeared. His heart leapt: it was Santarella, aglow against the horizon.

'Santa.' He whispered, wary that his voice might break the spell of her presence. He dared not move, lest she melt away, retreat into a world he could not enter. 'Santa,' he repeated, and the face lifted, light eyes meeting his. 'I wanted to see you again.'

The figure remained unmoving, close to him, silent. His eyes sought her face with its glowing calm. 'I wanted to see you. I don't know why – I felt somehow that if I could see you, speak to you ... it might make a difference.' He spoke in a low, soft voice, and his head bowed before her.

Santa's lips remained unmoving: she seemed to float in her silence, her spirit untouched by his voice, by the river, by the grasses and the trees.

Suddenly she drew away from him, as if her body had been lifted by a soundless breeze. 'Don't leave me!' he called out to her, his voice bursting through the stillness.

Santa raised her hand now, beckoning him towards her, and Francesco approached the white figure. She began to walk with slow silent footsteps at the edge of the river and Francesco walked beside her, fearful of coming too close, fearful of looking at the translucent profile beneath its dark mantle of hair.

He walked and stared at the ground before him. 'Santa, do you remember how I would study you in your mother's shop? How I used to follow you here to the river?' Santa made no sign of hearing his words. 'I always admired the way you were single-mindedly following a certain kind of life ... I didn't understand where you were reading your instructions, what signs you could see that were not there for me ...' Francesco felt the words bursting forth, as if her mere presence drew forth his confessions. 'I've started a new life, away from here. I'm married, Santa. And I'm now doing what I'd always wanted – publishing some wonderful works ... But something is missing ... It seems to me that you have found an answer.' He stopped in his tracks, but she proceeded.

'Wait, Santa, don't go from me!' he shouted as he rushed to reach her. 'Santa! Pray for me, Santa: I need ...'

He had reached her, and she turned. Her eyes shone bright, secret, and her lips parted as if to speak. Then she smiled, and for a moment, he did not breathe. But Santa moved away again, her figure gliding upon the grasses that sloped into the river.

'Santa!' he shouted, again moving after her. He strode behind her: the air seemed to transport her once more, distancing her from him.

'Don't go ...' he called out. But the figure, bright against the sky, continued to recede, till she glowed in the horizon like the first star.

Francesco stood still: he heard the humming of the air, the soft murmur of the waters. Somewhere beyond, the village voices raised in unison to prepare for tonight's feast. He was alone.

Francesco walked, immersed in thought. He moved away from the river, roaming the paths that brought him to the hills. What had he hoped to receive from her? Had he really believed that she would grant him a sign, make some symbolic gesture?

The last rays skimmed the hill above San Lorenzo, gingerly, like the village girls when they skated their feet upon the river's water, before immersing themselves.

He stared down at the village. Shadows were changing San Lorenzo, till it became a village of ghosts, where lost faces and figures merged with the blue that fell upon the fields and the narrow streets, in the arched courtyard doorways, beneath the bell tower and the sloping roofs.

Like winged creatures, angels or devils, the people of his childhood swarmed the air below him: Father as he called to them from the balcony; Mother as she sewed beneath the persimmon tree; Gianni er Brutto's arm hammering nails into wood. And Santa's pale figure, radiant against the dusk.

The air filled with their murmurs, with their gestures,

and their shadows fell upon every part of the village. The calls of the past echoed through the hills, but Francesco could not distinguish their words, could not heed their call.

The moon shone in the light sky, impatient for the last sun to dip beyond the hills. He stared down at the village, where the outline of the roofs and the Ferris wheel stood out against the sky. In the piazza, festoons of white light-bulbs linked the trees to the balcony of Vanna's inn, to the gutters of her roof, to the red, white and green tent of the shooting alley.

'Here I am.' The silence wrapped him tight. 'Where to now?'

Down below, the village began to prepare for the festa: laughter, chatter, hurried pacing filled San Lorenzo, weaving into an excited chorus. The thick air swelled, growing darker about him, as the windows below filled with mellow lights. Soon the road would fill, the narrow streets would be flooded with people. From the neighbouring villages, families and couples, youths and old men and women would come to San Lorenzo to honour the patron saint. And the windows below would grow dark, one by one, till all the villagers had poured out into the piazza, to celebrate as they had done for generations.

42

The piazza shone as if all the stars of heaven had fallen there. The stalls, the streetlights, the bar splashed their brightness upon the festa, while the Ferris wheel spun a luminous circle that moved faster and faster from earth to sky and back.

In this glow, the villagers paraded their Sunday finery. The people of San Lorenzo moved slowly, slowly: unhurried, they tasted every moment of the celebration. The women strolled lazily, like visitors to an unknown country; the men hung about in small groups, smoking and chuckling, and issuing well-worn quips about each other's expanding waist or receding hairline. Families exchanged formal greetings, acting like vague acquaintances and not lifelong neighbours.

The so-called 'summer people', too, were strolling through the village streets: they were the former inhabitants of San Lorenzo, those who now lived in Torino, in Genoa, or in nearby towns. They still had relatives in the village – parents, an aunt, a sister or a brother – and returned to the village for the feast day, for their summer holidays, for All Saints' Day in November, for a funeral. They lived other lives, inhabited new places, but still they returned, to the old world left behind.

And how the villagers showed off these relatives! They sported their nieces, nephews, children or grandchildren with the same pride with which they wore their finest earrings or showed off their new car. Franca Felici stood behind her daughter Mina, who'd come from Torino, and smiled and fanned herself, as if the mere presence of this gleaming city girl were heating the air. Nuccio the baker synchronized his every step with the long lithe one of his first-born – a cadet at the Academy in Cuneo. And even Old Rocco was beaming because his daughter, who'd broken his heart when she had married a Northerner, was here fussing about him, straightening his collar, making a neat triangle of his handkerchief.

From the other villages of the hills, from Castel d'Oro and Susa and beyond, came young people on their motorcycles, older couples and families in cars. Children rushed about, laughing, shouting, exhilarated by these bright lights, the late hour, their parents' unusual permissiveness.

The boards of the dance floor stretched across the piazza, gleaming beneath garlands of lightbulbs. At one end of the floor, the orchestra's chairs had been ranged in a semicircle. When the musicians finally made their appearance, in their ancient dinner jackets, the couples and families began to pour onto the dance floor to stake their claims to a set of chairs, a table, a bench. And while the musicians took out their instruments, turned their music sheets, and scanned the faces of tonight's crowd, their audience jostled to get a good seat, a better table, lest they miss a single note.

Now the piano player made his entrance: he was out of breath because his car had broken down in the midst of his journey from Castel d'Oro, and he'd been forced to walk the last mile and a half. In vain, he had tried to flag down the oncoming cars and motorbikes: no one had stopped, not even slowed down. Every single vehicle, it seemed, was bent on hurrying to the festa at San Lorenzo, bent on their enjoyment of a special night without a charitable thought entering their hearts. How he had cursed them, as he stood waving like a windmill beside the road.

The piano player snorted and scowled as his eyes searched the well-combed, over-dressed men and women who called out to one another from their little tables. How much of his life had been spent playing old-fashioned, sentimental music for these people? Was he destined to live this way for ever – his masterpieces unheard, his time taken up by village feasts ... But then: whether it was the sight of pretty Veronica admiring him from her father's table; or the excited whisper – 'The pianist is here! the pianist is here!' that now quivered among the seated figures before him; or perhaps the glimpse of an elderly couple whose feet tapped a polka ... he did not know why or how, but suddenly he felt music swell within him, and a good mood stir his heart. He smoothed talcum powder on his hands and smiled.

Vanna had decided that she and Claudio were to enjoy themselves tonight – 'Aren't we allowed to have our fun, too, once a year?' she had asked all who would listen – and she had had Grillo move dozens of bottles and hundreds of glasses out onto a makeshift bar (a narrow board astride two chairs) in one corner of the dance floor.

Behind the green and black bottles, polishing a glass with her breath and a towel, stood plain-faced Marta,

299

Nuccio the baker's daughter. She cast her sister Veronica a self-important smile, then resumed a serious expression to count the bills and coins strangers handed her for a bottle. Marta had volunteered to man the bar: she had been only too happy to avoid watching the village boys ask every girl but herself to dance; to avoid telling some out-of-town youth Veronica's name, or Lisetta's, or Sara's ... Tonight, right here, Marta was finally in the thick of things!

Grillo sat in a corner of his parents' bar, and plucked a few chords of his guitar. Tonight, after those old stooges had played their silly songs that said nothing about anything, he would take his turn. What had Gianni er Brutto said – 'Everyone's given a chance – and sometimes only one.' Tonight was his chance ... But would he dare? A fly buzzed by his glass. Grillo went behind the counter and replaced his guitar in its case. He suddenly caught sight of himself in the mirror that stretched behind the bottles: here he was, a sad face amidst the Campari, grappa, Strega, Martini bottles; amidst the stemless glasses that, despite Mother's frenzied polishing, still bore water spots; with the coffee cups and saucers that through the years had dwindled from a set of twenty to a mere seven ... Grillo swallowed hard. Was this where he, Grillo, belonged and where he was going to spend the rest of his life? He felt a great lump in his throat and saw the winter nights spent behind the counter, while his father smoked and watched over the hundredth game of scopa and his mother sat, in her slippers, thumbing through the popular magazines to see what other women, somewhere else, wore. Grillo took a deep breath and straightened his shoulders. No. He would do something, now. He would not spend the rest of his life behind this counter. Tonight he would sing at the festa.

Pina the former postmistress sat alone at a tiny table near the entrance. She watched Marta, and saw herself at that age: plain, flat-chested, ignored by men. Pina, stiff in her brown silk, sat and stifled a sigh: 'Get used to it my girl,' in her heart she addressed Marta, 'you'll have to live with it for the rest of your days ...' And for a moment, her heart tightened into a fist.

Old Rocco and Gianni er Brutto sat at a card-less table, drinking the spumante that Rocco's son-in-law had offered them ('the only thing he's good for, that nitwit') and roamed with their eyes over the gathering, and with their thoughts over the feste of long ago.

'Eh, do you remember the girls in our day, Gianni? Not like these skinny little chicks they have today ... at the feste – San Lorenzo, San Rocco, Sant' Anna, wherever – it was a pleasure to see those plump pretty turtle-doves ...' Old Rocco sipped the Spumante and tasted his youth.

'Yes ...' whispered Gianni, who remembered the way no girl had ever given him a second glance – and the one who had was a young thing at the festa at Castellazzo, who had sobbed: 'Poor boy, did you see, half his face has a brown blob on it!'

'Oh, what have we here? What's all the fuss?' Old Rocco, excited by the commotion, leaned over his table. 'It's the bishop, by God! The bishop!'

Indeed, there he was, mitre-less but splendid in his red and gold vestments: Bishop Natti. How regal his wave, to the left and to the right; how beatific his smile as he moved slowly through the crowds that parted like the

Red Sea before him. In his wake came his secretary, thin, forbidding, all in black, with Don Luigi waddling at his heels. A pace or two behind, came the mayor and his wife and son; and bringing up the procession was the marshal, resplendent in a twelve-button uniform.

'Oh my, oh my, the bishop's going to speak and seal our fate ...' Old Rocco winked at Gianni. 'And I have a funny notion that what he'll say won't be music to our mayor's ears!'

'Let's wait and see ...' answered Gianni.

The bishop, who seemed to skate along the polished wooden floorboards, now sat at the very centre of the long table that stretched behind the orchestra on a low dais. The Mayor Battistini immediately elbowed himself next to the prelate, bringing a heavy frown onto the secretary's thin face. 'Come here, come here, Anna,' the mayor barked at his hapless wife. Unperturbed, the bishop continued to smile, an other-worldly expression glazing his eyes.

'How wonderful he looks!' exclaimed Vanna beside her husband.

'How wise! How distinguished he seems!' echoed Pina from her lonely table.

'He'd better tell us what we want to hear, or else Battistini'll be in a fine stew!' spat out the butcher.

Above the festa, the red August moon shone bright. With her radiant face the moon tonight seemed as capable of giving off heat as the sun she had replaced. Indeed, the air that fell about the villagers was as warm as a shawl – and sweetly scented, with the eau de cologne worn on sunbrowned wrists and throats, with the burnt sugar smell of the candyfloss machine, with the faint odour of fields, grasses, fruit and flowers that fills any summer night in the countryside.

Alma and Francesco finally left their house and made their way to the festa. 'I resent the village festivity burying our mourning for our home ...' Alma had sighed as they settled down at a round table a safe distance from the piano.

'The festa takes place no matter what. And look how excited everyone is – it's probably in honour of the bishop, that's him up there, how self-satisfied he looks ...' Francesco felt tired and slightly on edge because of all the people, the lights, the warmth of the summer night.

'The bishop. Of course. Will he or won't he give a blessing upon the mayor's enterprise ...?' Alma's tone was cynical, but her eyes already shone at the kaleidoscope before her.

'Remember how we used to look forward to the festa? Me in my polished shoes, you with that ridiculous bow on your head ...' He was laughing now. 'Look: the Signorina Teresa – Alma, shouldn't we have her join us ...' He was already on his feet, holding out a chair for the frail figure in silk. She came towards them with a bashful air, the signorina, protesting that they needn't, really, spoil their fun by sitting with an old lady. But once she sat down, on Francesco's right, she opened her pastel coloured fan and bestowed a happy smile upon the proceedings. 'A festa is always a pleasure ... Even though, my dears, it breaks my heart to look across the hazelnuts and think that you will no longer be there ... when for generations our families have been neighbours ...' The signorina fanned herself mournfully.

'Yes.' Francesco cleared his throat. 'It's hard to believe.

303

But ... we couldn't afford to keep it on, though we were both ready to make almost any sacrifice ...' Beside him, Alma nodded but couldn't speak.

'And I suppose it's Franca, isn't it?' the signorina began, timid. 'Such a ... force of nature, isn't she?' The signorina looked frightened at the very prospect of the Felici tornado coming her way.

'I suppose it will be Franca.' Francesco sounded tired, already weary of the bartering that doubtless would take place.

'Everyone's here ... all dressed up ... and look at Bishop Natti ... we are all expecting the bishop to say he'll let us build a shrine ...' The signorina fanned herself thoughtfully. 'Though I don't think I really want a proper shrine and a million pilgrims pouring into San Lorenzo ... No I don't suppose I want any of that ...' The signorina's eyes closed, as if to keep at bay that vision.

The musicians continued to leaf through their music sheets, chatting among themselves. The audience, though rumbling and scuffling their feet, seemed to enjoy their wait: they were drinking in the strangers, comparing notes on dresses and hair styles, chiding their children, exchanging gossip.

Suddenly, the pianist raised his hands and banged down on the keyboard to strike the first note. A hush fell upon the audience, who stretched their necks to watch the musicians take up, one by one, the chorus of lively notes. The polka rose in volume, spun in the air, brought smiles to the farmers and their wives: feet tapped, tunes were hummed, eyes shone while a hundred memories of youth and summers stirred and skipped to the tempo. Who would begin, then? Who would open the dance?

304

And everyone looked at their partners expectantly, to see who would dare take the floor.

Suddenly, seemingly materializing from the air itself, there in the centre of the gleaming floor stood the Mayor Battistini. Chin raised, head thrown back in defiance, Bettino Battistini clapped twice and stretched out his arm to invite his wife to join him. In her seat, Donna Anna flushed a terrible purple, uneasy beneath the stares of half the village. Then, fear of Bettino being stronger than any other emotion, she joined him on the dance floor. The mayor placed his arm around his wife's waist, held her right hand as if it were an emperor's sceptre. Battistini scanned the audience with a tight smile of triumph, and then ... ooplah! the mayor hopped to the right, leading his wife with a pull. How quick they span, she looking suddenly as light and elegant as a ballerina, he as full of energy as a young boy again as he turned and skipped.

The sight of a dancing couple worked its charm: one by one, new couples took to the floor, taking sliding soft steps, turning and skating smoothly upon the wood. Middle-aged men turned their partners with quick, easy hands; thick-ankled, big-hipped women took light, small steps and gave coquettish little cries of delight as they followed their partners' next move. They danced, round and round, the women bending slightly back, away from the men, as if the couple were still at the courtship stage, while the men leaned closer and closer, to gain a better view of that white expanse of throat and bosom.

The dance floor was full, all in motion, with the colours of the women's dresses shining beneath the lightbulbs. Women danced with women, mothers with their children, men danced with tiny daughters who stood on their fathers' shoes.

Franca Felici and her brood began to spread out across the dance floor just as their property had spread out across the hills of San Lorenzo: her sons shone with perspiration as they swung and turned and held up their huge wives; her daughters-in-law glowed with the gold necklaces, earrings and bracelets they donned only on festive occasions. Shiny-eyed with excitement, her gold-toothed smile permanently crossing her face, her bracelets and earrings dangling, Franca Felici outshone even her heirs' brightness. With a little nod to her husband, who sat wrapped in his usual coverlet at the family's immense table, Franca skimmed the floor with dainty feet, swung from Beppe's right to Beppe's left arm, hopped as if she were a young girl. Poor Beppe tried to keep up with his mother's fast-paced mazurka, attempted to keep her from kicking up a leg in the air ... but to no avail. With wide-armed movements, Franca made space for herself and her son in the very centre of the floor. Laughter bubbled in her voice as she took up the folds of her violet skirt, the better to prance.

In vain, the former postmistress Pina stared at the straining buttons on Franca's back; in vain, Vanna raised an eyebrow as she and Claudio danced close to the irrepressible Franca; in vain, Battistini not so accidentally stood upon Franca's feet, in their new shoes from Alessandria: Franca Felici, as ever, ignored others and carried on exactly as she pleased.

'Will you dance like that when you're her age?' Grillo whispered into Veronica's throat while they turned round and round on the dance floor. 'Will you look like her son when you're his age?' murmured Veronica in reply. Grillo squeezed her tight and thought of how well they were dancing together. On and on Grillo and Veronica danced, embracing so tight as they turned that Nuccio the baker felt his heart skip a beat with anxiety for his daughter, and Vanna felt a pang of sweet sadness at the thought of her boy in love. And when they spun past the pianist, he missed a chord at the sight of the pretty girl so inflamed with happiness.

'Alma, Miso is trying to make his way to us ...' Francesco felt as if he should warn her. The signorina looked alarmed and fanned herself violently. But Alma remained calm.

'May I join you?'

Miso looked self-conscious, eyes settling on the signorina rather than on the Ferratis. His hair was still wet from his bath, combed carefully back. But Alma knew without looking that rebel curls would already be straying away from his collar. 'When did you arrive?' He had turned to Francesco as he sat down.

'This morning. Went through the bids. And tomorrow, I shouldn't wonder, we'll all come to your offices for you to draw up the contract.'

'Always at your service.' Miso smiled. But he was ill at ease, and kept shifting in his chair between brother and sister. Alma still didn't say a word.

'I'm going to get us some spumante. Signorina, you'll join us, won't you?' But the signorina was finding the tension at the table too much for her, and she stood now, her fan folded into a small baton. 'Oh, I couldn't possibly. But please, Francesco, will you help me make my way past all those people ... my legs feel a bit unsteady tonight

...' She held onto his arm with a tremulous hand, and heaved a sigh of relief at leaving Miso and Alma.

The orchestra was taking their break, and the musicians, hair flying and cheeks red, sat about chatting, comparing their impressions of this, the latest saint's day feast. Back at their tables, the villagers were quenching their thirst and trading gossip.

'That dress – that blue – it suits you.'

'You always knew flattery was the best way to my heart.' She smiled but her eyes fled his.

'If you need anything ... I mean, once you're in Torino ... or if you should wish to come back here to paint ...' He kept stumbling in his speech.

'Thank you. But the San Lorenzo phase of my life is now over.' Her voice was low and strained.

'Alma, I'm sorry. I tried. I promise you, I tried.'

'I know. I know. But in the end, I want too much and you are prepared to make do with too little. Hardly a good blueprint for a long-term partnership...'

'No.' He suddenly stretched out his hand and took hers.

The shock of his fingers laced in hers sent a shiver down Alma's spine. 'Miso, don't ...' The longing was still too close to the surface and the lightest touch would uncover it.

'We haven't had a dance...'

'The festa's only just begun ...' She smiled.

'My mother said that if you and Francesco want to come over for lunch tomorrow...'

'No thanks. It's very kind.' Alma felt at ease again: she remembered the dark and narrow world of his and knew she could never inhabit it.

'Here we are. Spumante. We seem to have scared off

the Signorina Teresa ...' Francesco sat between them, placed the glasses before them and uncorked the spumante.

'Cin cin to a glorious future.'

'Cin cin. To the two Ferratis. Happiness and prosperity to you both.' Miso raised his glass and met Alma's gaze.

'And what of the shrine? Shall we not drink a toast to our mayor's dream?' asked Francesco.

Miso laughed and shook his head. 'No, not tonight. We may bring him good luck.'

'The bishop's keeping us on tenterhooks ...' Alma was smiling now, as if in the sweet bubbles of the spumante she had regained her good mood.

'Goodness, he's standing – he's getting ready to deliver his speech ...' And Miso set down his glass and crossed his arms to listen to the prelate's speech.

It was true: Bishop Natti stood, tall, shiny, imposing, waiting for the talking to stop. On his left, the mayor was tapping the table with a spoon to silence the crowd. At either end of the grandees' table, the Marshal Ciuffi and Don Luigi sat bolt upright, tense and expectant.

'My dear brethren, the people of San Lorenzo. It has been an honour to be among you tonight. This is, of course, a special night for all of us, as we gather together to pay our tribute to the patron saint of this village. It is on nights such as this that the blessings of a peaceful and bountiful countryside are most palpable ...' The bishop droned on and on, and what became truly palpable was the frustration of his audience.

'When's he going to talk of the shrine?' The butcher elbowed Nuccio the baker.

'What of Santa?' murmured the former postmistress

309

Pina. Indefatigable, imperturbable, the bishop sailed forth on the sea of bucolic glories he was navigating with such tenderness. On and on the bishop spoke, equally touching for his sincere admiration of the life of the countryside and his complete oblivion to the impatience of his audience. Finally, red with suppressed rage, the mayor half-rose and whispered something into the bishop's ear.

'What? Oh yes, of course. I nearly forgot,' the bishop muttered. It took him a few moments to get back on course after the rude interruption, but once again he set forth. 'Your good mayor, the admirable Barone – no no of course, Battistini –' Here a great laugh from Old Rocco who had to be nudged into silence by Gianni. 'Your mayor reminds me of the matter of the visionary, Marina Ramoni, known as Santarella. My dear brethren' – here the bishop stretched up his hands, palms upward – 'I need not bore you with the details of how many claims my Archdiocese receives from young women (and some men too) who have seen Our Lady. Every day, someone in a village much like this one claims that she has had a dialogue with the gentle Mother of Our Lord, and that the spot where Our Lady appeared deserves to be turned into a holy site.

'Dear brethren, so many visitations are beyond the bounds of credibility! Imagine, if every visionary were given credence! Why, every village from here to Torino would house a shrine!'

The bishop here laughed at the folly of it all. His audience remained silent as the tomb. 'Now, as you well know, your mayor and your excellent parish priest, Don Luigi, have for some time sought my humble opinion on the matter of your young Santarella, and on her supposed visions of Our Lady. Don Luigi described to me how innocent and good young Santa is. But, my dear friends, when he told me that she won't speak – well, I can assure you, nothing further can be done. How could we, my fellow bishops, the archbishop even, decide that Santa truly speaks to Our Lady and San Lorenzo is a holy site when the girl refuses to talk to us?' Here the bishop paused and allowed the wisdom of his words to sink like an anchor into the sea of faces before him. 'Hold onto your faith, my friends, for that indeed is a good thing. Hold onto your great spirit. The dream of a shrine to Our Lady does you great honour. And indeed, it is a tribute to your faith. But I have come tonight to warn you that though we in the hierarchy find your faith very touching – and indeed, it is your simple faith that has moved me to come to this little village on this night of celebration – we must ask you to recognize that your shrine must remain a dream.'

A murmur rose like a whistling wind through the audience.

'What?!' At the bishop's side, the mayor shot up, face crimson.

'What?!' At his end of the table, the marshal broke into a violent coughing fit.

'How could it possibly be otherwise, my dear friends?' The bishop looked surprised at the effect of his words. 'How could we possibly build a shrine based on such flimsy evidence?'

The bishop sat down, regained his regal composure. But amidst his audience, all attempts at propriety had been abandoned.

'I don't believe it! No shrine!' The butcher Romeo thumped his table.

311

'It can't be true – after all those promises.' Nuccio the baker cast a venomous look at the grandees sitting at their table.

'No shrine! To think of the visitors who would have come here . . .' Vanna sighed and shook her head.

'It wasn't as though I was hoping to make money out if it, but . . . I would have been so proud to have a shrine honouring Our Lady here in San Lorenzo,' the former postmistress was leaning over the back of her chair to tell Rosa Felici.

'We've been had . . .' Claudio drowned his sorrow in the glass of spumante before him.

'That wicked wicked girl who wouldn't speak . . .' The postmistress looked up at the widow Lea's window.

'That wicked man who filled your heads with nonsense . . .' Old Rocco tipped back his wine.

'Well, the bishop's driven a nail into that coffin!' And Miso raised a glass to toast the mayor's defeat.

'Yes . . . I wonder what will happen now to Santa . . .' Francesco murmured. In the window above widow Lea's shop, he could see a dark figure – mother or daughter, he did not know whom – move within the well-lit room.

'The mayor had better explain himself!' Nuccio the baker was standing now, clapping to gain the villagers' attention.

'Yes! Come on, Battistini! Defend yourself!' At the grandees' table, you could see Bishop Natti sit, square-shouldered, serene, amidst the hullabaloo; you could see the Marshal Ciuffi sink into his chair, one hand twirling his moustache; and Don Luigi practically disappearing into his cassock, neck shrinking to nothingness as the accusations rained upon him; and you could see Donna

312

Anna place a protective arm around her son's shoulders.

But where, oh where, was Battistini? The mayor seemed to have disappeared.

'Battistini! Battistini!' Rocco was chanting, glass in hand.

'Battistini!' In chorus, Franca's brood sang out the name.

'Where's that thief?!'

'Where's that liar?!' The calls whistled through the air like angry firecrackers. The piano player looked about him to find someone who would tell him what to do. Was he to play? Should he drown out the catcalls with his music? He shrugged his shoulders at his orchestra. Above them, Don Luigi's bells tolled eleven.

The bells found the Mayor Battistini galloping to the safety of his courtyard. Once inside his front door, he bolted it, pressed himself against it, arms spread out in crucifixion, brow wet with sweat. 'My God, I'll rip that woman limb from limb ... I'll drag that girl's tongue out with a pair of pliers if need be ... How dare they?!' In the darkness of his home the mayor howled his anger like a wolf.

In his seat, looking as miserable as a glutton on a Lenten fast, Don Luigi heard the bells of his church and addressed his Maker: 'Why, Father, oh why? In You I trusted, as the Psalm says ... and yet ... You test me test me ... is this "an atoning sacrifice for our sins" as John's Gospel says?' He shook his head, so heavy with wine and regret. He dared not lift his eyes to the congregation before him. Out of the corner of his eyes he saw the marshal staring mournfully into his glass, one hand pulling at his moustache.

A few chairs down, he caught sight of Bishop Natti who was fanning himself with the programme Bettino had had printed. 'Oh, Bishop Natti, if only you knew how greatly you have disappointed your humble servant ...' Don Luigi whispered, tears filling his eyes. But the bishop did not heed his parish priest's moan, and continued to fan himself and to glide his gaze upon the crowd, like one of the dancing couples on the floor.

The bells brought a look of determination to Grillo's flushed face: he had danced with Veronica, and knew she loved him; he had drunk six glasses of spumante, and knew he was unbeatable; and he had heard one polka too many: there was nothing to do now, but try his luck, just as he had planned. With the musicians silent, the mayor nowhere to be seen, he could take over the microphone undisturbed. Striding like a conqueror, guitar borne high before him like a sword, Grillo marched past tables and chairs and people, onto the dais. He would cover himself in glory, now, make them all sit up and listen. And he'd move them like no one else had ... He grabbed a chair, kicked it near the microphone, placed his right foot upon it.

'It's Grillo playing! Grillo's playing!' His friend Bobbo alerted the audience from his perch on a chair. The people of San Lorenzo – those who were queuing at Marta's bar, those who sat moaning with their friends about the shrine and its demise, those who were fanning themselves after the heat of the dance floor – fell silent, the better to hear the local boy.

And Grillo played – oh, how he played: every song he had ever written, adding a verse here, leaving out a verse there, remembering a variation on one theme or adding a new ending to an old favourite ... he sang in his low, sad voice, and his eyes brimmed with tears because he had never once heard his voice spread out over a hundred people. He sang and sang, Grillo, and at their table Claudio burst with pride, and Vanna allowed tears to slide down her cheeks. And in the midst of her ice cream, with her father's eyes fixed upon her, Veronica shivered with happiness.

'Let's dance!' someone called out. And one after the other, the young people of San Lorenzo took to the floor. They swung and turned, and echoed every line that Grillo uttered.

'Come, you promised me a dance, remember?' Miso dragged Alma up from her chair and into the throng of dancers. They danced self-consciously, careful not to touch one another, smiling absent-mindedly at the crowd around them, pretending not to be embarrassed.

The music now changed, grew softer, slower, and Grillo's voice soared as gentle as a cloud above them: Miso pulled Alma closer to himself and she grew tense.

'He's got real talent, our friend Grillo.' Miso spoke somewhere above her head.

'Yes. He's good.' She smiled as he stepped on her toes and apologized.

'Alma – perhaps ...' he whispered in her hair.

'No, Miso, it won't work. I would have to give up too much. Now, shshshsh ... let's dance.'

Francesco watched his sister dance with Miso. He sipped his spumante and stared up at the widow Lea's windows, where he now spied two figures.

'Dottore Francesco?' It was Franca Felici, suddenly materializing beside him, two glasses of spumante in her hands. 'These come from your vineyards, the ones your father, may the Good Lord bless his soul, sold me six years ago ... Please,' she handed him the glass in her right hand. 'This one is for you.' She settled down next to him.

'The sale of the house – have you had a chance to decide anything yet?' Franca was leaning over towards him, and he could breathe in her eau de toilette and her spumante.

'Well, Signora Franca ... it is not difficult to see that your offer is unbeatable – no matter who offers what, you say you're prepared to top their bid. It will simply be a matter of what the other bids will be – from the butcher, from Battistini ...'

'Cin cin, Dottore, cin cin.' And Franca's gold tooth showed as she grinned at him. 'All my life I have wanted to live in the Ferrati house ... and now, just as I am ready to sit down and think only of my heirs, now I finally have my wish.'

On the dance floor, the couples stood still: Grillo's song had drawn to an end, and amidst the whistles of approval and shouts of praise from the audience, the young man strode off the dais into his parents' bar. The ancient musicians, slightly jealous of all the attention the young whippersnapper had won, now ehmmed and ahmmed in front of their sheets, and the pianist made a great show of stretching his hands across the keyboard before beginning to play.

Now Franca brought a finger to her lips and pulled at Francesco's sleeve: 'Look. Look over there.' And Francesco followed her gaze to find two black-clad figures, cases in hand, slip out of the widow Lea's back door and head towards the road to Susa. Francesco looked up:

darkness had fallen over the widow Lea's house, and the windows stood black.

'They're going – where? What will happen to them, to Santa?' he whispered.

'I don't know.' Franca stood up, and her eyes followed the two women's flight till they were hidden by the night. 'I must go back to my family, Dottore Francesco. But not a word about those two – they should be left in peace.' She pressed her hand onto Francesco's shoulder and winked. 'Goodbye.'

Alone, Francesco watched once more the couples who twirled to the waltz. There, amidst them all, he saw Alma and Miso come together, his sister looking up into the brown face. They moved slowly, out of step with the other dancers, forgetting to turn. How beautiful, Francesco thought: the darkness and the lights, the soft warmth of summer, the smiling faces. In the black sky, a red moon that glowed like a good omen. Everywhere he looked, he could see people's excitement: just as his sister could, the people of San Lorenzo were capable of shrugging off their disappointment and breathing in the strong scents of the August night.

He rose from the table and made his way past the Felicis' long stretch of chairs and figures and bottles, and past the makeshift bar where a girl stood humming to herself. In the street, people still milled, chatting and laughing. Above them, shiny and fast spinning as a great firework, the giant Ferris wheel reached for the sky. He wandered down the crowded street, looked about the bright piazza, filled himself with the festa. He saw Gianni er Brutto and waved, but the old man didn't notice. At every step, someone bumped into him, touched him,

317

called out – he welcomed the sounds, the sensations, as if in this manner the happy excitement could rub off on him.

He buried his hands in his pockets and moved forth, pushed by the current of passersby. Behind her stall, Morgana beckoned with long, lacquered fingernails. 'Come read your future, come sit with me and I'll show you what awaits you ...' sang out the red mouth. Francesco walked past a kissing couple, past an elderly woman and her troop of grandchildren. He was growing tired, now, and half his thoughts were already turning to Camilla and London and tomorrow's return, while the other half followed two black figures down the road to Susa.

In the bell tower, the bells boomed the half hour. He strolled past the sacristy door, and suddenly an impulse shot through him: he'd climbed the stairs to the bell tower so often, when he'd been a boy ... He unlocked the door of the bell tower and pushed his way into the dark damp stairwell. Slowly he climbed: the moon carpeted now three steps, now four, lighting his way. He reached the top, where he dislodged two bats with his presence. From without, the echoes of laughter and music of the little orchestra followed the moon beams into this darkness. Through the arched window he could see the piazza, the dancers, the Ferris wheel as it continued to spin. Beyond, the hills lay dark.

Suddenly, a long loud whistle broke the air: against the horizon white, yellow, green and red fireworks burst in the sky. One after the other, fireworks lit up the heavens and the hills, preceded by a hissing that overcame the orchestra's music.

'Fireworks! Fireworks!' The dancers spilled out onto the streets, excited, pointing up at the brilliant sky. Children ran and laughed beneath the bright sparks while their mothers called out their names and their threats.

Someone, he knew not whom, wrapped his arm around a woman and they began to dance out there in the street. Another couple began to sway, twirl and turn. Soon the streets moved back and forth to the rhythm of the orchestra's polka: people clapped, some singing snatches of old songs, some sliding into steps they thought forgotten. The indefatigable Franca, having drained her eldest of all energy, was now pirouetting in the arms of her second son, Checchino. Claudio and Vanna, too, had resumed their dancing, and Grillo, fame and glory forgotten, was searching for Veronica to join him in the old-fashioned waltz.

The old men stood side by side and watched and nodded their heads to the lively music. Old Rocco's eyes sought his daughter among the dancers. Gianni hummed: they had both sung this song in their courting days. 'In the end, has anything changed?' Gianni asked the other. And then, smiling: 'Let's go and reclaim the marshal, look how unhappy he is, defeated after such a long campaign!' The two slowly made their way to the grandees' table.

Among the twirling couples, Don Luigi was trying to make his way home, head hanging as heavy as an overripe fruit from its bough. In the distance he could hear Donna Anna crying frantically, 'Bettino! Where are you, Bettino!' He allowed the voice to wash over him, as he was trying to do with his own disappointment.

Francesco looked up at the sky that filled with light, and at the colours beneath him. Franca would buy the

319

house. Alma would return to Torino. And tomorrow, in London with Camilla, he would try to build a new life . . .

Now he spotted Alma and Miso, almost directly below him.

He watched as they danced in the midst of other couples, turning round and round. He watched them as they danced and danced and danced.

All Orion/Phoenix titles are available at your local bookshop or from the following address:

> Littlehampton Book Services
> Cash Sales Department L
> 14 Eldon Way, Lineside Industrial Estate
> Littlehampton
> West Sussex BN17 7HE
>
> *telephone* 01903 721596, *facsimile* 01903 730914

Payment can either be made by credit card (Visa and Mastercard accepted) or by sending a cheque or postal order made payable to *Littlehampton Book Services*.

DO NOT SEND CASH OR CURRENCY.

Please add the following to cover postage and packing

UK and BFPO:
£1.50 for the first book, and 50P for each additional book to a maximum of £3.50

Overseas and Eire:
£2.50 for the first book plus £1.00 for the second book and 50p for each additional book ordered

---

BLOCK CAPITALS PLEASE

name of cardholder ....   *delivery address*
....   *(if different from cardholder)*
address of cardholder ....
....
....
....
postcode ....   *postcode* ....

☐ I enclose my remittance for £..............................

☐ please debit my Mastercard/Visa (delete as appropriate)

card number ☐☐☐☐☐☐☐☐☐☐☐☐☐☐☐☐

expiry date ☐☐☐☐

signature ....

prices and availability are subject to change without notice